Heart
of the
Storm

By Ally McGuire

2024

Butterworth Books is a different breed of publishing house. It's a home for Indies, for independent authors who take great pride in their work and produce top quality books for readers who deserve the best. Professional editing, professional cover design, professional proof reading, professional book production—you get the idea. As Individual as the Indie authors we're proud to work with, we're Butterworths and we're *different*.

Authors currently publishing with us:

For more information visit www.butterworthbooks.co.uk

CATALOGING INFORMATION
ISBN: 978-1-915009-61-6
CREDITS
Editor: Nicci Robinson
Cover Design: Nicci Robinson
Production Design: Global Wordsmiths

Acknowledgements

Change is inevitable, and often uncomfortable. Goodness knows I've been through many changes in my life; who hasn't, by the time they reach this half-way marker in life? I find myself contemplating both change and chosen family, as well as the friendships that keep us going. The things on my mind often end up in my books, and that is very much the case here.

Those people around me, *my* chosen family, always serve as my inspiration. And on that note, I want to say thank you to the friends and family who continue to show up, those who make the effort to check in, and whose cheerleading keeps me writing even when it's an uphill struggle to get the words out. And as always, thank you to my wife, who just shakes her head when I complain about all the dialogue I have to write and who continues to fill my world with romantic inspiration.

Dedication

To my wife,
who always calms the
storm and holds me safe.

Chapter One

"THIS FUCKING PLACE." AMBER Archer scraped the bottom of her high heel on the curb, trying to get whatever godawful sludge she'd stepped in off the Louboutins that had cost her more than her monthly rent in New York. Her rental car was covered in a fine layer of the dust that seemed to drift in the air like a never-ending call toward climate catastrophe. If there was going to be an end to the world, she had no doubt it would start in a place like this, with its vast fields full of cows, quaint white houses big enough to hold a family of forty, and barns that looked like they were about to crumble to pieces beside tractors left to rust.

"Need some help?"

She looked up to see an honest-to-God cowboy looking at her, a wry smile on his lips, and his thumbs hooked in his belt loops. "Do I look like I need help?"

His eyebrows quirked slightly. "Well, ma'am, you're about to wear that coffee, based on the way it's tilting, and your car keys appear to be stuck in something you don't want to get on your fingers. Add to that the bag of Ms. Nellie's food in your other hand, and well..." He shrugged slightly. "Yeah. Looks like you could use a hand."

She'd rather eat raw kale than admit to needing help. "Nope. I'm good. Thank you. Off you go, back to your horse."

His expression turned a little less friendly. "Okay then. Have a good one."

He sauntered off, whistling some tune she didn't recognize, and got into a battered old truck. She waited until he'd pulled away and then focused. She set the bag of food on the roof of the car, followed by the coffee cup, which teetered slightly before settling. Hands free, she stared down at the car keys which were, in fact, mired in what was very clearly shit of some kind. She rifled through her bag, but there wasn't a tissue to be found. Okay, so she'd have to go inside to get one. She looked up as she stepped toward the door, only to find several people at booths watching what was unfolding outside. "God fucking damn people who can't mind their own business." No way would she go inside and listen to them titter at her behind their yokel hands.

So be it.

She reached down and plucked the keys from the shit pile and shoved the key into the lock. What cars didn't have automatic locks now? *Ones you rent in the middle of fucking nowhere.* She got in, threw her bag on the seat, and slammed the car into reverse, sending gravel flying. Coffee splattered over the windshield as the cup was launched off the roof, along with the bag of food she'd been looking forward to, even though it was deep fried and greasy. Gritting her teeth, she turned out of the parking lot and let the ruined breakfast land in the gravel.

Ten minutes down the road, she finally pulled over to start the GPS. She hadn't wanted to stop where people could still see her. As it was, her face probably matched the bottom of her shoes. "This fucking place," she muttered as she punched in the address from the attorney's paperwork.

Twenty minutes later, she pulled up at a gate just about fifty miles outside Louisville, Kentucky. A hinge was broken, and the gate sat almost forlorn, like it couldn't stay up under the weight of its abandonment issues any longer. "I know how you feel." She dug the key from the envelope and grimaced as the first hint of rain touched her skin. Her hair would become a frizzy nightmare if she didn't get inside soon. The sign reading Honeysuckle Bank turned over under her shoe, and it was missing a couple of letters. She managed to get the lock undone, though she couldn't imagine anyone wanting to get in who wouldn't just go over the gate, and wrestled it open enough for her to get the car through.

"Okay. It's fine. You can do this. You are worthy of success. You have what it takes to be powerful. You are a good person who deserves to have good people around you." She repeated the mantra from her self-awareness group therapy program and tried to believe it. She never had before, but maybe today would be the day.

The dense thicket of trees lining the driveway kept her from being able to see the house ahead, and when she finally did, she stopped to take it in.

It was pretty. *Really* pretty. And not in the shabby chic way either. A huge single pane of glass went from the ground floor to the second floor, highlighting the wide staircase in the middle. Large windows beside it on both floors would let in a wonderful amount of light. A covered, wraparound porch had some chairs on it that had clearly seen better days, and a vague feeling of being exactly where she was meant to be flittered through her mind, but she quickly shook it away. No time for that kind of sentimental nonsense.

She drove forward and parked in front of the two-car garage. The key for that was in the envelope too, but she wanted to get inside before the rain came and ruined her silk jacket, which hadn't been up to the cold wind at all, but it'd looked nice. She grabbed her small suitcase from the backseat and hurried up the stairs. The wind whipped at her hair, obscuring her vision so she tripped on the top step and stumbled forward, hitting her shoulder on the door just as the heel on her shoe snapped. "Fucking fuck this fucking place."

She got the door open and then slammed it behind her. It was like someone had thrown a blanket over the world, the silence was so complete. Sighing, she yanked off her shoes and threw them down next to her bag. First things first, she thought, and hunted out the thermostat. She hit the power button on the little white box on the wall, but nothing happened. She pressed another button, and then another, but nothing continued to happen. She rested her head against the wall. "I'm going to freeze to death in the middle of nowhere, and no one will care or even know until my body stinks up the place. *If* they can smell it over the cow shit."

She felt marginally better when her voice echoed back to her. She'd never really been one to talk to herself out loud, but it was better than the utter, intense feeling of isolation that assaulted her. She took out her phone and groaned. No reception. They could take pictures of galaxies a gazillion miles away in space, but they couldn't cover rural areas with phone signal.

Okay, so she'd look around, get a sense of the place, and then head back to the hotel in town. It hadn't been five-star, granted, but it had been clean, and she'd felt safe. It would do until she could get the heat on. Just as she was about to start up the stairs, there was a loud pounding on the door.

"Jesus H." She put her hand to her chest, her heart threatening to escape. She opened the door a crack. "Yes?"

"Hi, there. Amber, right? I'm Cornelius Atticus." At her blank stare, he said, "The lawyer who sent you all the paperwork and keys and such."

"Oh, yes." She opened the door wider. "Sorry, I didn't know you were coming."

His smile made his eyes crinkle deeply at the edges. "Hope you don't mind. I heard there was a visitor in town from the city, and I kinda figured it might be you, so I thought I'd pop in and see if everything was okay."

She motioned toward the thermostat. "There's no heat." The fact that he'd heard there was someone new in town made her stomach turn. How rare was it to see a new face here? Anonymity was a friend, and she didn't want to give that up.

He nodded and looked over her shoulder. "I can fix that right now."

She stepped aside to let him in and followed him into the kitchen, where he opened a cupboard and flipped a red switch.

She glanced over her shoulder to see the LED light flicker to life on the control panel. "That's great. Thanks." She bit her lip, unaccustomed to having to ask for information. But she never would have assumed that switch turned on the heat. "Anything else I should know? Is there hot water?"

He motioned. "Come on down. That can be a little trickier in this house. I warned Grant and Virginia that they'd need to replace that old boiler soon, but I don't think they ever got around to it."

As she followed him through a door and down some basement steps lit only by a single bulb hanging from a naked rafter, horror movie music played the theme tune to her inevitable and rather stupid death. She hung back by the stairs, watching warily as he went to a huge cannister looking thing and knelt on one knee beside it.

He opened a tiny door, grunted, and plunged his hand into his pocket. "Pilot is out. No surprise after all this time. It'll take a while for the water to heat up. Couple hours, maybe."

She huffed and glanced around, noticing the old-looking trunks and boxes stacked on tables and shelves against the walls. She'd have to deal with those at some point. She returned her attention to the lawyer. "A couple of hours for hot water? What is that thing?"

He laughed, and then sobered when he realized she wasn't kidding. "You've never seen a water heater?"

She shrugged, her jaw aching slightly as she clenched it around her words. "I live in a New York apartment. I use a light switch, and my lights come on. I turn on the hot water, and the water is hot. I've never needed to see where it comes from."

He nodded as though he understood, but there was a gleam in his eyes that also suggested he was trying not to laugh. "I can see how this would be a little befuddlin' then." He handed her the box of matches he'd used to ignite the pilot light. "Keep these. If it goes out, just turn that yellow knob, light the match, touch it to the metal bit inside, and close the door again."

She held the box of matches to her chest. "How will I know if it goes out?"

"Well, you won't have hot water, I suppose." He motioned toward the stairs. "You mind if I look around the house with you real quick? Just to make sure there isn't any damage or anything that needs fixin' before I leave."

There was no way on earth she'd tell him she'd be grateful for the company in the big, empty house. "If you must." She led the way up the cellar stairs, conscious of the fact that she was in her stockinged feet because she'd thrown off her heels. She probably looked ridiculous.

"Back here is the living room." He cut through the large, modern kitchen, past a dining table that looked like it had been made from an entire redwood tree, and into a huge open space. Another large window faced a forest beyond. The empty fireplace whistled until he reached in and pulled a lever.

She shivered at the trees now blowing wildly in the wind. "This looks like something out of a clichéd fairytale."

He laughed, and it echoed through the room. "It does at that. But in the spring and summer, it's the prettiest thing you'll see around here. Blossoms all over the grass right up to the tree line." He pressed a button and electronic shutters moved across the window, effectively blocking out the scene. "Grant and Virginia had this put in when they found it was too hard to draw the curtains across these big windows anymore. You'll find it that way in all the rooms."

Well, that was an unexpected touch. The house was far more modern than she'd thought it would be. Maybe it could be a good refuge after all. "Nice." She looked toward a white door pressed into a grass mound not far from the house. "What's that?"

He followed her line of sight. "That's your storm shelter. If you hear the tornado sirens go off, it's a good idea to hustle on in there. I spent more than one afternoon in there with your grandparents and my own family. We don't have a shelter at our place, so we hightail it over here."

There seemed to be an unasked question in there, like he wondered if she'd allow them that option. But he didn't ask, so she didn't answer. She didn't want to be locked underground with a group of people she didn't know. She followed him to a formal dining room, a cozy games room that had a massive TV and deep couches, and then upstairs to each of the four bedrooms. Every room was furnished and had shelves of things stacked every which way. A thick coat of dust covered the floor and showed tiny pawprints.

"Oh my God. Are there rats?" she asked, backing away.

He tilted his head and looked closer. "Nah. Those look like opossum. I'll get someone out to check the attic. Unless you want to do it now?" The look she gave him was enough to make him hold up his hands. "Right. Plenty of time for that later." He moved toward a corner of the master bedroom and stared at the ceiling. "You've got a leak. We'll need to get someone out."

The stain on the ceiling wasn't very big. Maybe two feet, if she had to guess. She was far more concerned about opossums playing roommate than a watermark on the ceiling. She followed him back downstairs.

"Did you want me to grab some wood for the fireplace until the house gets warm? I'd be happy to help."

She frowned at him and opened the front door. "I'm fairly certain that's not within an attorney's job description. But thank you for showing me around the house and getting the heat and water on."

He tipped his head and stepped onto the porch. "No problem at all. If you'll come by the office when you're ready, we'll finalize the paperwork and get it on the market if that's still what you want to do."

She looked beyond him at the desolate, gray sky and empty land that matched the feeling in her chest. "I think so. I'll be in soon."

He loped down the stairs to his truck. "Good luck!" he called and laughed as he jumped in and headed off down the driveway.

She closed the door behind her and looked at the house given to her by people she didn't know in a place she'd never been. Slowly, she slid to the floor beside her suitcase and broken heels, and with no one to judge her, no one to see, she let the tears fall. How had it come to this?

Chapter Two

"Pull!" Rowan Payton's muscles strained, and sweat dripped into her eyes, making them sting. "Nearly there! Pull!"

Slowly, the horse's front legs scrambled from the mud, the sucking of the muck around his belly barely audible over the swearing and heavy breathing of its rescuers. Ropes were drawn taut, and everyone stayed out of the way of the horse's tossing head and gnashing teeth. Once the belly was out, the hindquarters quickly followed.

"Fucking finally." Rowan dropped the rope and bent over, her hands on her knees as she gulped in air. The horse, exhausted from the struggle, also fell to his knees, head lowered.

"Can't thank you enough, Rowan."

She looked up at Fred Best, who'd called for help when his prize horse had gotten loose and then trapped himself in the lethal mudbanks of the swollen river. "You can thank me with some of that apple pie we had last week."

He slapped her on the back, and they watched as the vet coaxed the horse into the trailer. "I'll bring you twelve. You and your guys saved my hide."

"We saved the horse's hide." She finally straightened and stretched the spasm in her lower back. "Your hide is too tough to need saving."

He waved and jumped into the vet's truck.

She turned to her crew. "Nice job, everyone. Burgers at the barn tonight."

The team of eight made their way back to the various vehicles they'd come over in, and Rowan headed for her truck.

Kelly Marks, the local fire captain and her occasional fling, sauntered over. "Looks like you need a hot shower, cowboy." She leaned against Rowan's truck. "Want company?"

Rowan grinned and wiped mud from her face. "If you think you can get me clean before I get you dirty, you're on."

Kelly grinned and headed for her own truck. "See you there."

Ted, her ranch manager, waited by the passenger door. "Why do you look like you just came off some lesbian photoshoot, and I probably look like I've been dragged through a cornfield backwards? No woman around askin' me to shower with them." He ran his hand through his thick mop of gray-gold hair that was more than a little covered in mud.

"Because lesbians are supposed to be sweaty and muddy, I guess." She whistled softly. "It could have been a real tragedy if that horse had got sucked in. River will be rising any time now." She wasn't about to go into details about the fact that Kelly was a kind of pressure valve for Rowan and nothing more. A quick release without expectations was all she wanted or had time for.

He nodded and rested his head against the open window. "Fred couldn't take that kind of financial hit, that's for sure."

They were silent the rest of the way to the Willows, her family ranch and current home of the most well-respected racing horse stable in the country. The big white house with the navy blue trim came into view, and that sense of calm and rightness settled over her as it always did. Home was where her heart was, no doubt. The willow trees that lined the long driveway leading to the house, and which had given it the name, were blowing in the breeze, dancing as though welcoming her back. She'd never say that out loud, of course. They'd think she'd gone batshit soft.

"See you at the barn for dinner. I'll get the grill going now. I know how much you hate it when we run late." He waved and set off, brushing more mud from his hair. "Even though you're probably going to be late yourself."

She tossed her keys on the granite kitchen countertop and

braced herself as she opened the back door. A giant ball of fluff threw itself at her, paws on her shoulders and tongue ready to smear her face. "Hey, there. Missed me, didn't you?"

The 120-pound Newfoundland flopped at her feet and rolled, belly ready for love.

"Come on, Shift. Burgers in the barn tonight."

He shot up and ran to the front door, looking back at her as though telling her to hurry.

She laughed and headed upstairs instead. "Shower first. Then food."

Kelly was already in the shower, her long, strong body highlighted by the steam. "Took you long enough."

"Forgive me for keeping a lady waiting." Rowan stripped down and jumped in.

The sex was hard and fast. Kelly's long blond hair looked sexy as she threw her head back and moaned as Rowan fucked out the energy of the day. She was more muscular than Rowan was generally attracted to, but her femme side was strong enough to make up for it. Generally, Rowan liked her women on the soft, girlie side. But she was happy to oblige in the bedroom when Kelly came around. It wasn't like there were a ton of lesbians hanging around the town, after all. Kelly helped wash her down, but she knew full well that Rowan wasn't a receiver. At least, not for casual encounters like Kelly. When Rowan let someone touch her, she needed a connection. And that wasn't something she'd had in a long time and wasn't likely to have any time soon.

She put on a fresh white T-shirt, her comfiest ripped-up jeans, and her broken-in boots and felt like herself again.

Kelly, similarly dressed, gave her a quick kiss on the cheek. "Thanks for that," she said and grinned. "Let me know when you're up for another round." She whistled and gave a quick wave as she left.

Shift's big eyes followed Rowan around the room, tail occasionally wagging when he thought she was finally ready to head out. She squatted and gave his head a swift rub. "All right. She's gone, and it's just us, buddy. Let's go."

He darted from the room, his nails clipping along the hardwood floors as he raced to the front of the house. As soon as she opened the door, he was off, speeding toward the barn where the scent of cooking meat was already wafting through the air. She took her time following, as always noticing the state of the land around her. There were weeds in the potato patch, and the drainage in the reserve field looked like it couldn't cope with much more rain. The herd of Angus cows had been moved to the eastern pasture, but that too was wet as a sheepdog in a hurricane. Fortunately, the round pens for the racehorses remained in good condition, and since that was the primary reason for the Willows' existence, she was grateful for that small miracle. She made a mental note to get more sandbags when she headed to town again and remind everyone to be on the lookout for hoof rot.

The barn, named that solely because of the shape and not because it was used for animals, was full. Not just of her crew of twenty-six, but Fred's people were there celebrating too. Fred's wife, Rita, was busy cutting up a variety of pies. Clearly he'd passed the message on. Rita was known for having a stocked-up freezer of baked goods ready for any occasion from birth to death.

When she saw Rowan, she set down her pie cutter and came around the table. "Once again you've come through." She hugged her tight and placed a kiss on Rowan's cheek. "I don't know what we'd have done without you all these years." She cupped Rowan's cheek. "Your parents would be so proud."

Rowan's chest constricted, but she smiled. "Thanks, Rita. If it means you'll keep bringing us pie, I'll have to get your horses in trouble more often."

She snorted and headed back to the table. "Anything you need, you just ask, Rowan Payton. No reason to put anyone in danger over my baking."

Rowan nodded. "Yes, ma'am." She accepted a burger on a paper plate from Ted and took a seat next to Pam, one of her ranch managers. "All good?"

Pam took a big bite of her burger before answering. "All good. Vet says the horse is exhausted but will be fine. Was worried about leg injuries from the struggle, but there's nothing wrong." She looked sidelong at Rowan. "Cost us a day of harvest though."

Rowan sighed and continued to eat without answering. Each day they didn't get the field done was a day closer to the rain wiping it out. But there shouldn't be any emergencies tomorrow, and they'd manage it somehow.

She listened to the conversations going on around her, content to be in the background as everyone talked about the rescue, about farming, and teased each other about their shortcomings. The camaraderie was good, and spirits were high. It was a good way to head into winter. The thought made her glance at the old oak tree in the middle of the circular driveway. The leaves had gone from red to gold to brown, and now fell in silent loops to the ground. The tree was her guide to the seasons as well as to memories of her mom, who loved to sit in the swing attached to it.

"I'm heading to Power tonight." Pam stood and tapped some dirt off the tip of her boot. "Wanna go? Or did Kelly soothe the beast?"

Rowan thought about the shower and how disconnected she'd felt. "Yeah, I'll go."

Pam nodded and wandered off to chat to more talkative people, leaving Rowan to wonder who she'd meet at the only lesbian bar left in Louisville. She glanced at her watch. She had to be in the tractor seat by four in the morning, so it couldn't be a late night. Pam caught her eye and she motioned, and they left the gathering. No one said anything. She and Pam were friends, and it was well known they were both gay. And since neither of them had a partner, it made sense they went out together. No one had ever given Rowan any grief about it. And if they had, she'd have told them to find work elsewhere.

When they got to Power, the parking lot was already full of pickup trucks and a few regular cars. "Looking for anything in particular tonight?" Rowan asked as they got out of the truck.

"Girlie." Pam hitched her jeans up a little. "I want to tangle my hands in someone's long hair tonight."

Rowan made a noncommittal sound of approval. "Sounds right."

The band was already in full swing, and people were on the dance floor. Rowan breathed in the scent of women, all sorts, there to have a good time among people who knew the game. She smiled at more than one woman who'd given her the time of day at some point. A few had offered a second or third time around, but Rowan always let them know she wasn't looking for more than a bit of fun. The cowboy reputation still alive and well in Kentucky seemed to make that acceptable, so it was easy to find new partners without a lot of drama.

Pam slid a cold beer into her hand, tilted her hat, and grabbed the hand of a woman hovering nearby to lead her to the dance floor. Rowan laughed and shook her head. Trust Pam to be with someone within thirty seconds of them being inside. It wasn't long though before Rowan was leading a woman around the dance floor herself. But the woman was with friends and thanked her for the dance before heading back to her group. So much for an easy pickup.

She grabbed another beer and checked the time. Pam was nowhere to be seen, which meant she was probably out back in the alley or in the bathroom with her find of the night. She'd probably be ready to go soon. Rowan, tapping her foot to the beat, drank and perused the room. In the far corner, in the shadows, sat a woman alone. She couldn't have looked more out of place if she were a rooster among sheep. She looked stiff, one hand around a glass, the other flat on the table.

Intrigued, Rowan made her way through the crowd to the woman's table. "Hi there."

The woman looked Rowan over almost as though debating whether or not to answer. "Nope. I'm not looking for company. But thanks."

Rowan looked around. "Doesn't look like you have any company, so that's good." The woman's lips twitched a little, but the smile didn't fully appear. "But maybe you could use a friend?"

Once again, the woman looked like she was debating answering. Her red lips pursed, and her thick black lashes fluttered. "For a minute, I suppose."

"Rowan." She held out her hand, and the woman's return handshake was firm, her skin soft.

"And is this your normal hunting ground, Rowan?" She finally let go of her glass and motioned toward the bar.

"Well, as the only lesbian bar in a hundred-mile radius, it's the only hunting ground for a whole lot of women." Rowan wondered how soft that expensive-looking white blouse would be under her hands as she slowly pulled it from the woman's shoulders. "But I'm thinking this is ground you've never been on. What brings you to our little piece of heaven?"

The wry smile suggested the woman didn't see it that way. "Family business. I won't be here long, hopefully." She looked over Rowan's shoulder, her gaze shrewd and judging. "It's not really my crowd."

"And what is your kind of crowd?" Rowan sipped her beer and checked the time again. This wasn't going to be the woman to scratch the itch, that was certain. But it was a different kind of conversation to the one she was used to.

The woman stood, brushing off her skirt like she was trying to wipe away the stink of the bar. "The kind where there isn't sawdust on the floor or fiddles on stage." She tilted her head. "Nice to meet you. Thank you for being a *friend*."

Rowan tipped her hat and turned to watch as the woman moved fluidly through the room. Her classy outfit, complete with deadly looking high heels, made her shine like a diamond in a haystack. Rowan finished her drink, spotted Pam by the door, and headed out. At least she'd have good dreams tonight.

Chapter Three

"I'M TELLING YOU, ROWAN, she looked like she stepped from a ballroom into a slurry pit."

Rowan shook her head as she watched the horses loping around the ring. She leaned on the fence and tried not to notice the garlic on Cornelius's breath. "Can't believe Virginia and Grant left their place to family instead of making other arrangements."

He huffed, blowing another little cloud of garlic toward her. "I think Virginia always believed their kid would come around and come home. But after Virginia got sick, they quit talking about her at all."

Rowan hadn't ever heard the full story. Ranchers were a proud bunch, and when a story was too personal to share, everyone let it be and didn't get nosy. But they'd been kind people and decent ranchers until they got too old and sold off all the livestock, most of it to Rowan.

"Hey, boss." Ted came striding over, his hat pushed back off his face. "See the storm's edge?"

She turned and looked at the sky behind her. Sure enough, the line of clouds cut an edge between the blue above them and the black beyond. "Damn it all." She turned and gave a loud whistle, causing horses and riders to slow to a stop. "Get on in the barn and washed down." With a wave, she indicated the sky behind her, and the riders wheeled and headed out of the ring. It was only when she turned that she realized Cornelius was still beside her. "You come out just to gossip, Corn, or did you want something?"

He grinned and tapped his boot against the fence post. "Well, seein' as how you're neighbors, I thought it might be nice for you to drop on over and say hello."

She raised her eyebrow, waiting.

"Thing is, Rowan, she says she wants to sell. And that would be fine, except I don't think she really understands what she's got." Once again, he tapped his boot to the fence and averted his gaze.

"Corn, I've got a lot to do before the storm comes in. Spit it out."

He sighed and shoved his hat back on. "Jimmy Cartwright has been sniffing around. If it goes up for sale, there won't be anything I can do to stop that little shit."

"There it is. You want me to go flex my feminine wiles on her and get her to see the sense in keeping a ranch she won't know the first thing about. She didn't know what a water heater is, Corn. You think she's going to want to keep a 400-acre ranch?"

"Rowan, ain't no one ever accused you of having a feminine anything." He laughed just as the wind began to pick up. "But yeah, I want you to talk to her. Maybe she knows of a private buyer, and that might be better than selling to Jimmy. Hell, she won't know what she doesn't know, and maybe you can help with that."

She shook her head and pushed away from the fence. "I'll see if I have time. Let me get back to work."

He waved and half-jogged to his truck as rain started coming down in fat drops. Rowan jumped onto the quad and headed to the east pasture, where she helped the ranch hands drive the cows into the covered shelter area. Sheets of rain pelted the metal roof as she and the hands watched the field quickly develop puddles that turned into mini lakes.

"I thought the world was getting hotter, not wetter," one of the hands muttered as he pulled his jacket tighter.

She gave a quick nod and darted back to the quad. The ride back to the house was wet and muddy and full of swear words her mom would have kicked her ass for. Pam and Ted were sitting on her porch laughing as she ran up the stairs.

"You look like you got dragged behind a horse to get here." Pam squinted as though trying to see through the muck.

"Grab me a coffee, would you?" she said as she passed them on her way inside. "Then you can tell me why I'm paying you to sit on my porch."

When she came back down, the fire was lit, and Pam and Ted were lounging in the overstuffed chairs in front of it. A steaming mug of coffee sat in front of her favorite chair, and Shift's tail thumped a greeting from where he was splayed out in front of the fire. "Thanks."

Just as she was about to sit, her phone rang. She pulled it from her pocket and grimaced. "Corn—"

"Her roof fell in, Rowan." He sounded genuinely upset. "I saw a leak in the main bedroom, and it didn't look all that bad. But she just called in a panic saying there's water everywhere. I can't leave the girls at home in this storm, or I'd go out myself. You're the closest person to her."

Rowan sighed to the tips of her wool socks. "Yeah. Okay." She hung up before he could say anything else. She'd had enough of a description of the new owner earlier to know all she needed to. "Don't suppose you two want to go to Honeysuckle Bank and help a lady in distress?"

Ted shook his head emphatically. "I heard about her in town. Real high and mighty type, not a nice word to say to anyone. I say let the country rain wash some of the city off her."

Pam stretched her legs out in front of her. "I'm comfy. And you're more the knight in shining leather type anyway."

Rowan swore softly. "Feed my dog. And keep your phone handy in case I get stuck somewhere along the way." She grabbed her big canvas raincoat from beside the door on her way out. She drove slowly down the lane, watching the willows bend and flex in the now howling wind. Once she was out on the

main road, she took a left toward Honeysuckle Bank. The drive
was intense, and she had to skirt more than one tree branch as
well as a couple deer who darted in front of the truck and then
disappeared into the woods.

Honeysuckle Bank's long driveway, like hers, was lined by
trees. But these were old oaks, and one in particular looked like
it was leaning a little too far. She gunned past it and looked in
the rearview to see the bulge in the ground where the stump
was pulling away. "That's gonna be messy," she murmured as she
looked back at the house.

And promptly wished she'd brought backup.

A woman stood on the porch looking as angry as a hive of
bees poked by a bear. Arms crossed, she was also barefoot,
which looked especially strange given how cold it was. Rowan
climbed out and jogged up to the porch.

"It's about time." The woman turned and stomped inside. "The
lawyer said someone was coming to help, but he didn't say it
would take years for you to get here."

Rowan tilted her head and looked closer. "You're the woman
from the bar."

The woman froze and slowly turned to look at her. The now
familiar once-over made Rowan grin. At least she'd showered
and was wearing clean clothes. An hour ago, the woman
probably would have sent her packing and drowned in the house
instead.

"And you're not here to hit on me. You're here to fix my roof."

Rowan's grin slipped, and she leaned against the door. "I'm
not here for that. I'm here to see if you want to come to my place
up the road until the rain stops, and you can get back in your
house safely." She held up her hand when the woman looked like
she might pop a kidney. "What's your name, by the way?"

"Amber Archer." She practically bit out the reply. "And what
am I supposed to do about the fact that my house is flooding
while I'm over at Hot Cowboy Ranch?"

Rowan laughed and made a note of the name. "Well, with that description, I guess I can take a look inside." She took a step forward and raised her eyebrows when Amber backed up a step. "No need to be afraid. I'm a good guy."

Amber flushed a pretty pink and motioned toward the stairs. "It's the ceiling in the main bedroom."

Rowan walked past, making sure to get a little closer than necessary, and chuckled when Amber clearly fought not to step away. "Let's have a look."

The waterfall making its way down the stairs made it clear that Amber hadn't been exaggerating. Rowan splashed onto the upper level and looked into the bedroom. A jagged hole about four feet wide and two feet across was open right through the attic to the gray sky above, and a lake had formed on the bed beneath it. Thunder rattled the windows, and lightning flashed across the open space.

Rowan backed out and nearly knocked Amber over, who'd been standing just to her right. "Hate to say it, but there's nothing we can do right now. The storm is too strong to go up there, and if we close off the room, the water will sit in here and drip through the floorboards even worse than it's already going to. Better to let it make its way down the stairs. It's going to be a hell of a clean-up job."

"Thanks for that bit of country wisdom. I thought it was going to be simple." Amber spun and headed for the stairs.

"Hey now—" Rowan grabbed her arm just as she lost her footing on the slippery tiles and nearly went headlong.

"This fucking place." Amber wiped at her face. "Thanks." She tugged her arm out of Rowan's grip, grabbed the handrail, and slowly made her way down.

Rowan moved so she was going down ahead of her just in case she lost her footing again. "I could just carry you out to the truck if you want. Might be less dangerous."

"Try it, and you'll see I'm way more dangerous than a bit of fucking water."

Rowan tilted her head so Amber couldn't see her smile. The woman was a viper contained in five-foot-nothing of sexy fire. At the bottom, she waited as Amber grabbed a huge handbag, a small suitcase, and what looked like broken shoes.

"Lead on." Her words were hard, but the look in her eyes was water-soft, like she was seconds from crying.

"It's awfully muddy out there," Rowan said, looking at her bare feet. "Sure I can't give you a lift?"

Amber swallowed and raised her chin. "A little mud won't hurt, will it?" She looked out at Rowan's truck. "It isn't like that hasn't seen its fair share."

Rowan tugged the suitcase from Amber's hand. "All right then. Let's go before the roads get any worse."

She put Amber's case in the back and then opened the door for her. It took everything she had not to laugh as Amber's feet squished through the mud and the color in her face drained. Still, she held herself stiff as she climbed into the truck, her hair dripping wet, rain sliding down her face, and her feet cloaked in muck.

Rowan ran over and got in the driver's side. "We'll be at my farm in about ten minutes as long as there's nothing to clear on the road."

Amber gave no indication she'd heard. She just stared out the window. With no idea what else to say, Rowan headed down the lane. The tree she'd noticed earlier had tilted even farther, and the long arms of its branches were sweeping along the drive like a monster searching for a victim. "Hold on." She jerked the truck to the side and gunned it just as there came a violent cracking sound. The ground seemed to judder as the tree's roots gave way. It came crashing to the ground behind them, and one of the branches slammed into the tailgate.

Amber screamed and hid her face in her hands.

Heart racing, Rowan got the truck onto the main road and

forced herself to breathe. "Hey now." She lightly touched Amber's shoulder. "It's okay. We're all right. Just an old tree that decided it was time to stop fighting the storm, that's all."

Trembling, Amber lowered her hands from her face, and black smudges from her makeup showed the tracks of tears down her cheeks. "Thank you for coming for me," she said softly, wiping at her face with her jacket sleeves.

"No problem at all," Rowan said. "Welcome to Kentucky."

Chapter Four

AMBER COULDN'T HELP BUT wiggle her toes, the strange feel of mud between them something to focus on other than the state of her life right now. The wind outside mirrored the feeling inside her. She too wanted to howl and thrash and break things. Instead, she was on her way to a complete stranger's house, escaping from the death trap of a house that was her only connection to the world right now.

What a shitshow.

And to top it all off, she'd been rescued by the very cowboy she'd quite rudely turned down at the club while she was drowning her sorrows, and then spent the night dreaming about her anyway. Her mom would have called it karma. Her dad would have called it a weird coincidence and told her not to lose focus. She called it fucking irksome and inconvenient.

"You okay over there?" Rowan said, her hands firmly gripping the wheel and her eyes constantly in motion as she scanned the area around them. "There's a lot of sighing going on."

"Sorry. I've been told I do that without even realizing it." Amber wiggled her toes again, mud-slick but drying. "I was thinking about what a disaster this trip has been so far, and I've only been here for two days."

Rowan nodded. "Yeah, I can see how that would be. But I got to meet my new neighbor, and that's a plus." She shot Amber a quick smile.

That smile was *hot*. Volcanic, scorching, femme-melting hot. And those eyes made her think of the blue sky in summertime. She snorted at herself mentally. *Idiot. Who thinks like that?* "Great.

I'm with a crazy person who likes to meet their neighbors."

Rowan laughed, and it went straight to Amber's center. She shifted uncomfortably. Damn it. The last thing she needed was an attraction to someone right now.

"I'm guessing you don't talk to yours wherever it is you come from?"

"I can't imagine anything worse." Amber didn't miss the quirk in Rowan's eyebrow. "Why talk to people you don't know? Time is too valuable to be wasted on that kind of thing."

"Hmm. How do you get to know people if you don't talk to them?" She turned into a long driveway a lot like the one at Amber's new place, except the sign, The Willows, looked expensive, as did the open gate that wouldn't have looked out of place at a spa.

"The way normal people get to know other people. At a bar through friends, or at work. Or the gym, if it comes to that." She craned her neck to try to see the house. Rowan had said it was a farm, and she needed to know if she'd be sleeping in some kind of shack.

"Pretty small friendship circle." Rowan slowed when the tree line ended. "Just going to scan and make sure nothing is out of place."

Amber didn't respond. She was too busy being stunned at the beauty of the house in front of her. It was huge, with large windows, a big wraparound porch, and even in the rain, it looked like it might have been freshly painted the day before, so white did it look against the cloudy sky. The navy blue trim almost blended with the storm clouds. "That's gorgeous. And not at all what I thought a farmhouse would look like."

Rowan grinned as she pulled up in the driveway and hit the remote to the garage door. "Thank you. It belonged to my parents, and they really loved it. I keep it as nice as I can in honor of them."

That was more personal information than Amber knew what

to do with, so she didn't say anything at all. They got out and the garage door lowered behind them, muting the storm outside. Rowan pulled Amber's suitcase from the back and shook some of the rain from it. Amber stood there awkwardly, mud-caked toes raised from the cold cement floor.

"Right. Hold on a sec." Rowan set down the case and rummaged through a big blue container on the shelf. She held up a ragged old towel. "It's clean. Hop up on the tailgate, and you can clean your feet off."

Amber tried not to show her frustration. Sitting on a wet truck bed wasn't the worst part of the day, but it wasn't going to be the best either. She turned to lift herself onto it, but Rowan stopped her.

"Here. You're already wet through; no need to make it worse." She spread another towel on the truck bed.

Amber blinked back sudden and unexpected tears. "Right." More awkwardly than she would have liked, she lifted herself onto the truck bed that was higher up than it had seemed and took the towel from Rowan. The mud, mostly dry now, flaked off fairly easily, but the mud that had oozed through her stockings and between her toes was going to have to wait. Rowan, meanwhile, had begun to towel off her suitcase. She looked up and gave Amber that soul-melting smile.

"Ready to go on in? We'll get you set up in the guestroom and you can take a hot shower, if you want to."

Amber moaned. "That would be heavenly. I hate feeling this... grubby."

Once again, Rowan laughed. "Welcome to my world. I spend most of my days looking like something dragged up from the riverbed. Come on in." She held the door open, and Amber stepped past her, then followed her through an enormous, spotless kitchen that looked like something out of a cooking show and into a formal dining room. Beyond that was a large, cozy living room with two people and a dog sitting in front of a roaring fire. All three of them stood when they entered.

"Amber, this is Pam and Ted. They work and live here at the ranch. This is Amber, the new owner of Honeysuckle Bank."

The man came forward, his cowboy hat in hand. If she'd never seen a cowboy, she would know this was one just from the way he walked and the way he dressed. He kind of...ambled. Was that the word? She'd never seen anyone do it, but that's definitely what he was doing.

He held out his hand. "Nice to meet you. I knew Grant and Virginia well. Even worked for them every few years when they needed an extra body. They were good people. I'm sorry for your loss."

Amber shook his hand lightly. "No need to be sorry. I didn't know them." She glanced at the woman behind him. "Hi." She looked at Rowan. "Can I get that shower now?"

Rowan's expression was hard to read, but she shrugged. "Sure. Right this way."

She followed her up the stairs and tried harder than hard to keep from staring at the way the relaxed jeans hugged her hips and ass just right. People in New York would pay hundreds for that look, and Amber had a feeling Rowan simply wore her clothes that well.

Rowan opened a door and set Amber's case inside a large room. "Bathroom is right across the hall. Plenty of towels in the cupboard. Help yourself. I'm going to make some food, so if you're hungry, come on down and join me." She shoved her hands in her pockets and gave a slow nod. "Okay then."

Amber watched her head back down the stairs and then closed the bedroom door behind her. The bed was probably a king and would have taken up all the floor space in her New York loft. Here, there was still room for bedside tables, a big comfy-looking chair by the window, a full-length freestanding mirror, and even a dressing table. A beautiful painting of horses in a meadow hung over the bed.

She lifted her suitcase and placed it on the chair, not wanting to chance it getting the beautiful white bedding dirty, and opened it. She groaned.

Everything on top was wet. She pulled things out, dropped them to the floor, and found that the clothes in the middle were only a little damp. She could work with that. She pulled out a pair of True Religion jeans, a green Armani sweater she'd been told made her eyes stand out, and a pair of Tommy Hilfiger sneakers she'd bought in Paris when the ballet slides she'd worn had proved to be too thin for the Paris streets. Just because she was in the country didn't mean she needed to *look* country.

The shower was magnificent. Steam filled the room, and she leaned against the cool wall. Only then did she allow the day to really hit her. When she'd heard the cracking of the ceiling and seen the water cascading in, panic had been the only thing she could feel. Calling the lawyer had been something, at least. And he'd sent Rowan to get her, which had actually been really kind of them both. Rowan had driven out of her way to help a total stranger. Well, not a *total* stranger. Just one who'd blown her off the night before. She tapped her head against the tile wall. What was she going to do now?

The water began to cool. She took a deep breath and washed away the remnants of her makeup. Now, she was going to go downstairs and eat something. Then, she'd come up with a plan. She was good in a crisis, notwithstanding her reaction to the faulty roof, and good at planning. She could do this.

She wrapped the towel around her and gathered her clothes, then opened the door to head across to the bedroom. Rowan, her hand raised to knock on Amber's door, turned.

Amber very nearly dropped the clothes and towel and grabbed Rowan's hand to drag her to bed. The way she looked her over was how a woman dying of thirst might look at a glass of water. Rowan's jaw tightened, and she looked from Amber's feet to her eyes. Her hand flexed almost like she was going to reach for her.

Instead, she cleared her throat, looked away, and backed up a step. "Just wanted to tell you that dinner is ready. I thought maybe you'd fallen asleep, and I wanted to check before I ate without you."

Amber stepped closer, unable to help herself. The sight of a ruffled butch was always exciting. "I'd very much like to eat...with you." She allowed a breathy sound into her voice and tilted her head so her hair fell over her naked shoulder.

"Yup." Rowan backed away, gaze still averted. "Okay. Ready when you are. The food is, I mean. Ready." She turned and took the steps down two at a time.

Amber laughed softly and went into her room to change. Feeling human again, she headed down the beautiful woodgrain steps. The people who'd been in the living room were gone, but the dog was snoring away, belly turned to the fire.

"That's Shift." Rowan came in carrying two bowls of food. She handed one to Amber. "He's the best dog I've ever had. But he loves a good hug, so watch out if he gets excited." She looked Amber over as she sat down in one of the big, overstuffed chairs. "In fact, he might be taller than you when he stands on his hind legs."

Amber curled into the chair opposite Rowan. "I've never had a dog. But I like seeing them in the park when I go for my morning run." She sniffed the contents of the bowl. "Chili?"

"My mom's recipe." Rowan took a spoonful and murmured her appreciation. "Doesn't taste quite like hers, but it's close. Good for cold days."

Amber studied it and then winced slightly and set it on the table between them. "Thank you. I really don't mean to be rude, but I'm a vegetarian."

Rowan continued to eat, looking thoughtful. "I even put chicken and bacon on my salads. I'll go see what I have in the kitchen."

Amber shook her head. "Really, don't go to any trouble. If you have some bread, I'd be just as happy with toast."

Rowan shook her head and got up, still eating as she walked to the kitchen. "I can do toast, but it's not much of a meal."

She came back in shortly with another bowl of chili for herself and some toast on a plate for Amber.

"Thank you. I appreciate it." The bread was seeded, and the butter was saltier than she was used to. It was perfect after the day she'd had. They ate in silence for a while, nothing but the crackling of the fire and the snoring dog between them. Eventually, Rowan set her empty bowl down and stretched her legs out in front of her.

"So, Amber. Where do you come from?"

"New York. With the way people around here knew my grandparents, I thought you'd have known that." She smiled a little to take any sting from her words.

"Well, yeah. They said their kin was in New York. But that doesn't mean that's where you've come in from." She tilted her head. "Besides, it's better to hear things about people from the people themselves instead of from the rumor mill. What is it you do in New York?"

"I'm in finance. Stocks, that kind of thing." She didn't feel the need to go into the fact that she'd *been* in that field and was now somewhere outside it. Rowan wasn't that kind of friend. Yet.

"Numbers person." Rowan yawned behind her hand. "I do the numbers thing to run the ranch, but I couldn't do the kind of thing you do, where the numbers are theoretical instead of attached to actual things."

She would never admit it out loud, but Rowan's intelligent response surprised her. It wasn't correct, but it showed an understanding that most people didn't have even at that level. "Stocks are attached to things. Companies, usually."

Rowan rubbed at her eyes. "Of course. But my numbers are attached to things more immediately clear. Horses. Race winnings. Heads of cattle. Bales of hay. Things that are measured and sold at certain prices for specific reasons. Your math is bigger." She grinned and stood, running her hand through her short, dark hair. "Hope you don't mind, but I need to turn in. We get up early around here."

Amber, also exhausted from the trial of a day, stood as well. "I'm not much of a morning person."

Rowan motioned toward the kitchen. "I'll be long gone when you get up. Help yourself to coffee and more toast. I'll be back for lunch and if the rain has let up, we'll head back to your place to check out the damage."

Amber led the way up the stairs this time, and she would swear that she could feel Rowan's gaze on her ass. She put a tiny bit more sway into it, just in case. At her door, she stopped and put her hand on Rowan's arm. The muscle flexed under her hand and that flare of lust ran through her again. She shoved it away. "Thank you, again." She wanted to say more. She wanted to say she wasn't usually so bitchy, but that wouldn't be true, and why apologize for not coddling people?

Rowan's large, calloused hand covered hers. "You're very welcome." Her eyes moved to Amber's lips, and she stepped back, her hand sliding away. "Sleep well," she said, shoving her hands in her pockets.

Amber opened her door and gave her a final smile. "You too." She closed the door behind her and let out a whoosh of breath. Maybe this unexpected sojourn into middle America wasn't going to be such a bad thing after all.

Chapter Five

"YOU STAB THAT HAY any harder, it's going to take offense and stab you back." Pam leaned on her pitchfork and took a swig of water.

Rowan threw the pitchfork onto the mountain of freshly cut grass that would become silage after they wrapped it in plastic and let it sweat. "Being neighborly has its drawbacks."

Pam nodded sagely and threw Rowan a bottle of water. "I can see how having an impossibly hot woman of ice in your house would be a nuisance."

"She's the one who shot me down at the bar the other night. I told you about her on the way back." Rowan drank down half the bottle in a long swig. It was seven in the morning, but they'd been at it for hours. And this was only the third chore in a list as long as her arm.

Pam choked on her water. "That's one hell of a chance meeting. Least we know she bats for our team. That's one less thing to deal with when you put the moves on her again."

Rowan shook her head and started on the hay, this time with a little less vehemence. "Not a chance. She told me how she felt about this part of the world that night, and nothing I've seen since suggests she feels any different twenty-four hours later. And now that she might be a neighbor, I can't exactly bed down with her, can I? Say it was fun and then have to see her at the store or drive past her on the road all the time."

"I'm guessing she'd run you off it and not stop to check to see if you were dead or not." Pam started working beside her. "But damn, the nights could be something else."

"If I lived to see more than one." Rowan grinned. "She said

thank you. Seemed genuine enough. Still, though."

They worked in silence for another half hour, leaving Rowan to mull over what to do with her houseguest. Seeing her in the towel last night had nearly brought her to her knees. That auburn hair and those deep brown eyes that were as guarded as a stray dog's who hadn't been shown enough love had made Rowan want to wrap her in her arms and show her some of what she'd been missing.

Instead, she'd damn near run away like some teenager afraid of kissing a girl for the first time. Hell, she hadn't even run away back then, and she'd been kissing girls ever since. But not one like Amber. Not one filled with some of the Devil's own fire.

"Jackass."

Rowan looked up and saw Pam nod toward the ground. Rowan had been so lost in thought she'd driven her pitchfork into the ground once the hay was gone. "Houseguests," she muttered and hooked the tool into its space on the wall next to Pam's.

They left the hay barn together, and Pam waved toward the quad. "I'm going to go check on the stables. And I think you have a houseguest to attend to."

Rowan checked her watch. "She's probably not even awake yet. I'll come with you."

"Chickenshit."

She didn't reply as they headed toward the stables. Two trucks were parked out front, and Rowan sighed. "Fantastic. The Jessops are here."

Pam slowed the quad. "Want to pretend like there's an emergency somewhere else and skip this?"

Rowan shook her head. "Nah. Mom always said lies like that brought on worse things later. I'll deal with them, and it'll put me in the right frame of mind to deal with Amber after."

Pam chuckled. "All kinds of ice floating around the property today. Better you than me."

"Thanks a lot." Rowan left the quad and headed inside. The

three Jessops were standing outside a stall having an animated conversation. When the youngest Jessop saw her, she raised her hands.

"Finally. Rowan, tell my parents they don't have to come see me ride all the time. It's not like I can't handle Flying Fury on my own." Jessica Jessop flung her long blond braid over her shoulder and stood with her hands on her hips, a pose Rowan was familiar with.

"Rowan. Please inform Jessica that Flying Fury is a prize racehorse, and no matter who is riding him, we want to be here to see it," Mrs. Jessop said without looking at Rowan.

She looked at Mr. Jessop, who shrugged and gave a little shake of his head but didn't say anything. He tried not to when they were like this because then they ganged up on him as well as each other. She gave him a quick, sympathetic smile and moved to stand between mother and daughter. If there was one thing Rowan was good at, it was controlling the situations around her. "Jess, no teenager in the history of teenagers has wanted their parents around all the time. That said, you ride their horse, you have to deal with them watching. You want to have privacy, get a hobby that doesn't include something that they pay for." She saw the wind go out of Jess's entitled sails, and then she turned to Mrs. Jessop. "And ma'am, you know full well Jess is one of the best riders in Kentucky and would never do anything to hurt that horse. And no one here would allow it either."

Mrs. Jessop let out some air and lost about an inch of anger-height. "Of course I know that. It's the reason we board Fury here."

"Good. Jess, why don't you get on with getting Fury ready to head into the ring while I talk to your parents about the season? You're doing group canter today." Rowan opened the stable door, ushered Jess in, and gave her a quick wink as she slipped inside. She turned to the parents. "Let's head into the office."

They dutifully followed her down the long row of stables to the small office she kept at the end. It wasn't lavish, which kept folks from getting too comfortable, and that was the way she liked it. If she used the big office in the main building people tended to think she had more time than she did. They sat in the stiff-backed chairs across from her desk.

Mrs. Jessop glanced around the office. "We could pay to have this redone so it isn't so...basic," she said, a small curl to her lip. "Or we could meet in that gorgeous office you have in the reception building. I don't know why you'd want to keep it this way."

"Thank you for the offer, but that won't be necessary. I got a message from the trainer that you wanted to talk about the schedule." Rowan folded her hands on the desk and waited. She knew what was coming. It was always the same with people who'd bought their first racehorse and had no earthly idea what it meant to have one or what to expect. They all thought they knew best though.

"I read an article that said this is the best food for a racehorse. All the winners from Cheltenham use it." She handed over an advertisement for a food that promised "real results."

Rowan glanced at it. "That's subpar feed, Mrs. Jessop. It contains nitrogen rates that are far too high and way too little calcium. I'm willing to bet the article was written by someone invested in the sales of the food. You said you brought Fury here because you know we're the best racing yard in Kentucky. That means you need to trust us to know what we're doing."

From the pink in her cheeks and the set of her jaw, it was quickly clear that no one had basically told Mrs. Jessop to butt out of their business in her entire existence on planet earth. Mr. Jessop's smile slowly spread across his lined face like a tide coming in.

"Now. As the trainer told you," Rowan continued before Mrs. Jessop could launch into some kind of entitled whirlwind of misinformation-spreading, "we're introducing Fury to the other horses, and she's learning how to group canter. She'll get a few weeks off at Christmas, and then come January, her real training will begin. That's when the jockey you've chosen will begin working with her in earnest. And that's when we'll start to see what she's really got under the hood. Until then, there isn't a whole lot for you to do around here but watch and admire." She stood and held out her hand. "I trust that answers your questions?"

Mr. Jessop stood and shook her hand a little more enthusiastically than usual. "Completely. Thank you, Rowan. We trust you implicitly, and we'll stay out of your way."

Mrs. Jessop was slower to stand, and her expression suggested she wasn't nearly as trusting as her husband. "Thank you. I'll let you know when we have more to discuss."

Rowan gave a little wave as they left and then dropped into her chair, only to stand up again. There was no time to rest. She took the keys to the quad from the hook on the wall outside and headed toward the house to deal with her next issue. When she opened the door, she stopped to listen. Shift was nowhere to be seen, but she could hear music coming from somewhere in the house. Feeling ridiculous when she realized she was creeping around in case Amber was still half-dressed, she called out. "Anyone here?" And that felt even weirder, given that she lived alone.

Amber came to the top of the stairs, Shift standing beside her, his tail waving wildly. "Hey, honey, you're home."

Damn it all, why did that make Rowan's knees go weak? She'd definitely been living alone for too long. But two could play that game. "Thought I'd see what the wife was making for dinner."

Amber made a gagging sound. "You win. And if you saw my cooking, you'd know how extra gross that statement was." She came down the stairs barefoot. "Although I may have to steal your dog when I leave. He's the best listener I've ever known."

Rowan gave Shift a quick head rub as he went past, heading toward the kitchen. "Did you have breakfast?"

Amber stopped in front of her and had to tilt her head slightly to meet Rowan's gaze. "Two pieces of that really good toast and a cup of way too-strong coffee. Thanks."

"I've got some time right now if you want to check out your place. I called Corn on my way up to tell him to meet us there."

A flicker of disappointment seemed to pass over Amber's face but it was gone so fast, it was hard to tell. "Perfect. Let me get my stuff."

"About that." Rowan forced herself to say the words that her mom would have told her to say, despite her misgivings. "Your place may not be habitable for a while. Or at least, not tonight. You might want to stay here again until we get someone to at least cover that hole properly."

The way Amber's gaze swept over her told her in no uncertain terms it was a bad idea.

"Thank you. But I wouldn't dream of taking advantage of your kindness. I'll stay at the hotel in town." She waved. "Although, this is nearly as nice as a hotel in New York."

Relief warred with flattened desire, and Rowan hoped neither one showed on her face. "Well, the offer is there if you need it."

For a moment, it looked like Amber was going to say something, and then her expression shuttered, and she gave a quick smile. "Thanks. Be right back." She headed upstairs and disappeared down the hall.

Shift came and sat next to her and whined softly.

"Yeah, boy. I know." What she knew, she wasn't sure. But she kind of wanted to whine like that too.

Within minutes, Amber was coming down the stairs, and Rowan leapt up to take the suitcase from her. But Amber held on.

"I'm not some damsel from a tower who can't carry her own bags," she said, her tone covered in steel. "No need for old school chivalry here."

Rowan let go. "Understood." The ice she'd seen earlier had appeared as quickly as it had gone, and the chill was a good way to dampen the lust. She turned away and headed out to the truck, trying not to grimace as Amber clearly had trouble swinging the suitcase over the side, given her height to truck bed ratio. It finally landed though, and she didn't look at Rowan as she climbed into the passenger seat, clearly a little flustered.

She backed out and waved at Jess as they passed the ring.

"Beautiful horse," Amber said. "Is it special? I noticed when I was looking out the window this morning that there seemed to be a lot of them around."

"We're what's called a racing yard. Aside from all the normal ranch stuff, like cattle, we board racehorses. That one there is Flying Fury. She's young and not quite ready for the track, but I think she's got a good chance with the right trainer and jockey."

"That isn't her jockey riding her now?" Amber asked, looking back over her shoulder as they moved out of view.

"No, that's the daughter of the owners. Jess is a good kid. Raised with money, you know, so she's got that stereotypical bratty thing going on, but she's really good with the horses, which says more about her than the way she behaves with people. But her parents..." Rowan gave a low whistle. "I've seen plenty like them come through here, and they don't give Jess a lot of room to breathe. I know paying a half mil for a racehorse makes them think they can act however they want—"

"A half-million dollars? For a horse?" Amber blinked, her eyes wide. "Are you serious?"

"They can go for a lot more than that depending on breed." Rowan grinned. "Different kind of math than you're used to, isn't it?"

Amber tilted her head and looked out the window. "The only horses I've ever been close to are the ones the cops ride in the city. And they're pretty, but I bet they weren't that expensive. And that explains why your *farm* looks nicer than a lot of places I've been to in New York."

"Yeah, well, we take our horses seriously down here."

Somehow, it didn't feel like a compliment. She turned onto Amber's lane and grimaced at the tree blocking their way. "We'll have to walk from here. I'll call someone to come out and take this apart for you. It'll make good firewood once it's dried out."

They got out, and Amber hesitated. "Should I get my case?"

"Maybe hold off until we've seen the house. Then I can come get it for you if you're going to stay." Rowan grinned. "Or you can come back and get it yourself. Either way."

To her relief, Amber smiled back at her, and then they made their way around the huge fallen oak and toward the house. When it came into view, Rowan winced. "Damn."

It looked far worse in the light of day. Even more of the roof had caved in overnight, leaving wood beams exposed like a ribcage, showing the rooms beneath.

"Good thing I was going to sell it anyway, I guess," Amber said quietly as she stared at the house, her arms wrapped around herself.

"Come on. Let's see what the inside looks like." Rowan didn't have the heart to get into a conversation about selling or keeping what now looked like a disaster site. Before they could go in, there was a shout from behind them.

"Wait up!" Cornelius shouted as he exited the tree line. "I'm coming!"

"Cornelius the cornball," Amber muttered and turned away to unlock the door.

"Hey now. He's a good man." Rowan frowned at her. "He didn't need to concern himself with you when you called, you know."

Amber rolled her eyes. "I'm aware. And I said thank you already. He's just so...country."

"And what about me?" Rowan said, leaning against the porch post. "Is that how you see me?"

Amber turned back, her eyes flashing. "Why shouldn't I? You run a farm with cows and horses on it. You drive a beat-up old pickup truck. Everyone around here wears an actual cowboy hat and not even ironically. You're crazy fucking hot, but yeah, you're clearly very country."

Rowan nodded, any attraction she'd felt smothered under Amber's superior attitude. "Well, I think I'd rather be that than the kind of city you are." She turned away from her and smiled at Corn. "Thanks for coming out."

He nodded and wiped a bead of sweat from his brow. "No problem at all. Figure between the two of us we'll know the right people to get the work done, whatever it needs." He gave Amber a kind smile. "Must have been scary last night."

She gave him a tight, brief smile. "It was, yes. Thank you for calling Rowan to come to my rescue." She turned and went inside.

Corn looked confused, but Rowan just shook her head and followed Amber in. "Let's just get this done."

The three of them walked through the house, and Corn made notes on his phone about the nature of the water damage. Between them, they figured out who might be free to do the work. Amber was strangely quiet throughout, and by the time they made it back to the front door, Rowan wondered if she'd had some kind of meltdown that had trapped her sharp tongue.

"We won't presume to make any calls or decisions. Do you want to call the people we've talked about and keep us out of it, so you have total control?" Rowan asked. She kept her tone as neutral as possible, but Amber's attitude had pushed her buttons.

Amber's eyes were glassy, and she quickly looked away. "I know when someone has more connections and a better way forward than I do. I'd appreciate you making the arrangements, thank you. But if you could give them my number so I can talk about the cost of repairs and such that would be good."

Rowan nodded and headed down the stairs. "Corn, can you take Amber into town? No way she'll get that rental car around the tree. She's staying at the hotel. I'll leave her case next to your car."

"Uh, sure, Rowan. No problem."

She'd have to answer his questions at some point but right now, she just wanted to get away from the city girl who made her feel way too many things in too short a time. This was exactly the kind of drama she wanted to avoid. But as she glanced back and saw Amber standing there with her hands in her pockets, head bowed, she swore at her desire to turn back.

Chapter Six

"IT'S A NIGHTMARE." AMBER perched on the edge of the bed. "The hotel I stayed in before would have been fine. But it was booked for something called the Sleepy Hollow Hot Brown fest, which sounds horrifying, and that meant I had to check into a motel on the outskirts. The roaches may very well be bigger than New York rats."

"And we know how much you love both of those things." Craig yawned loudly. "But your tales of Midwestern woe are dull. If I were among a bunch of cowboys, I'd go full-on *Brokeback Mountain*."

"Why are we even friends?" Amber shuddered as a roach scurried along the opposite floorboard. "Working together for fifteen years doesn't create friendship."

"Because we're both bitchy, and we both like nice clothes." He took a slurp of something. "And now I have to drink my rhubarb gin martinis on my own because you hightailed it out of here with your tail between your legs."

Amber winced and pulled her knees to her chest. "Bitchy is definitely not a good look around here. People are so nice. I don't know how to handle myself. I'm not making a good impression, that's for sure."

"Ooh. Who were you trying to get to see you as something more than a New York elitist with a heart of ice?" He gave a mock gasp. "Have you met some burly cowboy lesbian who's going to make you go full rom-com?"

Amber yelped when a roach scurried over the tip of her shoe and started up the side of the bed. She leapt off it and grabbed her bag, which she'd set just inside the door. "I can't do this. I'll sleep in the rental car if I have to."

"For fuck's sake, babe. Come home. You can deal with the repairs and all that tedious shit from here while you look for another job." He took a noisy drink again. "Or go groveling back to the boss. You know how he loves a good grovel." He hesitated. "I mean, you could try. Or maybe give it some time before you step into his glorified presence again."

Amber stood outside in the mild humidity, the sun bright and the sky a beautiful blue. Funny how little she noticed the sky back home. But then, it was pretty much blocked out by buildings most of the time. She looked around and groaned. "I forgot that my rental car is stuck at the property. Why are things going from shit to shitty?"

He laughed. "Just wait till they hit shittiest. Then maybe they'll start to get better." There was a slight pause. "Seriously, babe. Come home. You shouldn't be alone during all this."

Every once in a while, they let their sarcastic façades slip, and his genuine concern brought tears to her eyes. "Thanks, Craig. I just... I don't know where home is right now." She looked at the pitted gravel parking lot, the sign with its missing letters in Motel, making it just tel, and swallowed against the urge to let the tears fall. "I need to figure some stuff out, and I can't do that there. A total change of scenery will help."

He sighed softly. "Well, it sounds like you've got the change of scenery all right. Call me if you really need me, and I'll come out. Okay?"

"I will. Thanks. Right now, I'm going to call around to find somewhere to stay." She hung up and then stood there, numbly cradling her phone against her chest. After the way she and Rowan had parted, she had no doubt there was no refuge on that front. Cornelius might know of a place, though. Maybe an Airbnb she hadn't come across or something.

She hit dial and pasted on a smile, hoping it might sound real in her voice. "Hi, Cornelius? It's Amber. I was wondering—"

"Hey there! How can I help, Amber? Everything okay at the hotel?"

She moved a little further from the peeling paint of the room door. "Actually, after you dropped me off and I went to check in, they told me it was full and called a cab to take me to the motel."

"Ugh. Say no more, miss. That should have been torn down and used for scrap years ago."

"Do you have any idea where else might be available?"

There was silence for a moment. "Well, you could get another rental car and head back to Louisville. This time of year there are a lot of harvest type festivals going on, but there are plenty of hotels there. It would be a bit of a trek back and forth until the house is ready, but at least there you'd have all your city comforts."

"Fantastic idea. Where can I get a rental car?"

He hesitated again. "Well, Louisville is the closest place to rent one."

She took a deep, steadying breath. This man was her only connection to human contact or what passed as civilization here. "So, to get a rental car to get back to Louisville, I need to go to Louisville."

"Yeah. Doesn't really sound like an idea, does it?" He laughed. "You could get a taxi or Uber back, but it would cost a good amount." He left the comment open, as though waiting to see if she was the kind to pay a ton of money for convenience.

"Well, it doesn't sound like I have a choice, does it?" The smile was gone, and her tone reverted back to the snappish one she never liked to hear coming out of her.

"I wouldn't say that." He cleared his throat slightly. "Rowan has plenty of extra rooms and isn't far from your place. I don't know what happened to set her off on the wrong boot, but she's never been one to hold a grudge."

Amber held the phone away from her and groaned before coming back on. "There are no rental places? No cabins, or cottages, or whatever they have here?"

"There are a couple, but they've probably been booked up for the festival this weekend. People come from all around."

She waited, but he seemed to have said all he was going to say. "Christ. Fine. Can you call Rowan for me?"

He chuckled. "How about I text you her number, and you can ask her yourself? Seems better not to be the middleman between two women who could both kick my butt right outta Kentucky."

She hung up and waited and when the number came in, she put her thumb over it to call but couldn't bring herself to do it. Throughout the night, she'd gone over not only what she'd said, but also how she'd said it. And shame flooded her from her toes to her perfectly dyed hair. What had she been thinking, saying that kind of thing out loud? It was one thing to think it, but how incredibly arrogant she must have sounded. Grovel it is, she thought, and hit the number.

"Rowan."

The sound of Rowan's voice made her shiver. Husky and low, she could imagine her saying perfectly dirty things in her ear. "Um, hi. This is Amber."

"Uh huh. What can I do for you?"

Fucking hell. This was far harder than she thought it would be. "Well, I'm at this motel, and Cornelius said there's nowhere else to stay, but you might have space for me..."

It sounded like Rowan was a little breathless, and she didn't respond for what felt like an eternity.

"You're at the motel?" She grunted and swore softly. "Sorry. Got my hands full at the moment. Yeah. You can come back and stay here if it doesn't offend your city girl sensibilities too much. There's a diner about fifty yards to your left. Head on over there, and me or one of my crew will come pick you up soon as we can get free."

Amber deserved the jab, and the relief she felt at being able to go back to Rowan's clean, beautiful home outweighed her desire to argue. "Thank you, Rowan. I really appreciate it. I'll be at the diner."

"Yup." Rowan hung up.

Amber rolled her bag behind her, trying to avoid puddles with rainbow oil slicks for the sake of both her luggage and her shoes, and opened the door to the diner. Her stomach rumbled loudly at the smell of bacon and maple syrup that was probably part of the upholstery. She hadn't eaten meat in years, but the smell of bacon still made her salivate.

"Have a seat anywhere. Be right with you." A woman with a tightly coiled bun, sensible white shoes, and a red and white checked shirt walked by with two plates full of pancakes.

Amber made her way to a booth at the very end so she could sit with her back to the wall and still be able to see the parking lot. She put her case on the opposite seat and rested her head against the booth. She tried to shut out the catastrophe that was her life.

"Looks like you need coffee." The waitress put a ceramic mug down and raised her eyebrows.

"Latte with almond milk," Amber said.

The waitress held up a pot. "Just coffee, darlin'."

"Of course." Amber took the menu and tried not to grimace at the sticky feel. "The pancakes you just served looked really good. No bacon though."

"You got it." She took the menu back. "Anyone joining you?" Her expression suggested people dressed like Amber, with a suitcase in tow, weren't the norm.

"I'm waiting for a ride. Rowan said she'd be here soon."

The waitress's smile widened. "Well, any friend of Rowan's is a friend of ours. She held a fundraiser for us a couple years ago when it looked like we might lose this place. Kept us going and then some." She tilted her head, her smile slipping a little. "Didn't know she had friends from out of state."

"Oh no, we're not friends." Amber rolled her eyes. "I mean, we just met. I've come down to deal with a property left to me by my grandparents, and Rowan has been nice enough to help me out." No need to tell the waitress that she'd insulted her multiple times already as well.

Understanding lit the waitress's eyes. "Hold on. Let me get your order in." She did as she said, then made a quick round of the few other occupied tables before she came back to Amber, who watched her the whole time, marveling at how easily she spoke to everyone and how she remembered everything they asked for. Had her own life ever been that smooth?

"Now." She pushed Amber's case farther along the booth and perched on the edge of the seat. "You're the new owner of Honeysuckle. Is that what you're saying?" When Amber nodded, she continued. "Your grandparents were fine people. Always in the middle of helping others, doing what they could for the community, making sure folks knew they mattered. Real fine. Shame about what happened with your ma."

Amber swallowed the sudden ball of emotion in her throat. "Yeah. Shame."

"You plan on doing anything with the land?" she asked. "I'm Fran, by the way. Don't mean to be nosy..." She laughed and smacked the table. "That's a downright lie. We're all nosy neighbors around here."

Amber gave her a weak smile. "I'm not sure about the house yet. The storm did a lot of damage. Cornelius and Rowan are helping me find people to fix it." It wasn't much of an answer, but she wasn't about to go into detail with someone who'd probably tell the people at the next table over everything she'd said.

Fran looked up as another couple walked in. "Well, if you need any food delivered to the workers or such, you just say the word, and we'll get it done." She squeezed Amber's hand. "When you've got family from around here, you're welcome to become one of us, you know." She shot off and greeted the other people, quickly asking about their kids.

Amber stopped listening and shook her head as she scrolled through her phone. Become one of them? God forbid. The thought of living in a place where everyone knew who you were related to, who was bonking who, and who didn't go to church last week was stifling all on its own. The actuality might kill her.

Fran slid the pancakes in front of her along with a huge bottle of maple syrup then topped up her coffee. "Enjoy. I'll come back and keep you company soon as everyone is settled."

Amber didn't get the chance to say that wasn't necessary, as Fran was off and serving again. The pancakes were fluffy and hot. She winced as she touched the maple syrup and used a napkin to pick it up, which stuck to it when she set it back down.

"Getting syrup on your fingers is one of the best parts." Rowan slid into the booth opposite her and set Amber's case beside the table. "Adds to the taste when you lick them clean after."

Amber continued to chew, grateful that she needn't respond to something that provocative. She set down her fork and cleared her throat. "I'm sorry. I didn't know you'd get here so fast. We can go."

Rowan held up her hand and settled back against the seat. "I may as well eat while we're here. The pancake recipe is a family treasure they don't let go of. Go on and eat. Mine will be here in a second."

Amber picked up her fork again, glad she didn't have to leave the excellent breakfast behind. "It sounded like you were busy when I called. Something bad?" It wouldn't hurt to seem interested in Rowan's affairs if they were going to get along.

"Nah. Just a horse being stubborn while getting its hooves trimmed. But one kicks you in the head, and you're going to know it." Rowan gave her a lopsided grin. "It's better my staff don't get kicked in the head."

"Are you involved in everything there? I mean, you're the owner, right? Don't you have people to take care of all the grunt work?" There it was again, that sound in her voice that was going to make her an absolute pariah here. She'd have to work on it.

"There's no grunt work on the farm, just work that has to get done." She smiled at Fran when she set down the plate with an extra high stack of pancakes along with a bowl of chopped pecans and strawberries.

"Mine didn't look like that," Amber said, looking at her nearly empty plate.

"That's 'cos I'm special." Rowan winked and dug into her food.

Somehow, Amber had a feeling that was true, but she'd damn well never say it out loud. "Rowan, I'm sorry about yesterday. I was an absolute asshat, and while I'd like to say that isn't my style, it totally is. But I'll try to rein it in while I'm here." Maybe it wasn't much of an apology, but she'd never been very good at them.

Rowan nodded and continued to eat as she looked at Amber thoughtfully. "You never got to know your grandparents, did you?"

Surprised at the change of subject, Amber shook her head. "No. Honestly? My mom told me they were dead. It was only when I got the papers from Cornelius that I found out it wasn't true." She hesitated. "Fran said they were good people."

"Mm." Rowan swirled a strawberry through the syrup and brought it to her lips. Her tongue darted out to catch a drip.

Amber nearly fainted.

Rowan grinned like she knew exactly what she was doing and ate the strawberry. "They were real good people. That's a hell of a thing to tell a child though. Do you know what they did at Honeysuckle?"

"No idea," Amber said, her voice less steady than she'd like. "But the land isn't covered by anything with hooves." She thought back to her first time inside. "Cornelius said something about a garden, I think?"

Rowan sighed happily and pushed her empty plate away, then winked at Fran when she came over and quickly refilled her coffee before heading off again. "They did have cattle. Big herds.

Some sheep too. Even a couple of ostriches for a while. They're mean buggers though. Nearly took off your grandfather's hand once. He got ten stitches in his thumb." She held up her hand and wiggled it.

"So what happened?" Amber found herself interested despite the story being about animals and yard work.

"They got too old to do it." Rowan shrugged. "Happens eventually. Farming is hard work. Physical labor that takes it all out of you some days. And although they had people to do the grunt work," she gave Amber that half grin, "they didn't like not being able to chip in. Eventually they sold off all the animals and turned to gardening. Like everything they did though, they didn't mess around. They grew enough food to take to the shelter in the next town over and for the people around here who could use some extra."

Amber frowned and played with her fork. They sounded like the epitome of good people. Not *her* people though. She wouldn't know what to talk to those people about, related to her or not. Neither, apparently, did her mother.

"Well, I better get back." Rowan stood and looked down at Amber's case. "Want me to grab that? Just a bit easier for me to reach the truck bed, that's all."

Amber appreciated the clarification. "That would be great. Thank you." Why did it feel like the words stuck in her teeth like shreds of toothpick?

Rowan threw some money on the table, and Amber dug in her bag for her wallet.

"Nope. Consider this your welcome to town breakfast." Fran pulled Amber into a tight hug. "Welcome home."

Amber couldn't do anything but give her a baffled smile and then followed Rowan to the truck. She looked over at Rowan when they got in, and Rowan laughed.

"You look like a cat faced by a racoon." She started the truck and headed away from the diner.

"I'm...I'm not used to being hugged." How weird did that sound?

Rowan gave her the side-eye. "As in by strangers? Or at all?"

"Who goes around hugging people all the time? God, please tell me you don't do that." Amber grimaced at the thought of having to hug more strangers. It didn't matter that for a nanosecond, it had felt nice.

"I hug everyone. All my ranch hands. My dog. The horses. Hugs, hugs, hugs." Rowan tapped her fingers on the steering wheel to the beat of the country song playing.

"You're making fun of me." Amber crossed her arms and stared out the passenger window.

Rowan didn't respond, and Amber assumed she was right. Okay, maybe she deserved it. She laughed softly. "I'm looking forward to hugging your dog again."

"Shift gives the best hugs." Rowan's tone was warm, the way it had been when they'd first met. "Amber, I'm sorry this is such a trial for you."

She looked over, once again surprised. "How can you say that when I've been such a bitch?"

Rowan winced. "That's a bit harsh, don't you think? You're under a lot of stress, and you're in a new place where you don't understand a lot of the customs. That's bound to make anyone a little cranky. Specially after your house melted around you."

Stunned at Rowan's generosity of spirit, Amber crossed her arms a little tighter and looked away. How did you even respond to that kind of...nice? She blinked back the unwelcome tears. She'd just ignore it until she could get back to the world that didn't care about her at all.

Chapter Seven

ROWAN PUNCHED HER PILLOW. Again. She flipped over to face the wall, then flipped back the other way. *Damn it all.*

She got up, slipped on her thick robe and slippers, and headed downstairs. With Amber across the hall, there was no escaping thoughts of her, even in sleep. Shift groaned and jumped off the bed to follow, letting her know he wasn't happy about the disturbance to his sleep. "You and me both, buddy." She ruffled his head and got another groan in response.

She warmed a mug of water in the microwave and slipped a tea bag in. Cold seeped in above her slippers, and she turned to light the fire.

"Fuck me backwards into next year!" She jerked, her hand to her chest. "You're a stealthy one."

Amber held up her hands, her eyes wide. "Sorry! Sorry. I didn't mean to scare you. I couldn't sleep and thought I'd get some water." Her gaze drifted downward and stopped at Rowan's slippers for a long moment before she began to laugh. She looked up. "Really?"

Rowan did her best to look offended. "You have a problem with my ducks?" She lifted one bright yellow slipper and shook the duck's orange beak at her. "I'll have you know they're the height of fashion here in Kentucky. On every runway. I might even wear them to the Derby."

Amber's hand was over her mouth, and her eyes were alight with genuine mirth. "I mean...I guess that makes sense. But I pictured you as more of a barefoot kind of cowboy. Or maybe those slide on things with plaid on them."

Rowan clucked and turned to get a mug out for Amber. She repeated the warming process, added a bit of honey to both mugs, and handed one over, all the while making note of the fact that Amber had been conjuring up mental images of her. "Despite your lack of taste, I'm going to invite you to drink tea by the fire." She set her mug down, started a fire, then settled on the couch. Shift jumped up and covered her feet, his muzzle resting on the duck's beak.

Amber curled up in the armchair. She was small enough to fit on it sideways with her knees pulled to her chest. She sipped the tea. "This is nice. What is it?"

"It's actually a blend your grandmother made for me. Lemongrass, spearmint, and green tea. Helps you sleep. Helps a stomachache, too." Rowan took a sip of her own, trying not to look at the way Amber cradled the mug and the way her lips touched the porcelain. "Want to talk about what was keeping you up?"

Amber stared at the fire as she drank her tea, and Rowan let her think about the question. She'd answer if she wanted to. But people were also entitled to keep their private thoughts private.

"Do you know what happened between my mom and my grandparents?" she finally asked, her voice quiet. She didn't look away from the fire.

It wasn't a surprising question, but they were finally being nice to each other, and Rowan didn't want to spoil it. But she wasn't one to run from the truth. "You want the polite answer or the real one?"

Amber's gaze flicked to her before it returned to the fire. "Do I seem like the polite type to you?"

Rowan chuckled. "Well then." She took a sip of her tea as she considered where to begin. "Your mom. What did she do when she got to New York? For work, I mean?"

Amber frowned. "She married my father. She didn't work in the traditional sense. I mean, she had me to look after, sometimes, but mostly I had a nanny while she did charity things and floated around the art world. Why?"

"Your grandparents never said anything about why the rift came about. But it was well known around here that she...well, she didn't take to farm work."

The sound Amber made was somewhere between a cough and a laugh. "No. I can't imagine she did."

Rowan nodded. So far, so good. "She liked dating. A lot. She didn't settle on any one guy, and your grandparents weren't always happy about that. She stopped going to church too, and that caused all kinds of gossip. I think sometimes your grandparents were embarrassed by her behavior."

Amber finally looked at her. "Because she dated a lot? That sounds awfully nineteen-fifties."

"It wasn't just that. My mom said yours was drinking, causing fights, running with a bad crowd. And she was always above this town. Said she'd get out and never look back. Sounds like she was mean as a viper stepped on by a horse." Rowan studied Amber's face, trying to see beyond the mask. But she couldn't. She settled back to watch the fire, content to let Amber ponder.

"And that's what she did." Amber sighed and set down her mug. "Was your mom a friend of hers?"

"I'm not sure your mom had many friends around here." Rowan hated how that sounded. "I'm sorry."

"Doesn't sound like she deserved any. And I don't think much has changed." Amber stood. "Thank you for telling me. I think that tea is working. Good night."

Rowan nodded and listened as Amber's soft footsteps moved up the stairs. Shift looked over the couch, then settled once Amber's door shut. Was Rowan right to have shared that information? It wasn't like it was a secret, and better Amber hear it from someone who cared. She snorted. Did she care? Why should she? Amber had been an ungrateful pain in the ass.

But Rowan had seen the tears well up in her eyes earlier. Had someone being nice to her been such a rare thing? That would be an awful way to live. "Come on, boy."

Shift jumped down and led the way upstairs. This time when Rowan fell into bed, sleep came quickly, though not without dreams of small, delicate hands and full, sweet lips.

***

Rowan walked the course with the jumping manager, Quin, measuring and triple-checking the jumps for height and stability. They were all set low to get the horses used to them, but they could still cause an injury if they weren't set up correctly. As they finished, Quin dusted off her hat on her leg and pulled it on again over her long, wavy hair.

"I hear you've got a houseguest." She checked something off on her clipboard.

"Of course you did." Rowan rolled her eyes. "It's been less than twenty-four hours. How could you not have heard?"

Quin shrugged. "Hear she's pretty too."

"Yeah? What else have you heard?" Rowan leaned against the fence. Quin wasn't one to be rushed, but she also didn't normally gossip.

"I hear she's uppity, not so different from her mama." She hooked her arms over the fence rail and looked at the course. "I hear she's having some trouble over at Honeysuckle, and there's someone real interested in taking it off her hands now that it's a mess."

There it was. "Who?"

"Same slimy toad who came here two years ago."

Rowan nodded, knowing who she meant. Jimmy was the one Corn had been worried about. "Have you heard about him making contact?"

Quin shook her head but didn't say anything more.

Rowan pushed away from the fence. "Thanks. Let me know

how the jump session goes, and if you hear anything more about our swamp-dwelling friend, give me a shout." Rowan walked off, thinking. She pulled out her phone. "Hey, Corn," she said when he answered.

"Well now, it's about an hour past when I thought you'd call." He laughed, making her pull the phone away from her ear.

"Yeah, well, you did send her my way. Again." She couldn't decide just how irritated she was or should be about that. "But that's not why I'm calling. I hear Jimmy is in town sniffing around Honeysuckle."

"Not surprising. I warned you." His tone grew solemn. "He wants that land real bad, Rowan. You had a chance to talk to Amber about it yet?"

"You mean between her telling me I'm too country and then calling me for a rescue from the motel? Not quite yet." She waved at a farmhand passing by. "I'm worried she'll get his offer and take it so she doesn't have to deal with the repair work."

"I can see why she would." He sighed. "Be a damn shame though."

"I'll see if I can talk to her at dinner. Maybe she'll see it our way." Even as she said it, she had a feeling that wasn't likely.

"Good luck. I've got a list of names for the repairs to run by you. Want me to come out today?"

Rowan strolled past the main reception building and nodded at the kids flowing off the school bus for their tour. "No. Give me another day. Come out for breakfast tomorrow morning. Maybe swing by Fran's and pick up some of those cinnamon rolls on your way."

He chuckled. "You got it."

Rowan spent the next two hours on paperwork, doing what she could not to get distracted by thoughts of Amber. Just when she'd decided it was time for lunch, Pam came in and leaned against the doorjamb.

"Firepits tonight?" she asked, her thumbs hooked in her belt.

Rowan frowned, feeling like she'd missed something, and then rolled her eyes. "Shit. The festival."

Pam quirked an eyebrow. "You forgot? When there's pumpkins lining every inch of the visitor area and enough scarecrows I'm beginning to think I'm a crow. I get so damn jumpy when they catch me out at night."

"Sorry. A lot on my mind." She stood and stretched the kink in her back. She caught Pam looking at her critically. "I've told you before you're not my type."

Pam snorted. "Like I'd ever ask. Aside from your body, I couldn't deal with your control issues."

Before Rowan could ask what she was thinking, a shadow appeared behind Pam and then Amber's head poked in the doorway beside her.

"Hey. They said I'd find you here." She smiled and looked between Rowan and Pam. "Am I interrupting?"

Pam tipped her hat back and shifted so she was still leaning against the doorjamb but was facing Amber. "No, ma'am. You're more than welcome. I'm Pam, the reason Rowan's place works like a well-ridden mare." She grinned and put out her hand.

Amber took it, her face turning a cute shade of pink. "If I'd known she kept this type of company, I would have come back sooner."

"Pam, don't you have work to do?" Rowan shot her a warning glance, which Pam barely saw because she didn't look away from Amber for more than a millisecond.

"I was tryin'. I asked about tonight, remember?" She still hadn't let go of Amber's hand and was stroking her knuckles with her thumb.

"What's going on tonight?" Amber asked, looking at Rowan and gently extracting her hand from Pam's.

Rowan finally let out a breath and wondered why she wanted to break every bone in Pam's hand. *Idiot*. "The reason you couldn't get a room at the hotel. The harvest festival starts tonight. It's tradition for us to go as a crew. We start here, carving pumpkins around the firepits, and then we take them down to be judged in the contest tomorrow."

Amber laughed. "Wow. How..." she trailed off when Rowan raised her eyebrows, "quaint. I'd love to see it. Can I come along?"

Before Rowan could answer, Pam jumped in. "The more the merrier. It will be good for you to get to know our little town. I'd be happy to show you around." She gave Rowan a wicked smile. "And you'll see why I win the pumpkin-carving contest every year."

"You win because you're always doing the judge, whoever she might be." Rowan came around the desk and stepped forward enough to make Pam move out of the way. "I was just coming to the house to have lunch. Interested?"

Amber nodded. "I'm famished."

Rowan motioned toward the house. "Go on ahead. I have to straighten a few things out here for tonight, and then I'll be up."

Amber bit her lip and looked down the row of horses. "I was hoping to get a tour. This place is gorgeous. When you said you had a farm, I thought it would be some rustic thing with cows." She looked down the row of immaculate stables, beautifully painted. "But this is something else entirely."

Pam started to speak, and Rowan pressed her bootheel into Pam's toes. "Why don't we do that before we start the party tonight?"

"Perfect." Amber smiled at Pam, a different kind of smile than the one she'd been giving Rowan. "I'll hold you to the promise to show me around tonight."

Pam grunted as Rowan pressed her heel down. "Can't wait."

Amber strode off through the stables, and Rowan and Pam watched her go. It wasn't until she was out of sight that Pam pushed Rowan off her toes. "Asshole."

Rowan turned to look at her. "Me? What about you? She's not some bar hook-up. She's the new owner of the Honeysuckle, and we definitely don't want her mad at either of us because we didn't call the next morning." She pointed in the general direction of town. "We both know how well that goes over around here."

Pam held up her hands. "Right. Okay, I hear you. And it's not my fault Becky May fell so hard for me that she had to leave town to heal her broken heart." She backed away, her hands still raised. "Know what I was going to say before that little bit of fire came over?" She waved one hand at Rowan's body. "I was going to ask why you're wearing your good belt and best jeans. Now I know." She turned around. "I'll get the firepits started early so we can get to the fair on time. I have a tour to give," she called over her shoulder and laughed loud enough to make the nearest horse snort.

"Jackass." Rowan gathered her paperwork and set off to the house, checking stalls and chatting with a few people as she went. When she got to the house, Amber was sitting on the porch, wrapped in a blanket, with Shift laying at her feet. Rowan climbed the stairs, trying to ignore the illogical feeling that said this was what happy could look like. "You seem comfy."

"I am. Thanks." She tugged on the blanket. "I hope this is okay. I wanted some fresh air, but it's chilly."

Rowan nodded. "You want to stay out here while I make us something?"

Amber stood and wrapped the blanket around her. Shift headed inside after stopping for a head rub. "No, I'll come keep you company, if that's okay?"

Rowan wanted to say it was more than okay, that she wanted Amber's company and hadn't stopped thinking about her. Instead, she led the way to the kitchen. "You like grilled cheese?"

Amber blinked. "You mean melted cheese in fried bread? I love it, but I haven't had it in about seven years. Not since my mom mentioned that my jeans looked tight. She said anything over a size four was too big for someone my height." She grimaced. "I haven't seen her in a long time because she'll be disappointed I haven't been that size for a while now."

Rowan stopped pulling things from the fridge and looked at her. "Your jeans would look just right no matter what." When Amber rolled her eyes, Rowan shook her head and went back to what she was doing. "No one should be judged as worthy of family relations by the size clothing they wear."

"Tell all of New York that." Amber watched as she spread butter on the bread and then cut thick wedges of cheese to put between them. "I'm already salivating."

Rowan liked the sound of that. "Well, you don't want to fill up too much today. Your mom ever talk about a hot brown?"

Amber blanched. "She never talked about where she was from. The only reason I knew she was from Kentucky at all was because I saw her birth certificate one day. But whatever it is, they couldn't come up with a better name for it?"

Rowan laughed. "When you grow up with it, you don't really think about it, but I get your point." She pressed the spatula against the bread, making it sizzle in the pan. "It's a hot sandwich like this but with turkey, tomato, Mornay sauce, cheese, and bacon. It's broiled all together and then topped with pecorino cheese, parsley, and paprika."

"That's...wow. That's a lot." Her eyes widened slightly when Rowan sprinkled parmesan cheese on the bread and then flipped it. "You just added more cheese."

Rowan shook her head. "You're clearly missing out on the good things in life." She flipped the sandwich onto a plate and handed it over. "Try it."

Amber pulled a piece off and eyed the string of melted cheese. She stuck out her tongue and captured it, then pulled it into her mouth.

Rowan leaned against the counter and tried not to stop breathing.

"Mmm." Amber closed her eyes and chewed. "That's amazing," she said after she swallowed. "Good thing I'm a vegetarian and can't eat your disgusting-sounding sandwich at the fair tonight."

"Your loss." Rowan took a big bite of her own sandwich and swore when it burned her mouth. "Tonight is mostly about dessert anyway. Tomorrow, you can get a hot brown for dinner over there. They make a vegetarian version, but I have no idea what's in it."

They ate in easy silence for a few minutes before Amber set her sandwich down and took a sip of the iced tea Rowan had poured her. "So, what's Pam's deal? I take it she's single?"

Rowan choked on her food and pounded her chest. After a long swig of tea, she nodded. "Yup. She's single."

"And clearly a lesbian. And yet..." Amber leaned forward, her crossed arms on the countertop pushing up her cleavage. "And yet, you don't want her asking me out. Why is that?"

"What makes you think that?" Rowan wasn't a good liar. She was shit at two things: poker and telling women she felt things she didn't. And obviously Amber was more intuitive than she let on.

"The fact that you crushed her toes before she could properly ask me out and the fact that you sent her a death glare when she was clearly coming on to me." Amber grinned and wiggled her eyebrows. "So? What is it?"

How the hell was she supposed to answer that? She wasn't even sure about the answer herself. Not the whole answer anyway. What she'd said to Pam was true, but she'd only come up with it in the moment as a way to explain her behavior. But there was more to it. She just didn't want to dig into what that pile of manure might be hiding. "I..." She stopped and blew out a breath. "Pam is good people. We went to school together. We came out together. We go out together." She tilted her head. "She was with me the night I met you at the club."

"She was?" Amber frowned, looking thoughtful. "I don't remember seeing her. And she's pretty memorable."

Rowan tried not to let that splinter get under her skin. "That's because she was out back with someone getting an itch scratched." Why did it feel like she was throwing Pam under the bus by saying so? It was true, after all. But she could hear the way it sounded.

Amber shrugged. "Isn't that one of the reasons we go to clubs? Why should that keep me from dating her?"

"Isn't a reason. You just said you hadn't seen her. That's all." Rowan's shoulders ached with tension, and she rolled her neck. "You can date whoever you want. It would just be a shame if it went bad and you didn't come around here anymore because it got awkward. Good neighbors are important, and you don't want to mess with that." It was another partial truth, but it would do.

Amber's gaze was searching. "Sure. That makes sense." She slid down off her stool and set her plate in the sink. Then she turned and moved into Rowan's personal space. "But just so you know, if there's another option on the table, I probably wouldn't turn it down." Her gaze slipped to Rowan's mouth, and her hand trailed over Rowan's forearm.

"Yup." Rowan backed up so fast she knocked the cutting board to the floor and then tipped the stool over when she went to pick it up. "Yup. Good to know. But for now, there's lots going on, and we need to get your house up and ready, and I've got to keep this place running like clockwork."

Amber's laugh stopped her rambling. "Wow. The women in New York would eat you alive." She smiled, and this time the seductive look was gone. "I'm messing with you. I'm not interested in dating anyone. I'm not even interested in just sex right now. You're right; I've got way too much on my plate. More than you know. But you're adorable when you're flustered."

Rowan rested her head on her forearms on the counter. "Well. Now that I know you're going to kill me, at least I can prepare."

Amber patted her shoulder. "I'll try to make it a fun way to go. For now, I've got some things to do on my computer. What time should I be ready for tonight?" She bit her lip. "Actually...I don't think I have anything to wear. And since the rental car is still stuck at the house..." She sighed, her shoulders falling. "I'll work it out."

"Hold on." Rowan pulled out her phone. "Hey, it's Rowan. No, no, Fury is fine. I have a weird favor to ask. A friend of mine needs a lift over to the mall to get some threads for the harvest festival, but she doesn't have a car right now. Would you mind—" She held the phone away from her ear at the response. "Great. I'll let her know." She shook her head and put her phone back in her pocket.

"You got me a chaperone?" Amber looked a little bemused. "I've never gotten in a car with so many strangers before. You couldn't take the time away?"

"She's a client actually. The one you saw riding the other day. Jess will help you get set up. Better than I could anyway."

Amber's eyes darkened a little. "Somehow, I doubt that." She backed up, and her expression eased. "Thank you. Really." She turned and ran up the stairs. "See you soon."

Rowan washed the lunch dishes and looked down at Shift. "We're in trouble."

Chapter Eight

AMBER TURNED SIDEWAYS AND admired the way the skinny jeans fit. Jessica had been a lot of fun to hang out with and would have been a massive hit in New York. Amber had even invited her to come visit when she was finally out of here and back home. She'd been a little disappointed to find out that no one really wore cowboy hats and cowboy boots to the festival. Here, those really were mostly for work around the farms or ranches. She'd seen a lot of baseball hats, although there was no way on earth she'd be caught dead in one. What was the point in spending two hundred dollars getting your hair done if you were just going to pull it into a ponytail and hide it under a hat? No thanks.

But the black, long-sleeve T-shirt with the compass logo had spoken to her, along with the puffer vest that hugged her curves just right. Paired with the calf-high black boots with a three-inch block heel, she felt a little more like she could fit in. Jessica had been so sweet and full of light and laughter, making Amber feel a bit old and more than a bit jaded. When she'd relaxed after realizing that Jess wasn't going to judge her like some socialite, they'd actually had a lot of fun.

"Hey, Amber?" Rowan called from downstairs. "I'm heading over to the barn if you want to come along."

Amber put her hand on her stomach and took a deep breath. She'd asked herself several times throughout the day why she doing this. Why get to know these people at all? Why bother going to festivals and dinners? She wasn't going to be here very long and would never see them again.

She sat on the edge of the bed. Was that true though? Who

knew when she'd get back to New York. Or anywhere other than here, for that matter. She blinked back tears when she heard Rowan's footsteps on the stairs. She dabbed at her eyes, pasted on a smile, and opened the door. "I'm coming. Just wanted to make sure I looked country enough to fit in." She grinned, hoping to take some sting out of it, though it was also kind of true.

Rowan looked her over, and her jaw clenched before she looked away. "Yup. You look...right." She turned and waved for Amber to come with her. "Others will be waiting on us."

Somewhat deflated at Rowan's response, Amber shrugged and closed the door behind her. "If you show up a little late, it gives you the opportunity to make an entrance. And you're the boss. Surely they don't expect you to be on time."

They stopped at the front door, and Rowan held open the soft new ankle-length jacket Amber had also bought today. She slipped her arms in and fluffed her hair so that it hit Rowan's face.

"Being on time shows respect." Rowan slid into a brown leather jacket that looked supple and soft. "My time is no more important than theirs just because my name is on the deed. Sounds like none of your parties ever get started on time if everyone is trying to make an entrance. I like things to be punctual and steady. I like knowing people can count on me to keep my word and be right there beside them."

They started off toward the barn. Amber wasn't sure what to say. It was true, parties *rarely* started on time, and everyone *did* want to get noticed. "It's just the way things are, I guess."

"Same here." Rowan shot her a quick smile. "Just the way it is."

Amber stopped and stared. "That's a barn?" The three-story building was a beautiful deep red with white trim and enormous open doors, where she could see firepits glowing in a long line between rows of tables in the dim light, as well as a kitchen at the back.

Rowan looked at it critically. "Well, it's what we call the barn. It was one, once upon a time. Then we converted it into a small restaurant, but it's mostly the staff who use it now that the main restaurant for the clients has been built. The few staff we have who live on site have places around the back, and they hang out often. And we use the barn for get-togethers like this one."

Amber followed her inside and took in the wood-paneled walls, the slate flooring, and the big chandelier hanging from the center of the room. In the city, it would have been too kitsch to be tolerated but here, it was just right.

"'Bout time." Pam waved from her place in front of the barbecue. "Ribs or steak?"

Amber grimaced. "Salad? Fruit?"

Rowan squeezed her shoulder and then headed off to talk to other people, and Amber felt like she'd been left alone at the ball.

Pam motioned with the spatula. "Well, there's pumpkin in the pie, and that's a fruit. There's potato salad over there, but I have a feeling that isn't what you were hoping for."

"Not really, no." Amber took in the table full of food. "If I eat any of this, I won't fit into my jeans tomorrow."

"Guess we'll just have to make sure you don't have to wear them." Pam winked and then laughed when Amber raised her eyebrows. "Just sayin' it would be an option."

"I think I'll pass on food now so I can have something at the festival." On any other day, in any other place, she'd have been on Pam's offer like an heiress on a diamond necklace. But her life was complicated enough, and Rowan's obvious discomfort with the idea made her extra hesitant. The miniscule connections she was making here were the only ones she had in life. She didn't want to mess that up.

Pam shrugged. "You're missing out, and it's not like we couldn't put some meat on your city-girl bones."

The words had barbs that Pam couldn't possibly know about, but Amber felt them all the same. "Yeah. Maybe." She looked around for someone else to talk to.

"We could take that tour right now if you wanted to." Pam set down the spatula and wiped her hands on a dishtowel beside the barbecue.

"Could we do it tomorrow? I'm a little tired from a long day, and I think I'd like to just stick around here." Amber gave Pam her best fake apology smile and fluttered her lashes, hoping to keep her from getting frosty.

"Sure, no problem." Pam turned away and fixed herself a plate of food. "Come on. I'll introduce to some of the others."

Surprised at the easy flow of her response, Amber's shoulders relaxed a little. They sat at a long table that could probably have fit twenty people, and Pam did just as she said she would. There was plenty of banter and talk about family, and Amber found she was content to listen instead of being the focus of attention for once. The last thing she wanted to do was talk about the grandparents she'd thought dead all this time. After a little while, she got up to get herself another glass of water.

"Going okay?" Rowan asked as she walked up beside her.

"It is." Amber took a sip of water and looked at Rowan over the glass. In the house, she hadn't taken the time to really look at her. Now, in the dancing firelight, Amber looked her over. Without her hat, her short hair was styled so it swept forward on one side, a piece falling over her forehead. Her shirt, a dark blue plaid, was buttoned to the second button, showing a black T-shirt beneath. An eagle belt buckle caught the firelight and drew Amber's gaze lower, to thick, muscular-looking thighs in relaxed jeans, with simple black boots.

Rowan cleared her throat, and Amber slowly lifted her gaze.

"Given our conversation earlier, that's a mighty unfair way to look at a woman." Rowan's voice was raspy, her tone low.

"I'm not dead, just not available. Looking is allowed." Amber's knees went weak when she met Rowan's dark gaze.

"Looking like that could lead to more than looking." Rowan stepped back, and her expression changed completely as she looked over Amber's shoulder. "Is it time?"

Rowan's ranch manager, Ted, slung his arm around Amber's shoulders. "It's time. You ready for the ride of your life?" he asked Amber.

Her gaze flicked over Rowan. *That would be the ride of my life.* "Sure am."

Rowan shook her head, blew out a big breath, and turned. "Hey, everyone. Time to head out. Remember your blankets and gloves."

"Blankets?" Amber frowned. "What for?"

Ted turned her gently toward the back of the barn, where everyone else was filtering out a rear door. "Come see."

Amber looked over her shoulder at Rowan, who stood watching them go with her hands stuffed in her pockets, her expression unreadable. "Are you coming?"

Rowan nodded slowly. "Right behind you."

Amber turned back and stopped abruptly when they exited the rear door. "Seriously?"

"Deadly serious. This is our tradition, and now that you're here, you're part of it. Up you go." Ted tapped his hand on the step stool.

"Ookay." Amber climbed onto the step stool and accepted someone's hand as she stepped onto the bed of the truck. Pam grabbed her waist and steadied her as she made her way between bales of hay and took a seat beside her. "We're going on an actual hay ride."

Pam twirled a piece of hay in front of her. "Three trucks. Two for everyone involved with the ranch, one for all the pumpkins we're entering into the contest."

Amber had forgotten the pumpkin carving. "I thought you were doing that tonight."

"We did it a little earlier today. While you were out shopping, I think." Pam nudged Amber's boot with her own. "Nice choice."

Amber felt the heat rise to her cheeks. At least *someone* had noticed. "Thank you."

"Believe me, I should be thanking you." Pam reached behind her and pulled a thick blanket forward. "You're going to want this. The ride isn't long, but it's cold."

Any other time, any other place. Instead of sharing it, Amber tucked it around her legs, leaving no room for confusion about whether or not Pam's hands were welcome to wander under the blanket.

The truck rumbled to life, and Rowan jumped up and took the seat opposite them. "Let's go!" she called out, and all three trucks began to move.

Amber didn't miss the quick look she gave Pam, who seemed to give an innocent one back. Soon though, sexual tension took a backseat to laughter and teasing as trucks from another farm joined theirs, creating a convoy of music and mirth.

"Fred's farm didn't start doing the hay rides until we did, and now it's a rivalry to see who has the most people and how many pumpkins we're bringing to the festival." Rowan's shoe touched Amber's, and she grabbed her hand to steady her when the truck hit a pothole. "We win every year, but it's all done in fun anyway."

Emotions were difficult things, in Amber's opinion. They often didn't make sense, so holding onto the ones that did was something she'd become good at. Sarcasm, snark, and a sense of superiority got her through most days. This...this was something else. Sure, she could sit there and make rude remarks, or at least think them, but it was hard to do in the face of people having such a good time and seeming genuinely happy.

It wasn't long before the sounds of the festival rose above the rumble of the trucks and the laughter around them, and she was strangely disappointed it was already over. People piled off, and Rowan jumped down and turned. She held up her hands, her eyebrows raised in question, and Amber smiled and nodded. Rowan put her hands around Amber's waist and lifted her down easily.

"Thank you," Amber said, looking up into Rowan's eyes.

"Uh huh," Rowan said, barely seeming to breathe.

"You guys need to move that little scene, or I'm not gonna get my pumpkin into the judging section," Pam said, nudging Rowan's shoulder with her knee.

"You mean you're going to miss your chance to woo this year's judge," Rowan said, letting go of Amber's waist and stepping away.

Pam jumped down and placed a sudden kiss on Amber's cheek before backing away from the truck with a cheeky grin. "For luck!" she said, then turned and jogged off to the other truck where people were unloading their pumpkins.

"Jackass," Rowan muttered.

"So," Amber said, turning and trying not to show that the kiss had disconcerted her, "show me what a hay ride leads to."

Rowan laughed and waved the way forward. "My pleasure."

The rest of the night was a whirlwind of new things. She watched Rowan toss rings around bottles like an expert, watched her shoot water into a clown's mouth like a novice, and then watched her throw a baseball at a metal plate until it dropped the poor sap in a box into a pool of water, for which she was awarded a giant dinosaur with googly eyes and a goofy smile. She presented it to Amber with a bow. "Consider it your first gift from the Willows."

Amber hugged the stupid thing to her and tried to blink away the inexplicable tears.

"Now." Rowan pointed to another booth. "It's your turn. If you can toss anything other than your hair, that is."

Amber pushed the dinosaur into Rowan's chest. "You doubt me?"

Rowan shrugged slightly. "I mean, I doubt you need a whole lot of eye-hand coordination in the city."

Amber picked up the five darts. "Have you ever tried to cross a Manhattan city street while drinking coffee? Or tried to read during rush hour on the subway while wearing four-inch heels?"

She threw the darts in quick succession, popping all five balloons in seconds. The carnival guy rang a bell and offered her a choice of stuffed animals. She pointed and then traded Rowan the cute dog for her dinosaur. "If you squint, it looks a little like Shift."

Rowan held it out, looking a little bemused. "I'm usually the one who gives, not the one who gets."

Amber couldn't help it. "Is that so?" she asked, her lips quirked and eyebrow raised.

Rowan looked around. "I need to sit."

"Wimp." Amber laughed. "Didn't you tell me about some dessert I had to try?"

Rowan rubbed her hand over her face and tapped Amber on the head with the stuffed dog. "Yes, I did. Come on." She led the way past other stalls where people were trying to win things they wouldn't have wanted to buy in a store and past more food stalls with long lines to the very end, where three stalls were set up by one company. "Kentucky bourbon pie is something that'll make you sad you weren't born and raised here."

Rowan smiled and chatted with the people around them as they waited, and Amber simply watched, taking it all in. People glanced at her, included her in tidbits of conversation, but otherwise, she was just another person in the crowd. It was an odd feeling. She didn't like being part of the background normally. She wanted to be noticed, because being noticed meant you were someone, and when you were someone, you could climb the ladder, just the way she had. When no one noticed you...what was the point of existing?

"Hey," Rowan said softly, touching her elbow. "You okay?"

Amber smiled. "Fine."

"I wanted to know if you wanted me to order for you or if you want to choose." Rowan's gaze was searching, like she knew Amber wasn't quite okay.

Amber looked over the menu. The pie was the main thing, but the toppings list was daunting. "Dazzle me."

Rowan grinned and ordered. They moved to the pick-up area, and she looked over. "Really. Are you okay? Is all this just too weird for you?" She motioned as though to take in the whole festival. Their number was called, and she held up her finger. "Hold that thought." She grabbed their tray and then led the way to an empty table away from the crowd. They sat, and she set a dessert in front of each of them. "Now. You were saying."

"I wasn't saying, actually." Amber poked her spoon at what looked like a sugar coma in a bowl. "Tell me what this is again?"

"Pecan pie, basically. But with chocolate chips and bourbon. I've got vanilla ice cream on mine, and you have coffee ice cream on yours. I've noticed how much you like your coffee." She took a big bite and closed her eyes. "The best in the state."

Amber took a much smaller bite of hers, and the sugary, nutty taste flooded her tastebuds. She took a much bigger bite, this time with ice cream. "I don't think I've ever had coffee ice cream this good. And I was raised on Morgensterns." At Rowan's blank look, she said, "The best ice cream in Manhattan."

"Well, ice cream is fresh around here. Newfield Dairy is just up the road, and they have the largest field of dairy cows in a hundred-mile radius. Can't get much fresher ice cream than that."

They ate in silence for a bit, and Amber tried hard not to let her mother's voice inhibit her enjoyment of the calorie-laden dish.

"Can I ask a real personal question?" Rowan pushed her empty carton away even though Amber's was still half full.

Amber hesitated. "You can ask. I may not answer."

"Fair enough." Rowan crossed her arms on the tabletop and leaned forward. "Why did your grandparents leave you the ranch instead of leaving it to your mom?"

"I would have thought that would be obvious." Amber tried not to let it bother her that the question hadn't been something more personal, about herself rather than her situation. "They didn't get along."

Rowan tilted her head. "Yeah, I get that. Did they really not talk in all these years? And why leave it to you instead of selling it or leaving it to a charity or something?"

Amber pushed the carton away, the sugar beginning to make her stomach hurt. "Honestly, I have no idea, Rowan. When I got the call, I was baffled. I mean, I thought they were dead. But Mom must have known when they died for real, right? Someone would have called her? But she never said a word, let alone went to the funeral. When I asked why she hadn't said anything, why she'd lied about them being dead, she asked why she should say anything about them since they didn't matter. That's pretty deep animosity. So, I have no idea why my grandparents didn't do something else with it." She swallowed against the lump in her throat. "It came at just the right time though."

"How so?" Rowan asked.

It was nice to be the focus of someone's attention this way. She wasn't looking at her phone, or over Amber's shoulder for someone more interesting. "I... Work got complicated, and I needed to leave. The call about the house came when I needed to get away for a while."

"Want to talk about what complicated means?" Rowan rested her hand lightly over Amber's. "I'm a pretty good listener."

Amber gave her a wry smile. "I don't doubt that, but today isn't about my tales of woe. You don't want to hear about my pathetic life."

Rowan squeezed her hand. "Do you always do that? Shut down when people ask real questions?"

"Why wouldn't I?" She slid her hand from under Rowan's, the desire to leave it there and take comfort too tempting. "No one actually cares. I mean, when you say good morning or whatever, and say, 'how are you,' you're not really expecting an honest answer, are you? The answer is always, 'good' or 'fine, thanks.' That's just how it is."

"Damn." Rowan leaned back and wiped her hands on her thighs. "That must be a lonely way to live. And a lonely way to... well, to think, I guess." She stood and held up the stuffed dog. "Since we're not talking about anything deep tonight, why don't we go see how Pam is fairing with her pumpkin cheating?"

Amber gathered her dinosaur to her and walked beside Rowan, but the fresh feeling from earlier was gone, replaced with the acrid tang of disappointment she usually felt when someone tried to get close. "Oh my God," she said, stopping and staring. "That's surreal."

Ahead of them was an archway made of pumpkins. Beyond it, pumpkins were stacked and molded into enormous shapes. There was even a full-size horse with a person made of pumpkins on top, except the head was that of a mannequin. "That's incredibly disturbing," Amber said, laughing.

"A riff on the headless horseman, I think." Rowan studied it, her finger pressed to her lips. "Quite the societal representation of turning things on their heads to expose underlying truth. We're all just fruit of the earth topped with a façade of a person."

Amber stared at her until Rowan began to laugh. "I thought you were serious for a second there," she said, then pointed. "Looks like Pam found her judge."

Sure enough, Pam leaned against a post, her legs crossed at the ankle and one hand resting on the wall above a pretty woman's head. The woman, with a T-shirt that read, "I'll judge your face," was looking up at Pam with an expression that made it clear Pam was in for a good night if she wanted one.

"Jealous?" Rowan asked, her expression neutral.

"First of all, that little dog has done nothing to you," Amber said, tugging at Rowan's death grip around the stuffed animal's neck. "Second, no. She's got the kind of bold flirting style that would do well in New York, but..." She shrugged and let go of Rowan's fingers. "Like I said, I'm not interested in anything at this point. And if I was, I'd set my sights on someone else entirely."

From her periphery, she saw Rowan glance at her, but she didn't look away from Pam. "She can flirt with me all she wants. It won't get her anywhere. So no, I'm not jealous."

"I... Cool. If you need me to tell her to back off, just say the word." Rowan went to shove her hands in her pockets and couldn't do it because she had the stuffed toy in one.

"If I need her to back off, I'm perfectly capable of telling her myself." Amber finally looked at her. "I'm not someone who needs to be rescued." At Rowan's small grin, she sighed. "I mean, not generally. I'm a big girl. I can handle myself when it comes to women."

"I'll bet you can," Rowan murmured.

"What about you?" Amber asked. "How do you handle relationships?"

"Are you asking if I'm in one?" Rowan gave her a cocky grin. "Would you be jealous then?"

"That's the kind of answer a player gives." Amber crossed her arms and shook her head at a pumpkin with a depiction of Dorothy's house being picked up by a tornado. "Answer?"

"I have an...arrangement with the local fire chief, Kelly. She's the only other lesbian in town aside from Pam. But it's casual. No commitment. Just blowing off steam."

Interesting. So Rowan didn't mind casual sex and could use it to blow off steam. That sounded promising if they ever crossed that bridge. She winked. "I like your style."

They wandered the huge pumpkin area, full of kids running through it and judges wandering around with clipboards. Lights flickered in the pumpkins and set off a warm glow and the smell of roasting pumpkin.

"Do you like Halloween?" Rowan asked. "Or don't you celebrate that in the city?"

Amber rolled her eyes. "You know, you're sounding just as judgmental as I did when I said you were country. And yes, we do celebrate. There are huge parties all over the city. Last year I went as a she-devil, tail and all."

"I'd ask to see a photo, but I don't think my heart could take it." Rowan sidestepped a child who ran past with a huge wad of cotton candy leaving puffs on everything it touched. "We have school groups come by, starting tomorrow around four. The staff hand out candy, and we dress up some of the horses. It's lots of fun. Then the kids hit the houses. It goes on for about four hours."

Once again Amber was taken aback by how different life here was. "They stopped doing trick-or-treating in the city when they found poison in some of the candy, and some kids got really sick. I think they just do little fairs at schools now or something."

Rowan grunted. "Sick bastards."

The rest of the night went by quickly and by ten, everyone was back on the trucks for the ride home. Everyone except Pam, but the truck didn't wait for her. Amber sat beside Rowan and didn't mind in the least when she draped a blanket over them and put her arm around Amber's shoulders when she shivered in the cool night air.

Back at the house, she stopped at the bottom of the stairs, the dumb dinosaur still clutched in her arms. She raised it slightly. "Thank you for a great night. I haven't had this much fun in a really long time." It seemed like there was more to say, but she wasn't sure how to put it into words.

Rowan, draped in shadow, perched on the back of the couch. "Me either. Thank you for being with me tonight."

Tension rose, but neither of them broke it until Amber stepped onto the stairs, and Shift slid past her and headed up. "Good night, Rowan," she said softly.

"Night." Rowan's husky voice seemed to fill the air.

With a shiver that had nothing to do with the cold, Amber headed to bed and wondered what the hell she was doing.

Chapter Nine

"YOU'RE NOT SERIOUS. ARE you serious?"

Rowan sighed and rubbed at the headache already fully settled in her temples. "Amber, it's not a simple fix. You need a whole new roof. It ripped up some of the plumbing when it came down, and now you need a new system. New floors, new carpet. The kitchen cabinets are all ruined..." She trailed off when Amber leaned against a tree, looking dumbstruck. "I'm sorry. I know it's a lot."

"I mean...it isn't a lot in comparison to what it would cost in New York. I pay more than that in rent for my studio in a year. But..."

"But it's a lot of money to have on hand."

Amber shook her head. "It's not that. I just..." She sighed and closed her eyes. "It was going to be my place to pull myself together. Now I don't have that. I guess I'll have to go back to New York while the work is being done."

Rowan mentally chastised herself for assuming it was about money. "You can stay with me as long as you need to. It's not like the house is crowded, and I'm gone most of the day. We won't get under each other's feet."

Amber shook her head and finally dropped her arms from around herself. "You don't need to coddle me. Maybe you could help me find a place for rent nearby though."

Amber's push-pull when it came to accepting help was more than a little baffling. Sometimes it was like she expected people to be ready to jump when she gave the word, other times it was like she wanted to do everything herself. "Well, let's see how fast they can get the work done. No need for you to stay on your own if you don't need to." She couldn't insist, and she'd probably be better off if Amber stayed somewhere else. But she couldn't let go of the idea of Amber staying at her place.

"I didn't even have a chance to really look around before it was all ruined," Amber said softly, as though she hadn't heard Rowan speak.

"We can go in now, if you want." Was that the right thing to say? She had no clue. Amber was quiet for so long Rowan wondered if she'd heard her, and then she shook her head a little before turning to her.

"You can't tell me you don't have work to do."

Rowan had so much work to do she didn't know how she'd catch up. "Not so much that I can't be here to help if you want it."

"Like I believe you. No..." She looked at the house. "I think I'll take my time and do it myself. Now that the driveway has been cleared, I can get my car out, so you're good to leave me here on my own." She gave a mock-worried look at the forest. "Unless you think the big bad wolf may come for me."

"You might find *I'm* the big bad wolf." Rowan grinned and backed up toward her truck. "If you need anything, give me a shout, and I'll come back. For now, I'll leave you to it." She stopped when she got to the truck. "Remember that the kids start arriving around four, so you'll want to be parked before they get there so there's no accidents."

Amber waved her off. "See you later."

Rowan turned the truck around and watched as Amber receded in the rearview mirror. Was she right to leave her there? It was just a messed-up house, and Amber had her car back. Somehow she felt like she was abandoning her though. "You're an idiot," she muttered. Amber had made it more than clear she didn't want a chaperone, let alone a protector.

The ranch was busy when she got back. They were making good use of the fair weather and cleaning out the stalls as well as the lower fields. She stopped at the various barns and groups of workers to check in and was satisfied all was well. When she got to the stables, she found plenty of owners with their horses and riders out practicing. She had a few quick discussions about how this horse or that one was coming along, and what horse she thought was looking good for the Derby the following season before she finally made it to her office.

She shut the door and breathed in the modicum of quiet before she sat down to check messages and do paperwork.

A knock on her door made her blink her tired eyes, and she saw that a few hours had passed. "Yeah," she called.

Pam opened the door, followed by Ted. They took seats across from her, looking more serious than they should.

"What's wrong?" she asked.

"Camden Market," Ted said. "Something is wrong with the foreleg."

Pam shook her head. "Not something. Same genetic issue her dam had. It's a weakness. I watched her buckle on the mats."

"Shit." Rowan leaned back and rolled the kinks in her neck. "Have you told the Garrisons yet?"

Ted shook his head. "That's why you make the big bucks."

"Think they'll put her down?" Pam asked.

"Yeah." Rowan pulled up her Excel sheet with all the client facts on it. "They put down the dam when they found the problem. They'll cut their losses and get another horse from the winter auction. Damn it."

"Can't we use her as a training horse? I mean, she can't race, but maybe for the younger kids?" Pam's leg jumped the way it only did when she was agitated.

"We can't afford to keep a horse we can't totally trust." Rowan frowned and pulled up Google. "But you know, I met someone at the rodeo last year. Lori something. I think she said she runs a home for messed-up animals out in Illinois somewhere." She turned the screen toward them. "Sanctuary. A home for ex-service animals. Camden isn't a service animal, but maybe she'll make an exception. Especially if they make a big donation to the Sanctuary that will make them look good in the society pages. It would be a win-win."

Pam's smile showed her relief. For all that she was cocky and acted like a tough guy, she had a definite soft spot when it came to the horses. "Think the Garrisons will go for it?"

"I don't see why they wouldn't." Ted stood up. "Won't make any difference to them how the horse is gone, long as it's gone." He gave Rowan a nod. "Good thinking. And good luck telling them."

Rowan groaned. "Thanks a lot."

They left, and Rowan was glad Pam didn't stick around to chat about the previous night. The way she'd come on to Amber had irked the hell out of her, especially since she knew Rowan wasn't happy about it. Granted, it wasn't her place, but she still didn't like it.

With a sigh she picked up the phone. Calls like this were the worst part of the job, but it was part of ranch life when you dealt with racehorses. They were all about racing, and if they couldn't race, then the owner didn't want them. It was often that cut and dry, and she hated that part of it. She checked the time. Only an hour before the kids got here. Was Amber back yet? She checked the phone, but there were no messages.

She's capable of handling herself. Rowan dialed the client's number but couldn't quite get rid of the feeling that something was off.

***

"All right now, just move slowly past the horses, okay? They don't like being scared, and we don't want to spook them." Rowan raised her voice and then laughed as the kids slowed and looked into the horse stalls as they walked through the stable to get to the other side, where the tables of punch and candy were set up, along with some pony rides and small game tables.

It was dark, and all the pumpkins were lit with electric candles so as not to upset the horses with smoke. Beyond the stables, it was spooky music, a fog machine, and a horde of sugar-fueled small humans. It made Rowan's heart happy to have the community around this way. Parents stopped to chat about the lessons that would start in the new year, clients stopped to talk about the races and what to expect, and her staff talked about the kids and clients they hoped would leave soon. It should've been perfect.

But Amber wasn't back yet, and it was taking all of Rowan's willpower not to go find her. She'd sent three text messages and called once but hadn't received anything back. Did that mean Amber was busy? Or was she in trouble yet again? Should she head over to check on her? Or give her the space she needed in order to do what she needed to do?

"I'll go check on her, if you want me to." Pam leaned against the barn door next to Rowan.

"What are you talking about?" Rowan's tone was far more abrupt than she meant it to be.

"You know full well what I'm talking about. You took her out to her place, and she isn't back yet, and you're worried. You hate being out of control, and this feels a lot like that. This is about the millionth time you've looked toward the driveway." Pam grinned. "You're not exactly an onion full of layers, buddy. You're more like...dough. Rolled-out dough. No layers. All there for people to see and read." She poked at Rowan's bicep, earning her a glare. "Like I said. You're busy here. I can go check on her—"

"I'll go." Rowan bumped her shoulder as she went past. "Make sure no kids get under my tires."

Pam laughed and followed her to her truck. Before Rowan got in though, headlights lit the driveway, and Rowan gave a sigh of relief.

Amber drove slowly, and Rowan and Pam each took a side of the drive to make sure no kids ran in front of her. As she passed, Rowan thought she looked a little odd. When she stumbled out of the car, Rowan's stomach dropped. "Jesus. Amber, what happened?" She wrapped her arm around Amber's waist when she swayed. "Pam, I saw Kelly over by the apples."

Pam looked at Amber then jogged off without a word.

"I'm thirsty," Amber said softly.

"Come on, darlin'. Let's get you inside, and we'll get you some water." The iron smell of the blood dried on the side of Amber's face made Rowan's pulse race. She was pale and filthy, her hair a mess and her makeup smeared as though she'd been crying. She trembled in Rowan's arms and when she didn't seem to have the strength to get up the steps, Rowan lifted her gently and carried her inside. The fact that Amber didn't tell her off about it was more worrying.

She laid her on the couch and knelt beside her. Smoothing the hair from her face, she said, "What happened?"

"Water?" Amber murmured, her eyes closed.

"Okay. But stay awake for me. Don't fall asleep yet." Rowan dashed into the kitchen and grabbed a bottle of water. When she came back, she found Shift lying with his head over Amber's feet, his big eyes watching her closely. "Good boy. You keep an eye on her."

She held the bottle to Amber's lips, and after the first bit went in, Amber raised her arm and took the bottle herself. She drank half of it before Rowan gently took it from her. "Don't take in too much too fast."

Amber let her head fall back against the pillow. The door opened, and Pam came in, followed by Kelly, who gently ushered Rowan aside and took her place.

"Amber, I'm Chief Kelly Ellis. Can you open your eyes for me?" She put her fingers to Amber's wrist and then checked the side of her face.

"I think I saw blood on the back of her head too, Kel." Rowan shoved her hands in her pockets, unsure what else to do and hating feeling so helpless. Injuries were a fact of life on the ranch, but she always knew what had happened and most often, why.

"Hey," Pam said. "I'm going to go out and supervise if you're going to stay here."

"Thanks. Let Ted know too, will you?" Rowan barely looked away from Amber. "I knew I shouldn't have left her there alone."

"Beat yourself up later. I'll help. For now, just be in the moment and do what needs to be done." Pam clapped her on the back. "She drove here, which means it isn't all that bad." She left with a promise to check in after the kids had left and before everyone else headed off to the festival.

"Rowan, grab some blankets. Do you have a heating pad? She's way too cold." Kelly continued speaking to Amber softly, but Amber wasn't responding with anything more than small sounds.

Rowan took the stairs two at a time and gathered armfuls of blankets along with the heating pad she hadn't used since she'd hurt her back a few years ago. She and Kelly got Amber covered. "Can you bring me your first aid kit? The wounds look pretty superficial. I think she's cold and dehydrated, mostly. But if she doesn't come around in a few minutes, we'll need to take her to the hospital to get checked out."

Rowan kept up the litany of swear words and self-recriminations in her head as she retrieved the emergency kit and got the fire lit. It didn't take long for the room to warm up, and after more water, Amber seemed to brighten a little.

"Can you sit up for me?" Kelly asked and helped Amber into a sitting position. "I want to take a closer look at that gash in the back. Can you tell us what happened?"

Amber took another long drink of water and hissed a little when Kelly started prodding. "I was wandering around the house, seeing if anything could be salvaged and loading some things into the car to bring back with me. I found some stairs and remembered they went down to a basement, where I'd seen a whole bunch of things. I wanted to see if it was just a big swimming pool, so I headed down."

"Amber—"

"Yes, I'm now aware it was a bad idea." She shot Rowan a warning glare. "The step gave way from under me, and I went down backwards first, and the step I hit with my head broke too. Then I tumbled through the hole and down to the ground followed by a couple more steps, but fortunately the pool of water, which it turns out is fairly deep, broke my fall. My phone is now at the bottom of my basement pond."

Rowan's stomach churned and threatened to bring up her dinner. Amber could have passed out and drowned.

"So, I was pretty out of it, but I managed to climb onto a table instead of lying in the water like a bleeding otter. But then I realized..." She shuddered.

"The stairs were broken, and there was no way out." Rowan squatted beside Kelly, and the knowledge that she was next to the woman she occasionally had sex with and near the woman she really wanted to have sex with made her itch a little. "I'm so sorry, Amber. I shouldn't have left you."

Amber held up her hand, which still shook. "Stop. I shouldn't have tried to go down there. It was stupid."

"So how did you get out?" Kelly asked, pressing a square of gauze to the back of Amber's head.

"Well, after a while I figured out that I needed to save myself. So I gathered up as much furniture as I could find and started stacking it like some crazy game of bridge Jenga. Any piece that slid out would bring the whole thing down. But I managed to get it over the steps that were left, and after a whole lot of attempts to get across the hole, I finally managed. It turns out my upper body strength needs some work." She closed her eyes and rested her cheek against the pillow when Kelly was done with the back of her head. "But then I was too exhausted, and to be honest, too woozy to do anything else. I think I passed out in the hallway for a while before I managed to get to the car. Thankfully I'd set my keys beside the door, so they weren't with my phone."

Kelly looked thoughtful. "If you passed out, Amber, you probably have a concussion. I think we need to take you in and get you checked out." She turned to Rowan. "Can you get her some dry clothes? I think I left some that might fit her in your bottom drawer."

"She's staying in my guest room. I'll go grab something." Rowan leapt for the stairs but stopped at Amber's voice.

"Can I just stay here? Rowan can wake me up every few hours to make sure I'm not dead, can't she?" Amber sounded genuinely upset for the first time.

Rowan moved back to her side. "Amber, I'll come to the hospital with you. But I'd never forgive myself if there was something more serious we missed." She took Amber's hand. "Please?"

Amber looked back at her, but it didn't seem like she could focus very well. "Fine." She squeezed Rowan's hand and closed her eyes again. "Promise not to leave me?"

The vulnerability, something Rowan hadn't heard before, made her ache. "I promise." Rowan ran upstairs and felt a little weird about going through Amber's clothes, especially the pretty lacy things that she should only have seen if she was pulling them from Amber's body. She grabbed the puffer vest Amber had worn the night before, along with a thick sweatshirt and jeans. She added a pair of her own thick wool socks, as all of Amber's were too thin to be of any use. She brought them down and stood with them in her arms, uncertain how to proceed.

Kelly stood up and gave Rowan a knowing grin, tinged with a bit of something else. "Let me handle it. Grab a go bag."

Both relieved and disappointed, Rowan ran back upstairs and packed a small duffle with a change of clothes for both of them, as well as some basic toiletries. When she came back down, there was some color in Amber's cheeks, and she was dressed in the change of clothes. But she looked exhausted.

Once again, Rowan carried Amber, this time to Kelly's car. And once again, Amber didn't complain. Rather, she wrapped her arm around Rowan's neck and snuggled closer.

"I'm still cold," she mumbled.

"Let me get you settled in the car, and I'll go back for blankets." Rowan gingerly set Amber in the backseat.

"I'll do it. You get in and keep her awake." Kelly turned and went back to the house.

Rowan got in the other side and then turned to put her back against the door. Gently, she pulled Amber over so she was settled against Rowan's chest. She wrapped her arms around her and winced at how hard Amber had begun to shiver. Quickly, she sent Ted a text to let him know she'd be off-site for a while. He'd take care of the rest of the night.

Kelly opened the car door and awkwardly draped the blankets over Amber, and Rowan tucked them around Amber's chin. She set off down the driveway, her hazards sending orange light flaring through the evening mist around them.

"Keep her talking, Rowan." Kelly looked at her in the rearview mirror, again with the look Rowan couldn't decipher. "We don't want her falling asleep until she's cleared."

Rowan shifted to nudge Amber awake again. "Hey. Talk to me. Tell me what you were thinking about when you walked around the house."

Amber groaned. "I'm so tired. I don't want to talk."

Rowan kissed the top of her head. "I know. But stay with me, okay? Tell me what you like most about New York."

The faintest smile touched Amber's lips. "The park. I love walking through it in the early morning before it's full of people. It's this beautiful oasis in the middle of the most chaotic city on earth."

"I'm pretty sure there are even more chaotic cities. What makes New York so crazy?" Rowan shifted again, not wanting Amber to get too comfortable but feeling bad about not letting her rest.

"The New Yorkers." Amber laughed slightly. "I mean, the attitude. You're never supposed to stop. Never supposed to let your guard down or show any weakness. You have to be ready for anything and everything and look like you know what you're doing all the time." Tears began to track through the dirt on her cheeks. "I never know what I'm doing. I'm faking it. It's so tiring."

It was probably the first moment Rowan had heard something genuine about Amber's feelings toward her home city. But she didn't want to make her sad, not when she was already beat up. "Tell me about your best memory."

Amber was quiet for a moment, and Rowan was about to shift again when she sighed.

"It's a random one. When I was in college, I got the chance to present a paper at a conference in Hawaii. I got some classmates to submit papers too, and they were all accepted. So we went as a group. It was May; the weather was perfect..." Amber drifted off until Rowan nudged her again. "I was twenty-two and on my own with friends on this gorgeous island. We went snorkeling, and I saw an octopus float by. I worked out on the beach every morning and watched the sunrise. It was such a magical week, and I didn't want to go home at the end of it."

"That sounds fantastic." It really did, and Rowan wished she'd been there with her at the time. "Have you been back since?"

Amber grimaced and turned her head. "I'm getting a super-sized headache."

Rowan looked up and was grateful to see the hospital just ahead. "We're here, so we can get you fixed up, okay?"

Amber didn't respond. Kelly pulled up in the emergency area, then jumped out and headed inside. She was followed back out with two people in medical garb, one of them bringing a wheelchair. Kelly opened the door, and Amber was alert enough to shuffle toward her. The emergency crew helped her into the wheelchair, and Rowan started to follow.

One of the nurses turned to her. "Are you family?"

Before Rowan could respond, Amber said, "She's my partner."

Kelly raised her eyebrows, and Rowan gave a small shrug.

"Okay. You can come along then." The nurse turned away, and they took her in.

Rowan gave Kelly a quick hug. "I'll call Ted or Pam to come pick me up when we're done. Thanks for everything."

Kelly squeezed her tight. "If you need anything, you know where I am." She paused. "It's nice to see you look at someone that way."

Rowan jogged after the nurses and Amber and followed them into a room that smelled like the expulsion of unpleasant things. Throughout the next several hours, Rowan waited while they poked, prodded, checked, and ran tests. She kept turning Kelly's words over in her head. How did she look at Amber that was different from the way she looked at Kelly?

"She's definitely got a concussion. The chief did a good job of cleaning the wounds, but we've put in three stitches. We're going to keep her overnight as a precaution and to make sure her body temperature stays stable. Visiting hours start again at nine a.m." The nurse's tone brooked no argument.

"I promised her I wouldn't leave her. Is there a waiting room I can sit in?"

The nurse rolled her eyes. "What's the difference between you leaving and coming back, and you leaving to sit in a waiting room only to come back later?"

"My word." Rowan wasn't about to be cowed.

"Fine." She shook her head. "We'll be moving her to a room in about twenty minutes. I'll point out the waiting room along the way."

An hour later, Rowan followed Amber's gurney to another

area of the hospital that smelled far better and was far quieter too. Amber had long since fallen asleep holding Rowan's hand and hadn't seemed to want to let go, even in her sleep.

"There you go," the nurse said, tilting her head. "You can stay in there. The cafeteria is open twenty-four hours."

Rowan stopped and watched as they continued down the hall and turned left, out of sight. She slumped into a chair and sent a text to Pam and Ted, letting them know Amber was in her room now and that she'd hopefully be back before work started in the morning. She closed her eyes, her phone against her chest, and fell asleep.

She woke when someone tapped her shoulder. She blinked hard to focus on a different nurse standing in front of her. "Is everything okay?"

"Everything is fine." The nurse nodded toward the hallway. "I was told Amber's partner was out here in the waiting room. There's no sense in you being in here. The Grim Reba is strict about visitors, but on the night shift, we're a little more sensible."

Rowan stood and looked at the nurse who was clearly family. "I really appreciate it." She followed her down the hall. A comfortable-looking chair was next to Amber's bed, along with a blanket and small pillow. "Wow, that's really kind. Thank you."

The nurse checked Amber's numbers. "If it were my girlfriend, they'd probably have to arrest me to keep me from her side." She glanced over at Rowan with a grin. "And you're not exactly a small doe, are you? They're lucky you didn't break some heads."

Rowan laughed softly and settled in the chair. "They're lucky Amber was too out of it to break heads of her own."

The nurse left, and Rowan took the time to study Amber. There were dark smudges under her eyes, but she'd been cleaned up. Her hair was still tangled, and Rowan had a feeling she'd be most upset about that when she came to.

"It's rude to stare." Amber's eyes fluttered open.

"When an angel falls from the heavens and lands in a hospital bed, it's hard not to."

Amber made a gagging sound. "God, that was the cheesiest thing I've ever heard anyone say."

Rowan grinned. "Oh, I bet I could do worse." She held Amber's hand. "I didn't ask before. Is there anyone I should call? Your parents?"

Amber shook her head and winced. "No. I'm okay, and you know this is the last place my mom ever wants to come to. And... we're not close. She'd consider it a hassle to have to worry about me. And Dad is probably away on business."

Rowan found that incredibly sad. Her parents would have been there in a heartbeat, no matter where in the world she might have been. "Okay. Friends? Lovers? An ex you're still best friends with, like any good lesbian?"

Amber closed her eyes, and tears slid from beneath her eyelashes. "There's no one. I mean, there's Craig, but he's not that kind of friend."

Christ. Rowan couldn't imagine being so all alone in the world. "Okay, well, I'm here."

"Thank you," Amber whispered. Her breathing evened out, and it was clear she'd fallen back asleep.

Rowan moved her chair closer so she could continue to hold Amber's hand, then covered herself in the blanket, tucked the pillow between her head and the bedrail, and fell asleep. There was no way on earth she'd leave Amber's side now.

Chapter Ten

"I'm NOT AN INVALID, Rowan." Amber gritted her teeth and forced herself to unclench the blankets. "If I want a drink, I'll get one. It was a bump on the head, not broken legs."

Rowan held up her hands. "Okay. Okay. I'll leave you to it. The doctor said I should keep an eye on you, that's all. I just—"

"You've done enough." Amber closed her eyes and rested her head against the pillow. "Don't smother me."

There was a moment of silence. "See you later. I'll leave the door cracked so Shift can go out if he wants to."

Amber waved but didn't say anything and a moment later, she heard Rowan's footsteps on the stairs. Shift raised his head and looked at the door. "I'd like it if you didn't leave too," she whispered and ruffled his head. He lay it back down on her leg and gave the kind of sigh she wanted to.

Rowan had been amazing. No doubt. She'd been kind, gentle, and had offered to get Amber anything she wanted, including a replacement phone which had already arrived. And yeah, it was nice. But it also wasn't something she could afford to get used to. The accident had shown just how alone she really was in the world, and she wasn't about to start depending on people. She cradled her phone against her chest and hit Craig's number.

"How is my lovely fish-out-of-water country bumpkin doing?" he answered in a sing-song tone.

Amber began to cry. And then she began to sob. She couldn't speak into the stunned silence that followed. She heard typing and a printer.

"I've booked my flight. I get in tomorrow morning, and I'll rent a car. Send me the address you're at right now."

Without saying anything, Amber moved the phone from her ear and sent a text with the address. "You...you don't..." She hiccupped and tried to breathe.

"Shut up. You know I love this kind of drama and imagine the stories I'll have to tell when I get home."

She took a shaky breath and wiped at her eyes with the back of her hand. "I don't know if there's a hotel room available. There's a big festival here. I'm staying with Rowan."

He gave a little whistle. "We have some catching up to do. We'll figure out where I'm staying tomorrow. Babe, just hang in there, okay?" His tone gentled, the snarky teasing gone. "I know you think you're alone, but you're not. Do you want to talk things through now or wait until I get there?"

"Given how snotty I'm about to sound, we should wait."

"Okay. I'm going to go get some new jeans. I'll text you when I'm on my way from the airport."

They hung up, and Amber curled against Shift. She hadn't asked Rowan if it was okay, but surely she wouldn't mind Amber having a friend over at a time like this? Maybe it was a little presumptuous. She picked up her phone again and sent Rowan a text.

My friend from New York is coming to see me tomorrow. Hope that's okay.

It wasn't asking so much as telling. But it wasn't like she'd tell Craig he couldn't come.

Fine by me. You okay?

Amber swallowed against a new wave of emotion.

You've been gone for six seconds. I'm fine.

Amber waited, but there was no response. She shouldn't expect one, and it wasn't something she'd ever tell someone, but Rowan's concern had made the whole thing bearable. Even the part where she'd been taken care of by Rowan's...situationship woman. Kelly. She was gorgeous, and she hadn't even been in her firefighter uniform. She was tall, and strong, and pretty. Everything Amber always wished she was but would never be. How could she possibly compete with that? Thankfully, she hadn't been around in the short time Amber had been there. Would she come back around when Amber left? It was a stupid line of thought. Why should she care who was with Rowan?

But right now, she was safe and warm, and just as she'd promised, Rowan hadn't left her side the entire time she was in the hospital. When Pam had shown up at the hospital to pick them up, there'd been no flirting or flippant comments, just gentle concern. Amber had wanted to snap at her, both of them, and tell them to stop treating her like she was breakable.

But she hadn't, because deep down she didn't really want them to stop. She felt...broken.

"What is wrong with me, Shift?" she whispered, stroking his head and looking into his big brown eyes. "Don't answer that. There isn't enough time in the world." She settled back and checked the time. She couldn't have another pain pill for at least two hours. Boredom was going to set in fast at this rate. With a sigh, she closed her eyes and let the feeling of safety steady her breathing.

A sound woke her, and she looked around, confused for a moment about where she was. Rowan stood in the doorway, her gaze searching.

"Sorry to wake you, but we're having dinner, and I wondered if you wanted to join us?"

Dinner? Amber looked at her phone. "I've slept all day?"

Rowan tilted her head. "Looks like it."

Amber groaned as the headache came to full strength. "Clearly I didn't take my pain pills."

"Shouldn't take them on an empty stomach anyway." She made a vague motion at the hall. "Need help coming down?"

Amber shook her head and swung her legs out of bed, only to grit her teeth as the room tilted. "I'll just take it slow."

Rowan seemed like she was going to argue for a second, then she shrugged. "Okay. Give a shout if you change your mind." She backed up and then turned and walked away.

Amber refused to let the tears fall. *Stop feeling sorry for yourself. It's a fucking bump on the head.* She took a couple long, deep breaths and then pushed herself to her feet. Slowly, with her stomach lurching and her head throbbing, she made her way to the bathroom. After a quick, hot shower and brushing her teeth, she felt marginally better. Steadier, anyway. She put on sweats and a sweatshirt, figuring no one expected her to look her best anyway, and headed for the stairs.

Rowan was just cresting the top of them. "Hey. Was just making sure you were okay."

"Sorry. I needed a shower." At the top of the stairs she grimaced as they seemed to move from side to side. "And if you really want to help, I won't stop you."

Rowan's eyebrow twitched. "Well, thanks for doing that for me. It'll make me feel better, for sure." She held out her arm.

Amber hooked hers through it and gripped the rail as they took it slow down the stairs, and she didn't let go once they headed to the dining room. Pam and Ted were already there, eating. They both stood when she entered.

"I honestly thought people only did that in movies," she said, giving Rowan's arm a grateful squeeze as she let go of it and slid into a seat.

"We're just big on respect here," Ted said. "Old habits that we teach our kids so manners stick around."

"This smells wonderful," Amber said, because she couldn't think of a response to Ted's comment. People in New York had manners too. They were just a different type.

"Rowan's special Mexican chicken." Pam used a dish that hadn't been touched yet and put a portion on a plate. "She won't share the recipe, so we just have to bug her to make it. She made yours with some kind of vegetarian fake chicken. Can't imagine it'll be as good, but I guess you'll be used to that."

Amber inhaled, and her stomach rumbled in response. She took a sliver of avocado and a few spoonfuls of what looked like rice with beans in it. When she noticed the quiet, she looked up to find them watching her. "What?"

"You know you could eat more than a sparrow," Rowan said. "That's not a whole lot of food to keep you going."

Amber went to shrug, but the tightness in her shoulders stopped her. "I've always been one for small portions."

"Okay then. Just so's you know, there's plenty, and no one here is going to tell you not to have more if you want it." Rowan gave her a quick smile before digging into her own half-eaten meal.

Their conversation picked up again, and Amber was content to listen and zone out as she ate, catching occasional bits before drifting off to think of her own problems once more.

"So your friend is coming over?"

Amber looked up, brought back from her musings. "Craig. We work together, kind of, and I called him today." She teared up and set down her fork. "Honestly, I don't even know why I called. We go out and stuff, but we don't have heart-to-heart conversations or anything."

"You mentioned him in the hospital." Rowan's expression wasn't hard to read. It was like she was looking at an abandoned puppy.

"Yeah. I told him I don't know where he'll stay because of the festival, but he said he'd figure it out." Amber hadn't explored Rowan's house and had no idea if there were more bedrooms. It looked huge from the outside, but she couldn't expect Rowan to offer—

"I've got two more guest rooms. They haven't been used in an age, so I'll need to clean them up, but that's no problem." Rowan served herself another piece of chicken and a side of rice.

"I don't want to put you out. It's enough that you have me staying here, isn't it?" She continued to eat, taking small bites, dragging it out.

"Well, you do seem to take a whole lot of energy." Rowan winked at her when she looked up. "One person or two, doesn't matter to me. And it will be good to know that someone is watching out for you, stubborn as you are."

"Well, if she needs watching over..." Pam gave that flirty grin of hers and wiggled her eyebrows.

"You have work to do." Rowan waved her fork at her. "Not to mention you'll be busy meeting up with a certain pumpkin judge to say thanks for the trophy, won't you?"

Amber had completely forgotten about it being Halloween. "Did the kids have a good time last night?"

"Best year yet," Ted said, pushing away his empty plate. "Every house in town is decorated. Kids will have gotten enough candy to last them till next Halloween."

"You coming to watch the music show tonight?" Pam asked, looking at Rowan. Her gaze flicked to Amber and back again.

"Subtle." Amber leaned back, glad that the food seemed to have helped with the headache a little. "Don't stay home on my account."

Rowan yawned. "Nah. I'm wiped out from work this week. I'm going to stay in and watch a movie."

Ted and Pam got up and started clearing the dishes. When Amber went to help, Rowan waved her away. "Guests don't do dishes."

"But Ted and Pam can?" she asked, relieved she didn't have to move around.

"They're not guests. They're family. And locusts, based on how much they eat whenever they come around." Rowan grinned and handed Amber a cold bottle of water. "Doc said you should hydrate."

Amber nodded and took it without complaining or saying she could take care of herself. It was just a bottle of water, for fuck's sake. She thought about Rowan's comment about the way she shut down every time she was asked personal things. What Rowan didn't realize was that Amber had already shared more with her than she had with anyone else in years.

She watched as they moved around each other, the banter light and sporadic as they cleaned up. After Ted and Pam left, Rowan leaned against the counter and looked at her.

"How bad is it?"

"What?" Amber said, frowning.

"The headache." She motioned at Amber's face. "The lines around your eyes are tight, and your shoulders are practically touching your ears."

Amber's eyes welled up. "I feel like I hit my head on some stairs and then nearly drowned."

Rowan came over and knelt in front of her. "I'm good with my hands. What say we get settled on the couch and watch a movie, and I rub some of that tension away?" She looked into Amber's eyes. "I know you can take care of yourself. But that doesn't mean you always have to."

"Thank you," Amber said softly.

Rowan stood and put her hand out to pull Amber up. "I get to choose the movie though."

Amber rolled her eyes and moved to the couch, not as unsteady as she'd been earlier. "So long as it's not something ridiculous."

Rowan grabbed the remote, handed Amber a blanket, and then sat sideways on the L-shaped couch. "I watch only serious, highly acclaimed films that are in the running for Oscar nominations."

Somehow, Amber doubted that. She sat between Rowan's legs and groaned as the film started. "Street racing?"

"The special effects are fantastic. Totally unbelievable and absurd, and I can't get enough." She started rubbing Amber's shoulders. "Tell me if the pressure isn't right or you need to shift."

At his name, Shift jumped up onto the other section of the

couch, and they laughed.

Amber murmured appreciatively as Rowan began a gentle but firm massage of her neck and slowly, the headache began to recede even more. She pretty much ignored the movie in favor of falling into Rowan's touch. But in this position, Rowan couldn't go much further than the top of her shoulder blade, and she wanted more. Leaning forward, she pulled off her sweatshirt so she was in just the small cami beneath it, then she flipped over and draped herself over Rowan's lap.

"Um," Rowan said, clearing her throat. "Whatcha doin'?"

"So you can get the rest of my back," Amber said, her voice muffled by the blanket under her face.

"Yup. Right. Okay." Her strong hands began kneading Amber's back.

"That's amazing." Amber sighed happily at the tense leg muscles under her and the strong hands moving over her skin.

"Head any better?"

"If I say yes, will you stop?" she asked, tightening her hold a little.

"Not if you don't want me to." One of Rowan's hands left Amber's back to stroke her hair. "But you're missing the best part of the movie."

"I'll live." Amber closed her eyes, even the crashing and revving sounds from the TV not keeping her from drifting off under Rowan's ministrations. The feeling of security wasn't one she'd allow herself to get hooked on, but for now, in this moment, it was good.

It seemed like only seconds later when Rowan was gently shaking her shoulder. "Sorry. I fell asleep again."

Rowan continued to stroke her hair. "It's fine. The movie is over, and my legs are asleep, and that position probably isn't great for you."

Amber moaned as she pushed herself up, only to end up on all fours, face-to-face with Rowan in the flickering firelight. Rowan's eyes darkened, and her gaze moved to Amber's lips.

"Amber—"

She moved, pressing her lips to Rowan's, unwilling to think or wait.

Rowan's hands buried in her hair and pulled her close, and Amber moaned in a whole different way this time. She shifted so she was straddling Rowan's lap and ground down, pressing their bodies together. Rowan's tongue pushed for entry, and Amber granted it. Rowan moved one hand out of Amber's hair and settled it against her lower back, pulling her closer as she raised her hips.

Amber kissed her back, harder, as Rowan's hand slipped up her cami and caressed the underside of her breast. She released the kiss and gasped as Rowan's fingertips brushed over her nipple. "Take me to bed," she murmured as she went in for another kiss.

Rowan stood, and Amber wrapped her legs around her. Their lips hardly separated as Rowan climbed the stairs with Amber in her arms. She kicked open her bedroom door and set Amber on the edge, then slowly pressed her onto the bed, her solid body causing a flare of desire Amber hadn't felt in far too long.

Rowan's phone buzzed. She glanced at it on the night table but quickly turned her attention back to Amber, her hot mouth trailing down Amber's neck.

It buzzed again, lighting up the dark room.

"This better be important," she muttered. "Sorry." She picked it up, her bodyweight still on Amber, her hand still moving over Amber's breast.

Then it stopped, and she pulled away. "How bad?"

Amber bit her lip and sat up, looking around for something to cover herself with. The feeling of vulnerability wasn't one she liked.

"Okay. I'll be down in ten." She hung up and looked at Amber. "I'm sorry. There's an emergency down at the stable. Since everyone is out at the festival, it's only me."

Amber shrugged. "It's not like I'm going anywhere. Probably wasn't a good idea anyway." She stood, her arms wrapped around herself. "Good luck with whatever it is."

"Amber, wait—" Rowan held out her hand.

"No, really." She ducked around Rowan and slipped into the hall, then opened her bedroom door. "No big deal. See you in the morning." She closed it behind her and slid to the floor.

"Fuck," Rowan whispered just loud enough for Amber to hear, then headed downstairs.

Amber hugged her knees to her. What was she thinking? She was a guest in Rowan's house, and she had nowhere else to go. If she messed this up, she'd be sleeping in a ruin with no roof, or she'd have to go back to New York and the untenable situation there. But God, how amazing had it felt to be locked in her arms? Her mouth so hot and inviting, and her touch so...real. Her whole focus had been on Amber. She wasn't looking in a mirror or checking herself out. She was sexy in her loose T-shirt, and Amber wanted to get under it and see the body beneath.

But that was downright stupid. She wasn't in a position to have any sort of situationship, physical or romantic. It was good that the call had put a stop to it.

She rested her face on her knees and let the tears fall. Logic simply didn't make the feeling of being alone any easier.

Chapter Eleven

ROWAN WATCHED AS THE foal stood on shaky legs and nuzzled its dam. She wiped the sweat from her brow and shook out the aches in her biceps. The sun was just coming up, and it had been a long, stressful night.

Pam came in with two cups of coffee and handed one over. She looked tired but far more relaxed than Rowan felt.

"Nice of you to come by," Rowan said, taking a swig of coffee and appreciating the hit of caffeine.

"Hey, I offered. You said not to worry about it." She leaned against the stall door. "Looks like you guys did just fine."

Rowan rested her face on her arm and smiled as the foal investigated its new surroundings. "Looked pretty dire for a while there. Mare went into labor, but nothing happened. The foal was backwards. Took us a long time to get her turned around, and the mare was pretty stressed."

"You would be too if someone was reaching around inside you and messing with things." Pam hooked her boot on the rail. "Speaking of, I had a damn good night."

"You're disgusting, and that's a gross segue." Rowan shoved her slightly, and Pam had to hold her coffee up to keep from spilling it.

"Yeah, well, with a woman like Amber around, I was all worked up with nowhere to put it." She shrugged and stroked the foal's head when it came to inspect them.

At the memory of their make-out session, Rowan sighed. "Yeah."

"Isn't her friend coming in today?" Pam said. "You sure you

want him here? He can stay with me."

"Thanks for the offer. But it'll be good to have someone watch over Amber until her head has healed. She was a mess of headache and exhaustion last night." No need to mention that she'd rubbed it out and continued massaging even after her hands had begun to cramp because she liked having Amber lying on her that way, liked the way her skin felt under her fingertips, liked the way she was so soft and sweet when she was sleeping. Nope. Didn't need to say any of that.

"All right. Well, let me know if you change your mind." Pam stretched and backed away. "I'm going to get a couple hours' sleep. You should too. You look like something out of the manure pile."

Rowan flipped her off and continued to watch the beautiful new foal. Had Amber been right? Was it for the best that they'd been interrupted? *Who the fuck knows?* Would it really have been so bad to wake up beside her this morning? What if they started down a road that would take them somewhere together? *And what if it all went to shit, and she burned your house down?* Amber had a temper, but was she that kind of woman? It wasn't like Rowan knew her well at all.

But now she had to go back to the house and face her. What was there to say? Slowly, she trudged to her truck and drove back to the house. No lights were on, and the house was silent when she entered. Not surprising that Amber would still be asleep. Rowan took a quick, scalding hot shower to get off all the gunk that came with helping a horse give birth, then threw on her shorts and T-shirt and went to bed.

The pinging of text messages on her phone woke her too soon, and she groaned as the muscle soreness hit her. Helping a foal into the world was hard work, and her body let her know it. She grabbed her phone and squinted at it with sleep-filled eyes. There were messages from Pam and Ted about everyday things, a message from Kelly asking how Amber was doing, and a message from Amber asking if Rowan wanted breakfast.

She let her head hit the pillow. Why was the most complicated thing about her life right now the woman she'd unintentionally taken in for the foreseeable future? She texted back that breakfast would be great. Sighing, she shuffled out of bed and into the bathroom, where a hot shower only helped a little, given that the smell of Amber's floral shampoo continued to hang in the air, teasing her like a reward just out of reach.

Dressed and mostly awake, she headed downstairs and took an appreciative sniff. Her stomach grumbled loudly in response. She turned the corner, smiling at the country music playing quietly, and had to stop for a second. Amber danced around the kitchen, singing into a spatula. She was barefoot, and a toe ring glinted in the light as she moved. It was...perfect. Her thick, wavy hair hung loose down her back and swayed in time to her not terribly graceful dance moves. She lifted her arms in victory at the end of the song, and her shirt rode up slightly to reveal a small tattoo on her lower back. She bowed, as though to an audience, and Rowan started breathing again. She clapped. "I'd pay for that performance any time."

Amber spun around, her eyes wide and her cheeks growing pinker by the second. "Oh my God. How mortifying. How long have you been watching me?"

"Long enough to know you'd give any country diva a run for her money." Rowan grinned and looked her over. "And long enough to know you've probably got a story to go with that bit of ink on your back."

Amber covered her face with one hand and pointed at the oven with the spatula with the other. "By all that's holy, please open that and put some food in your mouth so you stop talking."

Rowan laughed and opened the oven door. "You made pancakes in the oven?"

"Obviously not. I made them in a pan and then kept them warm for you in there." Amber pushed over a plate and a bowl of cut strawberries. "Ted brought these by, and I thought I'd do something nice for you. No big deal. It's possible they're not even edible, given my history with cooking."

Rowan stopped piling the clouds of heaven on her plate. "It is a big deal. And I appreciate it. Thank you."

Amber shrugged and looked away. "I already ate. I was too hungry to wait."

Rowan sat at the table with her plate and a cup of coffee. "Understandable. Will you keep me company?"

For a moment, it almost looked like Amber might say no, but then she pulled out a chair and cupped her mug in both hands.

"I'm guessing we're not going to talk about last night, given the way we dodge things. So tell me about your friend coming in." Rowan tried to slow down as she ate, but the pancakes were damn good. "I thought you said you didn't have that kind of friendship."

"We don't." Amber turned the mug in her hands. "Well, I didn't think we did. But when I called, he didn't hesitate. I mean, I guess I'd do the same for him. I don't know why I didn't think he'd really care."

There was no question that Amber's stuff probably had to do with the mother who sounded like something out of an old horror film, but it wasn't her place to say it. "Well, I'm glad he proved you wrong. Before I head to the stable, I'll get the room fixed up." She frowned. "You're not driving to the airport, are you?" She motioned at Amber's head with her fork. "Probably isn't quite safe yet."

Amber huffed and gave her a look. "I'm not dumb, Rowan; I'm not going to risk getting behind the wheel and killing someone. No, he's renting a car at the airport. And if you don't mind, you can tell me where the sheets and stuff are, and I'll make the bed. It isn't like I have a lot to do today."

"Going a little stir crazy already?" Rowan grinned and took her empty plate to the sink. "You can always come help muck out the stalls if you want something to do."

"An answer springs to mind but it isn't polite, so I'll keep it to myself." Amber smiled, and it lit up her eyes.

"Good call." Rowan checked her watch. "I'll put the sheets and towels on the bed and then head out. We've got a busy day ahead of us with some horses being put through their paces. Feel free to come down and watch if you want to." She turned to head upstairs, her mind already on the work ahead.

"Rowan?"

She stopped and looked over her shoulder. Amber looked small, almost timid, at the big dining table.

"Thank you." She pressed her lips together and then looked at Rowan. "I haven't really said it properly. Thank you for letting me stay with you, for coming to my rescue, for not telling me I told you so." She swallowed and brushed away a tear. "My life is a tsunami of shit, and it's like you came into it just when I was about to go under."

Rowan wrinkled her nose. "That's kind of a gross metaphor, but I get it. You're welcome, Amber." She wanted to say more, but now wasn't the time. Instead, she gathered the things needed and put them in the extra guest room, and when she headed out the front door with Shift running ahead of her, Amber wasn't anywhere to be seen. *Probably for the best.* Amber's presence made Rowan not want to do much else than be near her, and that wasn't a good way to stay in business.

The rest of the morning at the racing yard passed swiftly, between conversations with clients about their horses, watching the horses canter in groups, and watching as some foals began the breaking-in process. Some clients wanted better rugs, better food, better stable hands. One client wanted her horse moved to a different stall because she was convinced the horse beside hers was giving off bad energy. She checked the solarium, the horse walker, the salt box, and the vibe plates to make sure everything was working. It was a better spa than was available in some hotels, and clients always made sure their horses were getting the benefits of the royal treatment.

For the most part, everyone seemed happy. From the grooms to the trainers to the owners and riders, the energy was high as the end of the season approached.

She'd just managed to sit down in her office when Pam came in and closed the door behind her. "Have you met Amber's friend yet?"

Rowan looked at her suspiciously. "No. Why?"

"It's lunch time. You should go have lunch. In fact, I'm hungry. Let's go have lunch at your place." Pam opened the door again and motioned.

"What's wrong with you?" Rowan's stomach grumbled. "I want to know why you're acting weird."

"I just..." Pam grinned and shook her head. "You'll see. Come on."

They got in the truck and headed back to the house but no matter what Rowan asked, Pam just shook her head. It was good to see that a fire was going, but she was surprised Amber had lit it.

"You lit the fire," she said. "That's how you've already met the friend."

Pam nodded, still looking mischievous. "I popped by to check on her since you were slammed. Didn't want her dying of that head wound on us."

"Sure. That's why you stopped by." Rowan rolled her eyes and parked in front of the house. They headed inside, and Rowan followed the sound of voices to the living room. "Hey. We came by for lunch."

Amber looked up, her smile bright. "Hey. This is Craig."

He got up from the couch and turned around. "I've heard so much about you."

Rowan held out her hand and kept her expression neutral. "I'm looking forward to hearing more about you. Want lunch?"

The four of them headed into the kitchen, and Pam glanced at her, grinning.

"You didn't want to tell me that Craig Caswell was in my house?" Rowan hissed.

"I didn't. But buddy, your poker face is better than it has ever been." Pam whistled softly. "I'm impressed."

The three of them sat at the table together while Rowan started getting out the fixings for sandwiches. *Not exactly movie star food.* She gave a mental shrug and watched them surreptitiously as they chatted. Pam wasn't nearly as controlled as Rowan had been and asked Craig all kinds of outrageous questions about his co-stars in the movies he'd become known for. The first openly gay action hero was the hottest thing in Hollywood, and he was getting a lot of work. He answered them all, and she realized his tone sounded familiar. It was the same tone Amber had used when she'd first arrived. A kind of snarky, fake blasé sound that made it seem like nothing mattered or was of interest. She also realized that Amber had lost some of that tone in the few days she'd been there, but now it was back again in full force.

She set sandwiches on the table. "Sorry it isn't more interesting, but lunch around here is better for the horses than it is for us." To be fair to both Amber and Craig, neither one said anything about carbs, or cheese, or whatever else it was that New Yorkers didn't eat. "How did you two meet?"

Craig rolled his eyes and waved almost dismissively. "She was my accountant. Kind of. I mean, who gets all that money stuff, especially when there's so much of it to deal with?"

"I thought you said you dealt with stocks?" Rowan didn't miss the tiny tightening around Amber's eyes.

"Oh, she does that too." Craig cut off Amber as she started to speak. "But she doesn't do it for just anyone. She's a wealth manager for the stars. You've never met anyone who could make taxable income disappear the way she does."

Amber flinched. "That makes it sound super shady. It isn't. It's just understanding how money can ebb and flow in the right ways. It's about taking care of the client, so they have the money to live comfortably even when there's no work."

He reached out and took her hand. "And that's exactly what you've done for me." He turned to Pam and Rowan. "I was a little out of control after my first film. My lifestyle manager convinced me to talk to Amber's firm, who reps a couple of my friends, about being a little wiser with my money. I didn't understand a lot of it though, so instead of having my manager explain it to me, I insisted on meeting Amber. We've been besties ever since."

"And I got him to sell the helicopter." Amber smiled, but she still looked sad.

"Which was a guy magnet, let me tell you." He shrugged. "But she was right. I'm getting more work than I can handle right now, but what happens when the wrinkles set in? Who knows if they'll still want me under the bright lights. Amber has made sure I won't have to work again if I don't want to."

"And you can do your job from Rowan's house, Amber?" Pam looked between them. "I'm surprised they don't want you in the office for that."

Rowan stood, scraping her chair back noisily. "Sorry to interrupt, but we need to get back to the horses." She hesitated. "Craig, do many people know where you are?" At his confused look, she sighed. "Am I going to need to worry about lots of people showing up to get your autograph?"

He laughed. "Do you think I told the world I was going to hang out at a farm in Kentucky? Not really my style. You don't need to worry. My agent got me the rental car, and I picked it up from a space, not a person." He squeezed Amber's hand. "I'm just here to support Amber in her time of need. But if you have any gay or gay-ish cowboys around, feel free to send them my way."

Rowan nodded and pushed Pam forward when she was about to speak again. "I'll keep it in mind."

"Oh, and thanks for letting me stay. This place is simply divine. Like something right out of a romance novel." He wiggled his eyebrows, and Amber shook her head.

"Okay. Yup." Rowan nodded and backed out. "We'll see you if you're around for dinner."

She and Pam left, and Pam gave a low whistle once they were in the truck. "Isn't he a peach?"

Rowan tapped the steering wheel. "He's about what I thought he'd be, to be honest. Just this side of arrogant and that side of narcissism."

"I know we don't know Amber very well, but it's hard to imagine her running with that crowd." Pam lowered her window and took a deep breath of chill air. "I mean, it wasn't hard to picture when she first got here. But a couple days in, and she seemed a little less...*that*."

Rowan agreed, but like Pam said, it wasn't like they knew her. Hell, she barely seemed to know herself. "Well, it makes it easier to curb the attraction. I don't want someone who isn't genuine and sees life as a half-full glass other people need to fill." She pulled up in front of the stables. "I need to go make sure the restaurant is good for the Harvest Grand and meet with the marketing team. Want to have dinner with us tonight?" It felt strange to use a plural when it came to asking Pam to come over.

"Raincheck. I'm meeting Julie for dinner at the Cricket." When Rowan gave her a look, she said, "The pumpkin-carving judge."

Rowan grunted. "Wow. More than two nights with the same woman. Watch out, or you'll get a reputation as a stayer."

Pam's expression turned serious. "There are worse things. Might be nice to come home to someone some days, you know? And I think you feel the same. Maybe you need to let go of some of that control freak in you and let someone in. Other than Kelly, who you just let out again. Not unlike Shift, really."

"I'm not a control freak. I'm organized and dedicated, qualities you lack on all levels." She shooed her out of the truck. "Go. Some of us work for a living."

Pam got out and headed into the stables, and Rowan drove up to the restaurant. At two in the afternoon on a weekday, it was pretty quiet, which she was grateful for. She checked her watch. Five minutes until the meeting would start. She slipped into the kitchen, said hi to the staff, grabbed a Coke, and then went into the conference room. Three of her crew were already waiting, notepads and stacks of paper ready to go. She sat and exchanged pleasantries and checked her watch. It was one minute past. "Is Steve joining us today?"

Just then the door opened, and Steve came rushing in, his young face flushed. "Is it true?" he asked as he slid into his seat, his eyes wide. "Please tell me it's true."

With a sinking feeling, Rowan narrowed her eyes. "What's true?"

"That Craig Caswell is here on the property." His gaze searched her face, and he gasped. "Oh my God, it's true. He's been my idol ever since he came out after doing *Bullet Craze*. He—"

"How did you find out?" Rowan asked, tapping the table to get his attention.

"Someone at the airport saw him getting into a car, and they followed him to the ranch. They Insta'd about it." He didn't seem in the least perturbed by that.

"Creepy." Sally, the restaurant manager, seemed far more put off by it. "That's going to change our order numbers for sure. Will he be at the event?"

Rowan groaned and rested her head in her hands. "He's here to see Amber, the new owner of Honeysuckle. He said no one would know he was here."

Steve shook his head. "Celebrities like that can't just *go* places." He looked around the table, as though waiting for agreement, then sighed. "Don't you see how huge this could be for us? If we get him to say he likes this place on social media, the Willows will blow up."

"We don't need it to blow up. We already board all the horses we can handle, and the tours are always full. We're doing great with people who actually care about horses. We don't need people here just to gawk at a celebrity."

Steve deflated and sat back in his seat. "So I can't post about him being here?"

"No. If things get crazy, so be it. We'll deal with it. But until then, I want him and Amber to have the peace and privacy they need to get her back on track. Now, let's talk about the Harvest Grand, please."

The conversation turned to more important things, and Rowan wrote down all the expected numbers as well as any requests they had. Steve was able, barely, to talk about his plans for promoting the charity event they held every year. When the conversation was finished, she was pleased with where everything was at and confident the event would be as great as it always was. She scheduled another meeting prior to the big day so she could make sure everything was as it should be.

Back in her truck, she closed her eyes. It'd been a long day, and she wanted to go home and relax. And maybe if it had just been Amber there, it wouldn't feel like a chore. But with two of them there...well, it just felt like too much. She pulled out her phone.

Dinner in the barn?

Ted texted back almost right away. *Seven.*

She nodded. She didn't mind spending time alone, but tonight she wanted someone to distract her from her houseguests. She sent a text to Amber.

Eating with my crew tonight. Feel free to raid the fridge or have something delivered. But maybe you could be the one to answer the door if you do that? See you later.

She winced at how formal it sounded, but the footing had become unstable. Being out of control brought up memories she wanted to keep buried.

Chapter Twelve

AMBER SET HER PHONE down and sighed. "Guess we're on our own tonight."

Craig stretched and nuzzled Shift's fur. The dog had gone straight to him and decided he was a lapdog for the foreseeable future. Craig didn't seem to mind at all. "Well, that's probably a good thing. We can talk things through without you worrying about being overheard by that tall drink of lesbian cowboy out there."

"She's definitely that." Amber smiled a little. "We had a mini make-out session the other night. If it hadn't been for a farm emergency, I would've woken up next to her."

He tilted his head, the façade he kept up around people gone. "Would that have been a bad thing?"

"My last foray into romance didn't end well, did it?" She snuggled into the big chair and wiped away the start of tears. "That literally ruined my life. And Rowan already has someone she has casual sex with, and I don't think she's looking for another. She's not like us."

"Who is?" He shrugged. "But let's be honest now that there's no one to hear us be real. We'd both like someone who wanted more than a fling or arm candy. For me, that's a long way off, probably. But, babe, maybe this is your chance for something different."

She laughed and wiped away more tears. "It couldn't be more different if I moved to the moon."

"Have you called Bea yet?"

This time, her sigh came with a churning stomach. Craig had

met her mother several times, and even he'd been unsettled by the vitriol and bitterness she exuded. "Not yet. I saw a text message from her yesterday that just said, 'Well?' and I didn't respond. She'll be thrilled that the house has fallen apart. Just like part of her must be thrilled that my life is a mess."

He grunted as Shift stretched out and settled again. "This dog is definitely size proud. He doesn't care at all that he's crushing me." Craig didn't move him though. "I wish I could say that wasn't true, that you're wrong about her, but you're not. She'd be the kind of villain we couldn't cast because no one would believe in someone so awful." He struggled to reach his phone and then held it up. "Let's order dinner."

Amber nodded and closed her eyes, content to let him handle it. Only vaguely did she realize he called his lifestyle manager instead of just pulling up a delivery app. Why did that seem odd? She'd only been in Kentucky a short time, and yet she already felt like her way of life wasn't normal. Whatever *normal* meant.

"It'll be about an hour. He's having Thai food brought down to us from Louisville." Craig moved, and Shift groaned and slid off him, going to the door and looking back at them. Craig got up and opened the door. "I assume he knows what he's allowed to do and where he's allowed to go." He looked back at Amber. "Should I go out with him?"

She shook her head. "He'll scratch to come back in, although it sounds more like a knock with those giant paws."

Craig settled back onto the couch. "So. What are you going to do next? You always work better with a plan. What's the plan?"

He was right. Not having a plan made her feel lost. "Okay. The house has a lot to be fixed, but Rowan and Cornelius—"

"Honestly?" He grinned.

"Honestly. Rowan calls him Corn. I call him Cornball." She grimaced. "Although Rowan got pissy when she heard me say it. I get the feeling they're protective of their people down here. Anyway, they've already got someone lined up to get the work done, and I think it will start tomorrow or the next day. Depending on how fast they work, I shouldn't have to stay with Rowan for very long."

He looked at her sympathetically. "And that probably makes you a little sad too, I'm guessing?"

She groaned and ran her hands through her hair. "And how stupid is that? I've known her for a few days, and yet I can't stop thinking about her. She held my hand at the hospital, and I swear to you, it was the first time I felt like someone was really there for me."

His eyebrows rose.

"Other than you, obviously." She plucked at a loose string on the blanket draped over the back of the couch. "Although I have to admit, I wasn't sure you'd be there. Not after everything that's happened."

He leaned over and squeezed her knee. "I get that. Your parents didn't exactly instill a huge sense of self-worth in you. But I meant what I said to cowboy beefcake. You're my bestie. The only person who gets me and wants to be around me for me. And I feel the same about you."

The dam broke, and Amber began to sob. Craig pulled her out of the comfy chair and onto the sofa and held her until she cried herself out. The doorbell rang and she stood. "I should get that. We don't need the delivery driver fainting at the sight of you."

"I do have that effect on people. I'm going to the bathroom." He stretched and headed down the hall.

Amber opened the door and smiled at the delivery driver, although her eyes felt swollen and sore. "Hi. Thanks for this."

He nodded, looking puzzled. "I can't say as we've ever had someone pay this much to get food delivered so far from the city. There are places closer, you know."

She gave him a quick smile and took the bag of food. "I wasn't in charge of this one. Thanks again." She was about to close the door when Shift bumped the driver aside and came in. He led the way to the kitchen, his nose in the air as she placed the big bag of food on the island.

"I'm pretty sure Rowan doesn't give you this kind of food," she said. The scent of lemongrass and peanut sauce made her mouth water.

"Oh my God." Craig came in and plucked a spring roll from a cardboard container. "I'm so hungry."

Amber found the plates and reflected again on how natural it felt to be moving around Rowan's kitchen, almost like she belonged there.

They ate at the dining room table, and Shift lay at their feet, his big brown eyes looking up at them hopefully. The door opened, and Rowan came in. Her jacket was slick with rain, and she shook it out before hanging it on the peg beside the door, and then placing her boots side-by-side neatly on the shoe rack beneath it.

"Hey there." Rowan looked at the dishes on the table and the mess on the countertop. "Looks like you found food."

"I'll clean it up, I promise." Amber motioned with her fork. "Help yourself. We've got a ton." She really, really wanted Rowan to sit with them and talk in the easy way they'd been talking before Craig's arrival.

"Thanks, but I already ate with the crew, and I have to be up early." She gave a brief nod and headed toward the stairs, then stopped. "I had a text from the roofing team. They're going to start in the morning and get it done as fast as possible. There's talk of a storm coming in, so they want to get it covered up at least before the rain hits."

"Thank you." As much as she wanted to talk more, there didn't seem to be more to say. "Goodnight."

Rowan looked like she was about to say something, then just gave them a quick smile and headed upstairs.

Craig shook his head and slurped in a noodle. "If I were you, they'd have to drag me away from this place. I'd stay until I knew for sure this wasn't where I wanted to be."

"Two days ago, you were telling me to come home and deal with the house from New York." She took her plate to the sink and began closing up cartons. There was enough for leftovers the next day. Maybe Rowan would eat with them then. "You're fickle."

"I'm practical. And two days ago, that was practical advice. Today, after being here and seeing this place, I'm being more practical." He finished eating and got up to help her clean. "I have an idea. Take me to see the house tomorrow, and we'll meditate on it. See if the answers come from the Divine."

She thought about that as they cleaned up. "I like that idea. Do you mind driving? I still have a headache." Even admitting to being less than capable made her feel a little ill.

"Of course I'll drive. I mean, the openness of the roads here and the ability to see the entire sky gives me a touch of vertigo, but I'll put up with it just for you." He wrapped her in a hug and kissed the top of her head. "I'm sorry you've felt so alone, babes. But you're not, okay? I'm here, and I'm willing to bet that Rowan and all the people around here will be on your side too."

She sniffled, but she was all cried out. "Thank you," she murmured into his shoulder.

They finished cleaning up and then went to bed. She lay there for a long time looking at the ceiling, seeing patterns created by the shadows thrown by the moon nightlight in the corner. *A plan.* Craig was right. She couldn't let life just happen to her; she had to create a path and drive her plan forward. The problem was, she had no idea what she wanted, so how could she plan for what was essentially just a big question mark? She rolled over, hugging the stupid fairground dinosaur to her. What would she have done without Rowan? It was a question she didn't want an answer to, and an option she couldn't make a habit. Eventually, she'd end up alone. Better to not get attached than to hope people didn't let you down one day.

***

Amber was disappointed that Rowan was gone when she came down for her first cup of coffee, but it wasn't surprising. She really was up and out at the butt crack of morning, and although Amber had heard Rowan's door open and close, and Shift head downstairs, she hadn't even cracked her eyelids to see the time. For a brief moment, she imagined Rowan coming in, closing the door behind her, pulling the comforter from Amber's body, and then lowering herself into bed on top of her.

Then she fell asleep and had very nice dreams that left her aching and in need.

Which was why she wasn't in a great mood when Craig came in dressed only in tight boxers.

"Ew." She threw a dishtowel at him. "Have some decorum. You're not in your own house."

He half-heartedly threw the dishtowel back. "Fine. Give me a mug of go-juice, and I'll cover up my fantastic body that I spend an inordinate amount of time on, just so I don't offend your sapphic sensibilities."

She handed over a steaming mug of coffee, and he shuffled back upstairs. Shaking her head, she pulled a blanket around herself and took her coffee out to the porch. It was cold enough to see her breath, and the last leaves on the big oak tree were barely hanging on. Curled up in the big chair, she sipped her coffee and thought about the day ahead. It was good that she and Craig were going to the house. It would give her a sense of purpose, a focus. Better than sitting around the house all day thinking about the things she could have done differently so she wasn't in this mess in the first place. Her phone buzzed in her sweatshirt pocket, and she shifted around to get it, trying not to expose any flesh to the cold morning air.

Have you forgotten how a phone works? Or who brought you into this world?

Perfect. Nothing like a passive-aggressive text from her mother first thing in the morning. She tucked the phone back into her pocket. She'd respond later, after she'd been back to the house. At the sound of a vehicle, she leaned forward and looked down the road to see Rowan's truck headed their way. It brought an instant smile to her face, and the feeling of excitement at seeing someone was altogether disconcerting.

Rowan jumped out and then went and opened the passenger door. Shift jumped down and ran to the porch. "Hey. Down."

He stopped short of jumping on Amber, his tail wagging like crazy as he whined.

She smiled up at Rowan. "Thanks. He might have squashed me and ruined this beautiful blanket."

Rowan took the seat next to her. "I was definitely more worried about one thing than the other."

"You're back early. I didn't think I'd see you until later." It sounded inane even as she said it. Surely she used to be more articulate.

Rowan stood abruptly. "Hold that thought and let me get coffee. Need a top-up?"

Amber held out her empty mug, and Rowan headed inside. What did she need to say that made her seem almost nervous? Was she going to ask Amber to leave? Was she going to say it wasn't working out? The thought made it hard to breathe.

"Here you go." Rowan handed her a full mug and took a seat again. "Look, Amber—"

"I'm sorry." Amber blinked back tears. "I know I'm a pain in the ass, and Craig and I don't really fit into this world. But I don't want to go." She swallowed hard and dashed away tears. When had she last cried so often? *Weakness is only good if it gets you something.* Her mother's voice echoed in her head.

"Hey now." Rowan set down her mug and moved to kneel next to her. "I wasn't going to say anything like that." She ran her thumb over Amber's cheek, wiping away the tears. "I was going to ask if I could come with you today. To see the house."

Amber sniffled. "You were?"

"It's just that it's not my place, and you're not one to take kindly to people jumping into your business. But as I've been reminded lately, I'm a bit of a control freak, and I feel like I should know how things are going over there, because I'm the one who suggested this team for the repair work." Her eyes seemed to search Amber's, like she was looking for acceptance. Or maybe refusal.

"I should say no. I should tell you that I'm fine, and I've got Craig here." Amber hiccupped softly and flushed. "But the truth is, I'd really like that."

Rowan blew out a breath. "Then we're good." She moved away and picked up her mug again. "Want to tell me what's got you so on edge? Or is it just...well, everything?"

Amber wished she'd chosen the two-seater swing instead of the deck chair so she could sit closer to Rowan. When had she become such a needy mess? *I've always been a mess.* "I guess everything, like you said." Her phone buzzed again, and she grimaced as she pulled it out.

You're pissing me off. They were my parents, not yours.

She handed the phone to Rowan, who scanned the texts and handed it back. "Your mom?"

"Ah, the queen of all bitches." Craig came out, fully dressed and looking far more alert. He took the seat opposite. "Do you know the first thing I ever heard her say?"

Rowan looked like she might get up and leave again as she glanced at her truck. "What's that?"

"She said, 'I'd make a far better friend to you than my sad sack of a daughter. At least she makes it look like you've got a social conscience though, hanging out with people beneath you."

Rowan's head snapped back, and she looked at Amber. "Is that true?"

Amber nodded, unable to figure out why on earth she was so mortified. It wasn't like she'd been the one to say it. But she'd never been able to shake the feeling that it might be true.

Rowan looked at Craig, her eyes narrowed. "And how did you respond?"

He sipped his coffee, taking a moment to look at her over his mug. "I told her she wasn't the right kind of bitchy, and that her daughter had more class in her toe ring than Bea had ever seen in other people, given that she didn't have any herself." He laughed, but it lacked humor. "She looked like I'd hit her in the face with a wet gym sock."

"It was the first time someone stood up for me." Amber could still remember that moment and how it had made her feel.

"It won't be the last." Rowan finished her coffee and moved toward the door. "You deserved better."

She went inside, and Amber smiled at Craig. "She's coming to the house with us."

He grinned and wiggled his eyebrows. "Looks like she can't stay away from you after all."

Amber stood and nearly tripped on the blanket as she shuffled inside. "I need to go get ready. I'll be down in fifteen minutes."

He gave her a queenly wave, and she headed upstairs. Behind her, she heard Rowan go back out on the porch. What would they talk about? Would they talk about her? About her shortcomings or issues? No. Rowan wasn't like that, and she had a feeling Craig wouldn't ever say anything bad about her. She got ready as fast as possible while still making sure her hair and makeup were just right. She put on the clothes she'd worn to the festival and had to admit it was nice not to worry about whether or not they were the right fashion for the day. Rowan genuinely didn't care, and Craig might make a sarcastic remark or two, but she could handle that for the sake of comfort and warmth. She turned sideways and looked at the cut on her temple. It was itchy and scabbing, and she'd done her best to hide it with makeup. The one on the back of her head had started to itch so often, it made her feel like she had fleas. Just another reminder of the potholes that were strewn across her path. *Stop with the pity party.* She headed downstairs.

She opened the front door, and they stopped talking. Craig looked strangely serious, and Rowan looked like she was thinking about the nature of time and space. "Am I interrupting?"

"Not at all." Rowan stood and pulled her keys from her pocket. "Did you want to drive and for me to follow you guys over? Or you can ride with me. Whichever you're happy with."

She looked at Craig. "I'm good to ride with Rowan if you are. These roads are beautiful and wide, and I'm convinced something is going to jump out in front of me any second."

"Only if Rowan promises to take us to lunch after. I'm already hungry, and I need to take full advantage of the time away from my trainer." He looked at Rowan expectantly.

She ran her hand over her hair and looked away. "Craig, I'd like to, but it's not like you're a low-key guest."

He handed her his phone, open to a social media page. "I think that wet cat has run howling from the sack, my love."

Rowan scanned it and sighed, then handed it to Amber when she held out her hand. "Guess so. Lunch it is."

Amber flipped through the app that was ablaze with speculation about why Craig would be at a racing farm in Kentucky, who he was visiting, and whether it might have to do with a new movie. Floods of comments and people saying they might head to the little town to get a glimpse of him filled the feed. She handed the phone back to him and noticed he didn't seem in the least perturbed. But why would he? This was his life, after all.

She followed them to the truck, and he got in the backseat. She couldn't help but wonder what Rowan was thinking, but it felt intrusive to ask. Fortunately Craig was never one to enjoy silence.

"Tell me about your farm," he said, leaning forward between them.

"Well," Rowan said, tapping her fingers on the steering wheel.

"We have just over two thousand acres of land. We raise cattle in the eastern section and have a few barns down there. We stable some of the finest racehorses in Kentucky, and most of the business is built around them. We have a guest house, two restaurants, and several of the staff live on-site." She glanced over as though to see if they were still listening. "My parents started it when they first got together, and I took over after they passed."

"Can I ask what happened?" Amber wasn't sure what the boundaries were. She'd never have asked something so personal in New York. But again, this place made her feel like the rules were written on a different chalkboard.

"Mom got cancer." Rowan tapped a little harder on the steering wheel. "Too late to do anything about it. We got her through as best we could. After she passed, Dad lost his compass. One day, he gave me a hug, told me he loved me and was proud of me, and that he was taking a trip." She shrugged, and her jaw clenched. "I got a call from the place they'd gone on their honeymoon to say he'd died in a cliff accident."

Cold swept through her. "But it wasn't an accident."

Rowan glanced at Amber, and there was still pain in her eyes. "Nope. He loved her with every blood cell in his body, and when she was gone, so was he." She put the truck in park. "Let's go see what's going on."

Amber blinked, unaware they were already at the house. Rowan got out and headed quickly toward the guy standing next to his truck. She looked over her shoulder at Craig, who looked equally shaken.

"Damn." He visibly shivered a little. "That's someone who knows love like we never have."

Amber nodded and got out. Words weren't really available for the kind of thing Rowan had shared so openly. She walked up beside Rowan and the guy she was talking to, with Craig strolling behind her. The guy glanced at him, and then did a comedic double take before looking at Rowan.

"I knew you were keeping different company, but not how different." He held out his hand. "Peter."

Craig shook it and didn't let go right away. "Craig."

Amber cleared her throat as the moment lasted too long. "Amber. The one whose house you're fixing."

With a last glance at Craig, he looked at Amber. "Sorry. Little starstruck. Nice to meet you, Amber. Come on over, and I'll talk you through what we're doing."

Together, they went with him and listened as he explained how they were going to do the repairs. Three guys were already on the roof, pulling out wet wood and tossing it to the ground below.

"How soon do you think you can get it done?" Rowan asked, her arms crossed as she watched the work in progress.

"I think we can make it livable by next week. You said Cory's crew is coming in to do the plumbing? They're good and they're quick, and I think we can work alongside them after we pull out all the wet stuff." He turned to Amber. "We noticed some pictures and such that survived, and I had the guys put them over there in case you wanted them."

Amber looked at the pile of things on a tarp. "Thank you. I'm not sure how I'll get them back to Rowan's though. Not to mention I'll just have to bring it all back. Maybe you should have asked me before doing it."

Rowan's sigh was almost imperceptible, but it was there. "Thanks, Peter. I'll grab my tarp from the back and put the stuff on it so she can go through it at my place."

He nodded, but the lightness had gone from his expression. "Right then. I'll get on it with it." He looked past Amber at Craig. "I'd be happy to show you around town, if you're staying a while." The look in his eyes suggested the only part of the town they'd see would be his bedroom.

"I don't know how long I'll be here, but I'll call you if I need a tour." Craig grinned, and his biceps flexed a little in his thick, long-sleeved shirt.

Peter left, and Amber shook her head. "You could get laid at a Mormon convention."

"Who says I haven't?" He hooked his arm in hers. "Let's see what we've got."

The three of them carefully entered the house, which didn't look quite as bad now that some clean-up had begun.

"I'd forgotten how pretty this place is," Rowan murmured as she moved through the living room.

"You've been here before?" Amber asked. "I mean, I know you knew them."

Rowan smiled. "You've seen a little of what our community is like. They were my neighbors and used to enjoy having dinner with my parents. I think my mom replaced yours a little, in that they had a daughter they could be around. When she was dying, your grandmother was amazing. She brought all kinds of homemade soups, things my mom could swallow without a lot of work."

How strange to think she shared genetics with such kind people. "You know, I've never asked how they died. Do you know?"

Rowan stopped in front of a painting on the living room wall. "Your grandmother painted this."

It was a watercolor of the trees and house, and it exuded the kind of calm that surrounded them. "It's nice."

"They got into a car accident." Rowan crossed her arms and kept staring at the painting. "A bad storm rolled through when they were on their way back from Louisville. They went to see a movie they'd been looking forward to for ages. A flash flood caught them and swept the car into the river."

"Jesus." Craig turned and headed for the stairs. "This place is just a fucking Disneyland of family stories."

Amber agreed wholeheartedly. "That's really awful. I can't imagine."

Rowan nodded, her expression solemn. "Yeah. But when we found them, they were holding each other. And the whole town turned out for the funeral. I could take you to the cemetery, show you where they're buried, if you want."

Amber swallowed. "No... I've always hated the thought of a huge area full of people buried beneath it. It's not like they're there anyway."

Rowan waved toward the stairs. "Let's go make sure Craig isn't having sex on a beam."

The light comment broke the tension, and Amber felt like she could breathe again. Without thinking, she slipped her hand into Rowan's as they climbed the stairs, and Rowan gave it a squeeze. They made their way from room to room until they got to the main bedroom. Craig stood in front of the giant window, looking at the forest beyond.

"Amber," he said, glancing over his shoulder. "You'd be fucking crazy to give this place up. Look at the light and the way it hits the trees. I've never wanted to live outside the city, but this is something else. We could even tell a location scout about it and get it used in a film."

She and Rowan stood beside him, and she rested her head against Rowan's shoulder. The noise from the workmen and the hole in the roof didn't take away from the beauty, it was true. "Rowan, you said your ranch is two thousand acres. How many does Honeysuckle have?"

"Four hundred." Rowan looked down at her. "Your grandparents used to have about the same as me, but when the time came for them to retire, they sold off a whole lot to me, though someone else wanted it real bad. The guy that owns the next farm over is..." She shrugged and looked back out the window. "I don't like to speak ill of people. I imagine you'll meet him soon enough."

"How many Manhattan city blocks is an acre?" Craig asked, finally turning away from the view and looking at the room critically.

"Well, I don't know what a city block measures, but I read somewhere that Central Park is a little over eight hundred acres, and one acre is a little over a football field, give or take. Does that help?"

Amber finally released her hold on Rowan's hand. "I have land half the size of Central Park and more than four hundred football fields?" At Rowan's nod, she said, "And you have two and a half times the land of Central Park?"

Rowan laughed. "You look a little surprised."

"Given that her apartment is smaller than your living room, it's more surprising she hasn't passed out." Craig moved back toward the hallway. "Just so you know, I'm claiming that back bedroom for all eternity. You'll have to hang my name on it. I'll have the plaque sent from my next dressing room."

Amber laughed, an unfamiliar giddy feeling rising from her chest. She had her own home. And land. She couldn't touch both walls by stretching out. It was paid for, and all she needed to do was handle the repairs. For the first time since she'd arrived, it really hit her. This was *hers*.

"You okay?" Rowan asked softly.

"I..." Amber shook her head and allowed herself an unfiltered smile. "I guess it just feels real for the first time."

Rowan leaned against the doorframe, her arms crossed, and her head tilted. "Well, it might be a good time to think of any changes you want to make so it really feels like your own. Get all the building done at once."

Excited, Amber hurried into the hall and looked into each bedroom, thinking about what she'd change or keep. She took out her phone and started typing in notes and taking photos, sometimes talking out loud about what she was thinking, sometimes just moving from room to room, lost in her own thoughts.

"I want them to tear out this wall." She pointed to the wall between the kitchen and living room. "I've always loved the idea of an open plan, where someone, not me, obviously, can cook while guests hang out and chat."

There was no response, and she turned around to find Craig sitting on the windowsill paying no attention whatsoever, and Peter and Rowan looking down at a clipboard as Peter sketched.

"Hello?" Amber put her hands on her hips. "Is anyone listening?"

Peter held up the clipboard to face her. "Something like this?"

She took it from him and motioned for the pencil, which he handed over. "I'd move this over here. And make this bigger, if we can. And I'd like a downstairs bathroom too, so no one has to go upstairs. Maybe here." She continued to sketch and then handed it back to him.

He looked it over with Rowan looking over his shoulder. "We can do all this, sure. But it'll mean you either need to wait to move in, or you move in and live with construction all around you."

"She'll wait till it's done," Rowan said without looking up.

"Will I?" Amber saw Craig's head turn at her tone. "I don't remember making that decision."

Rowan rolled her eyes. "Amber, why would you stay here when my place is free and without construction noise?"

"Because this is *my* place, and I'll decide what to do and where to live." They stared at each other for a moment before she turned to Peter. "I'll make that decision once the roof is done, so if you could call me and let me know, that would be great." She dug a business card from her pocket and handed it over.

"Yes, ma'am." He waved the clipboard and backed out of the room, but before he left, he looked over Amber's shoulder. "Remember my offer about that tour."

Craig shot him a megawatt smile and waved.

Rowan shoved her hands in her pockets. "Want me to get the tarp for the pile of stuff out front? Or do you want to carry it by hand back to my place, so you don't have to accept help?"

Amber gritted her teeth. "The tarp would be great."

Rowan turned and left without another word, and Craig gave a low chuckle from his place on the window seat. "She doesn't know you well enough to know how you feel about someone trying to control you."

Amber rolled her shoulders to ease the tension. "She will. Unless she kicks me out on my ass because she can't tell me what to do." Her phone started buzzing insistently, and she pulled it out. "Shit."

Craig patted the window seat. "Let's get it over with."

She sat beside him and answered the video call. "Hi, Mom."

"Don't pull that shit with me." Her mom's pinched, Botoxed face filled the screen. "Why haven't you responded, you ungrateful little shit?"

Craig squeezed her hand. "Always good to see your acidic expression on screen, Bea."

"Uh. You've got that ass-grabber with you, but you couldn't take a second to talk to me? Same selfish thing as always. What's going on with the house?"

"Why do you care?" Amber asked, looking up at Rowan who moved into the doorway and leaned against the frame. When she motioned as though to leave, Amber shook her head and held up her hand to get her to stay. If Rowan wanted insight into her, this was how she'd get it.

"Because they were my parents, and that house should rightfully be mine. But as usual, you've gotten the best of things, haven't you?" She frowned and touched on the side of her eye, as though to make sure there was no wrinkle in the Botox. "You don't have the first clue about living there. Sign it over to me, and I'll give you thirty percent of whatever it sells for."

Craig scoffed, and Amber squeezed his hand to keep him quiet. Rowan's expression remained neutral. "That's very generous, Mom, to sell my property for me and give me a little of it. I think I'll pass."

"You'll change your mind when you get tired of the country yokels. You think your movie star friend is going to come see you when you're surrounded by cow shit and rain?" She looked away and faked a yawn. "I suppose there were photos of me everywhere. I want them, just so I can remind myself how far I've come."

"Actually, there weren't any photos of you anywhere." Amber took malicious pleasure in the truth. "If I didn't know this was your parents' house, I wouldn't have known you'd ever lived here at all."

"You're a liar. You always have been, and thanks to your escapade at work, you've proven me right."

Amber flinched and felt the blood drain from her face.

"That's right, I heard about you slutting around with a client and what it cost her." Her smile was something out of a horror movie. "Sell the house and give me my cut, Amber. I'm entitled to it. I'll have my lawyer call you." She ended the call.

Amber lowered her phone slowly and nearly dropped it from her shaking hand.

Rowan squatted in front of her and took it, then set it aside to hold her hands. "I promised you two lunch, and I'm starving. Can we go?"

She nodded, grateful for Craig's arm around her shoulders and Rowan's touch. She always felt unmoored when she talked to her mother, but this had been particularly awful.

Craig kissed her cheek and stood. "Come on, babes. We both need carbs to soak up all that acid." He left ahead of them.

Rowan pulled her into a hug. "I'm so sorry," she whispered against her hair. "But I've got you."

Amber leaned into the embrace and took a long, deep breath. "I'm so glad the two of you were here." She pulled back. "I wanted you to hear. To understand. I don't mean to be so..." She shrugged.

"I get it. And believe me when I tell you that I see something you don't. But hopefully you will." She draped her arm around Amber's shoulders, and they headed to the truck. Rowan waved, and Peter waved back from his place on the roof.

Rowan opened the passenger door, and Amber hesitated before getting in. This was her house. She had a place in the world, and she wouldn't give it up. Not yet. "A year."

Rowan looked puzzled. "A year for what?"

"I'm going to give myself a year to figure out who I am and what I want. A year of living away from the city, away from my mother, away from my toxic career. After a year, I can decide where to go next. But for now, this is where I want to be."

Rowan nodded, looking thoughtful. "A year sounds good."

Amber got in the truck, and Craig squeezed her shoulder but didn't say anything, for which she was grateful. She wanted quiet and some time to think, but now she had a plan. And as Rowan got into the driver's seat beside her, that plan felt like the best one she'd ever made.

Chapter Thirteen

A YEAR. ROWAN COULDN'T get the phrase out of her head. A year sounded like a long time, and it sounded like barely a moment. Soon enough, Amber would be in her own place, and it had been good to see Amber so excited about it as she'd figured out how to put her stamp on the space. Rowan had thought, for a second, that she'd really come around to staying. But she hadn't. She was just using it as a place to heal, a stopgap on her way to a new life elsewhere.

And why was that a bad thing? Rowan had already decided not to take things any farther with their attraction. Amber's life was complicated and messy, and that was the last thing Rowan wanted in her neat, orderly life that was scheduled to the last minute of the day. Having a solid neighbor and friend for a year should be a good thing. And it was.

But damn it all, holding Amber in her arms after that call from one of the most vile people she'd ever heard speak had been like holding something precious and breakable. And Amber had been right. It gave Rowan understanding of Amber's baggage like nothing else could have. Lunch had been a lighthearted affair, with Craig keeping up conversation using tales of stunts gone wrong and locations he'd loved. Amber had come out of her sadness for a moment or two to laugh.

When Craig had been noticed and started getting requests for autographs and selfies, Rowan had taken the time to ask Amber if she was really okay. She'd said she just needed time to think, which was fair, but Rowan had hoped for more. When they'd got back to the ranch, she'd gone to work and left them talking in the kitchen, and when she'd finally come home late after dealing with some stable issues, they'd both already gone to bed. That meant she and Shift sat on the porch as she drank a cup of herbal tea and unwound from an intense day.

As always, she was gone before they got up, and even now, helping with the cattle far from the house, she wondered what was going on and if Amber was okay. Having her attention divided wasn't a good thing, and she wasn't sure how to fix it. The rumble of a quad pulled her from her musings, and she looked up to see Pam driving with Amber and Craig with her.

"Hey. They asked if they could come see the master farmer at work." Pam grinned and hopped off. "I told them you weren't nearly as impressive as some people think you are."

"Fuck off." Rowan peeled off the thick rubber gloves and tossed them in a nearby bucket. "I would've seen you at lunch."

Amber seemed to be taking it all in as she looked around. "Craig needs to get back. He's been asked to do a read-through for another movie."

He pressed his hand to his chest. "I wanted to say goodbye. Take good care of our girl."

Rowan pulled him into a sweaty, smelly hug and didn't let go right away as he squealed. "You bet I will."

He made a gagging sound as he smelled his sleeve. "You've ruined good cashmere."

"I have a feeling you have more."

"I'll give you a ride back to your rental car. Amber, you coming?" Pam asked.

"Um...no." She looked at Rowan. "Can I keep you company for a little while?"

Surprised, Rowan waved Pam off. "I'll bring her back. Make sure Craig leaves as pretty as he arrived. I don't want anyone saying we don't treat our studs well here."

He scoffed and actually blushed a little. "I'll call you in a couple days, babes. Take care of yourself, and call me if you need me."

He and Amber had a long hug, and then he gave a little wave as he and Pam drove off.

Amber sat on a bale of hay. "I wanted to say thank you."

"For?" Rowan pulled her gloves back on and picked up the shovel to keep mucking out the drainage ditch.

"For telling Craig that reminding me of things my mother has said isn't always useful."

"Ah, that." Rowan glanced up from her work. "He told you."

"He did. And he said I seem happier here. We're so used to being a certain way, you know, so no one can hurt us or get attached. It was easy to slip back into it when he got here."

"But?" Rowan wondered if this was the best way to have a real conversation. One of them busy and one of them talking so it didn't feel so intense.

"But." Amber twirled a piece of hay between her fingers. "But I actually like how nice people are here. I mean, it's hard to get used to, and I don't think I'll ever lose my edge."

Rowan continued digging and waited for more.

"Also, my mother tried to control everything I did. She always has. And my only way to survive it was to refuse to allow anyone else to tell me what to do, ever." She finally looked at Rowan. "Please respect that."

Rowan stopped shoveling and leaned on it. "I can try." She smiled at Amber's expression. "When my mom was dying, I realized I needed to control everything around me. I couldn't help her, and I couldn't save my dad. But I could keep everything running perfectly so they had nothing to worry about. I still work that way."

"So we might butt heads sometimes."

"Like bulls in a ring, I imagine." Rowan laughed and threw the gloves in the bucket, then put the shovel and gloves on the quad. "But we'll work it out. Ready for lunch?"

Amber nodded and got in. "Can you show me around a little first? Two thousand acres is a lot."

"Sure thing." Rowan's stomach growled, but she ignored it. She talked a bit about the areas they were passing. "This is my favorite place on the farm. No one really comes up here but me, I don't think."

"Wow." Amber got out of the quad. "You've got your own lake."

"Can't have Central Park without water." Rowan grinned and sat on the old wood bench facing the big body of water. "It's natural, but I had some fish put in a while back to keep the algae down. We used to be able to ice skate on it in the winter when it froze solid. Winters aren't as cold now though, and the ice isn't thick enough. It's still nice to come and find peace though."

"What's that building?" Amber pointed toward a small cabin.

"Boat house. I've got some kayaks and such in there. Haven't had a chance to use them in years." The wind ruffled her hair, and she looked up at the sky. "Storm's coming in. We should head back."

Amber frowned. "How can you tell?"

"See that edge right there? Where the clouds look like someone has dragged their finger through them? That's rain coming our way." They got onto the quad, and Rowan started down a middle road that would take them back faster.

"Can we come back here one day?" Amber said, looking over her shoulder. "I love sitting by the water in the park."

"I'd like that." The first raindrops hit them just as they pulled up in front of the house and dashed inside. "Let me get cleaned up, and I'll make some lunch."

It looked like Amber was going to offer to help with clean-up, based on the look she gave her, but then she shrugged a little and turned away. "See you soon."

Rowan rested her head against the shower wall. Damned if she didn't wish Amber was in there with her. Visiting the lake with her had been a bigger thing than Amber could know. But there was no reason to add more emotional stuff onto what they'd already shared. She finished showering and tried to ignore the throbbing need between her legs. She could take care of that later, when visions of Amber on her back would take her over the edge in no time.

When she got to the stairs, she inhaled and smiled. She found Amber in the kitchen, biting her lip as she flipped the grilled cheese over. The bread slid off, and she poked it back into place. When Rowan laughed, she shook her head. "You made this look easy."

"There's a knack for it." She moved behind Amber and pressed her chest to Amber's back. Then she reached around and put her hand over Amber's. "Hold the spatula like this," she said softly, next to Amber's ear. "Press it to the pan so it gets hot, and the cheese starts to melt."

Amber's breathing increased, and she pressed back into Rowan's body.

"Now slide it under, like this," she said, "and flip it fast, so it doesn't lose any heat."

When Amber shivered against her and pressed her ass against Rowan's crotch, she swore and spun her around. She wrapped her hand in Amber's hair and pulled her in for a kiss hotter than the pan behind her, and then she moaned as Amber wrapped one leg around hers, pulling her even closer.

The smoke alarm started screaming, and Rowan jumped back. Shift began barking at it and between the two noises, Rowan was slammed back to earth. Amber moved out of the way and started wafting a towel under the alarm, and Rowan took the blackened sandwich off the oven and tossed it out the back door for the animals to munch on. It steamed in the cold, and she drew in a breath of rain-scented air before going back in. She needed to get herself under control. Why the hell was she doing things she'd told herself she wouldn't do?

Amber already had more bread and cheese on the counter, and she giggled as Rowan nudged her out of the way. "Don't trust me now?"

"You should sit yourself right over there, or we're going to have to eat the next batch of charcoaled bread." Rowan pointed with the spatula.

"I was behaving myself. That was totally your fault." Amber slid onto a stool and rested her chin in her hands.

"I take full responsibility. I couldn't help myself, and I apologize." Rowan shook her head as she put an unburnt sandwich on the plate and handed it over. "You make me crazy and seeing you standing in my kitchen makes me a little nutty."

Amber bit into her sandwich and nodded approvingly. "I like that kind of crazy."

Rowan plated her sandwich and moved to sit beside Amber at the counter. "Yeah, well, now we know for sure that it can set fire to things."

Amber sobered a little and didn't say anything. They ate in silence for a few minutes before Rowan said, "Can I ask you about something I heard yesterday?"

Amber nodded but didn't look at her.

"Your mom said something about a woman, and how it messed things up for you. What was that about?"

Amber kept eating and didn't respond, but Rowan was happy to wait.

"Craig told you that I was a wealth manager. I worked with what we call HNW clients—high net worth. People with a lot of money to invest and who like to be really involved in where their money is going. It isn't rare to get close to your clients."

"Like you did with Craig." Rowan said, taking their empty plates to the sink.

"Right." Amber accepted the glass of iced tea Rowan offered her. "I got too close to a client and ended up in a fling with her. She was seeing several other people, but she was adamant that I not see anyone other than her. For a while, I was fine with that. I was really into her, and even my mother was impressed that I'd made it into that crowd."

Rowan couldn't imagine being fine with that kind of situation at all, but she held her tongue.

"She wanted to make an investment and instead of doing my due diligence, I basically just acted like a normal girlfriend and let her do it. I was distracted and overwhelmed by her, and... well, I just fucked up. She lost millions when it turned out the investment wasn't sound, and she went mental. She had a full-blown screaming meltdown in my office, which a firm partner had a front row seat to, and then she said I'd seduced her and ruined her. She posted on social media platforms and tagged in other financial houses to let them know I was a liability, just to make sure everyone knew I was shit at my job."

"Fuck." Rowan leaned back. "That sounds like chaos."

"It was. It is." Amber shrugged, but the pain was clear in her eyes. "They fired me for inappropriate conduct and dereliction of duty the next day. The world of high finance is weirdly small in New York, and it pretty much means my reputation is shot. I won't get another job in that sector before the sun explodes."

"And that's why you've got your year here."

Amber brushed away tears almost like she was irritated with them. "Like I said a while back. This came at just the right time. Exactly when I need to change my entire life."

"Well, it's a good place to do it."

"What about you? You know my entire sordid story. What's yours? Why do you live in this gorgeous house all by yourself?"

It was a fair question, and one Rowan had been asking herself lately. "I've had a few long-term relationships. One with a woman who loved horses and everything to do with them, so we matched well in that area. But she met someone else when she was in England for Ascot, and that was that. She came back, packed her stuff, and moved to the UK the following week."

"I guess you can't help who you meet." Amber shrugged. "I'm sorry that happened to you though."

Rowan fed Shift a piece of crust, and he set his head on her thigh. "We all have breakups. Wasn't nearly as dramatic as yours. I had my own place in town, but I spent a lot of time here. Once my mom got sick, I sold my place and moved back here to help out. Then there wasn't a spare second for relationships, and since they've been gone, I haven't had the time or the energy for it. I go to the bar for a quick hook-up once in a while, but that's about it."

"It doesn't sound like you're happy about that way of life." Amber held her hand. "Are you lonely?"

Rowan nodded slowly. "I haven't had time to be lonely for the most part, but yeah, lately I find myself wishing I had someone to come home to." It felt a little too big of an admission for the middle of the day with the scent of burned bread lingering around them. "I think I'll know when the time is right. I still have a lot on my plate running this place."

Amber looked like she was going to say something, then stopped and frowned. "Work can really take over our lives. I spent ten years at that firm, hardly ever taking a day off, killing myself for people who sent me packing without so much as a good luck." She looked into Rowan's eyes. "I'd hate for you to wake up one day and know you dedicated everything to this place and lost out on someone to share it with."

"Sounds like we both have some stuff to work on." Rowan stood and stretched out the kinks in her back. "I need to get back to it. You have any plans today?"

Amber's face lit up. "I'm going to do some online shopping for the house. I have an image in my mind of what I want it to look like."

"Nice. Have fun." Rowan backed away, aware of the fact that she wanted to kiss Amber before she left. "Look. I don't want to send you mixed signals." She shoved her hands in her pockets. "I think you're incredibly beautiful, and I'm so attracted to you, it's painful. And that's making me do things and think things I probably shouldn't. But you've got a lot going on right now, and if it didn't work out between us... Well, I'd hate to ruin your fresh start."

"And you have this place to run, and I'm not planning on staying forever." Amber's expression turned wistful.

"Yeah." Why did hearing it out loud make her chest ache? "It's the heart of the storm, where cold air meets hot and causes all kinds of problems."

"Are you the hot or the cold air in this metaphor?" Amber smiled.

"Depends on the day." Rowan grabbed her raincoat. "See you for dinner?"

"We've got a ton of leftover Thai food. I'm capable of reheating that, if it works for you?"

"Perfect." Rowan stopped as she opened the door. "Friends?"

"Friends." Amber's expression was serious. "I don't have nearly enough of those."

Rowan nodded and headed into the storm. The rain felt cleansing and cooled the chaotic feelings rampaging through her. She had work to do. And Amber would be waiting in the house at the end of the day. Friend or not, that felt pretty damn good.

Chapter Fourteen

AMBER PULLED UP OUTSIDE the diner and thought of how different things had been the last time she'd been there. It hadn't been long, and yet it felt like months. Could life really change so fast? She wouldn't have thought so, but here she was, buying food for the guys working on the farmhouse that was now hers. And tonight, she'd have dinner with Rowan, which she was looking forward to far more than she should be. She pulled up her hood against the driving rain and dashed to the door.

The bell tinkled as she entered, and Fran looked up from the table she was serving. "Well, burn my britches. I wondered if you'd be back." She came over and pulled Amber into a hug, then held her at arm's length. "But you didn't bring that hunk of a man with you."

Somehow it was hard for Amber to picture Craig as a hunk of anything, but that probably came from knowing him so well. "He had to head back for a movie thing, sorry."

Fran finally let go. "Next time, you bring him here for some real food." She held up a menu. "Did you want to look? Or are you just having the pancakes?"

Amber laughed. "Thanks, but Rowan made me a grilled cheese not long ago. You mentioned helping feed the workers at Honeysuckle, and I wondered if I could take you up on that?"

Fran hurried around the counter and pulled a sheet of paper and a menu from under it. "Here's what we can do in big batches. You tell me what you want and when you want it."

Amber sat on a stool and looked it over. She chose a variety of sandwiches and sides as well as some cake. "Can we do it tomorrow? The weather should be good, so they'll be there working."

"We can do that for you. But you have to do something for me." Fran removed a dome glass top from a pie plate. "I need you to try this cinnamon pecan pie and tell me what you think. I'm trying a new recipe." She plated it and then poured a cup of coffee to go with it. "Then we'll settle up."

Amber's initial reaction was to say she couldn't have pie for no reason and that she hadn't been working out enough to merit it. But she stopped herself and simply picked up the fork. That was her mother's voice, and she needed to work on getting it out of her head.

"Well, I was hoping I'd get to meet the new girl in town."

She looked up from the pie at a guy who looked like a caricature from a comic book. His slicked-back hair held enough grease to run a car, and his white suit was rumpled and didn't at all go with the alligator-skin boots.

He held out his hand. "Jimmy Cartwright. I'm your better neighbor."

Amber waved her fork. "Sorry, my hands are sticky." Somehow, she didn't want to touch him at all. "And I'm pretty fond of my neighbor."

"Well, I imagine you'll be mighty fond of me too, once you get to know me." He perched on the stool next to her. "I'll have what she's having," he said to Fran.

"We're all out." Fran poured him coffee that splashed a little over the cup, causing him to move his white cuff out of the way.

Amber could see half the pie still under the dome. So other people felt the same way about him. Good thing to know some instincts were still intact.

He frowned at her and then turned his big fake smile back to Amber. "I figure you've heard of me. I'm a big deal around these parts."

She shook her head and kept eating. "No one has mentioned

a Jimmy. In fact, no one has mentioned me having another neighbor, and I hadn't thought to ask."

His cheeks turned a mottled red, and the fake smile looked a bit more like concrete. "Well, then it's extra good we've run into each other here." He pulled a brochure from the inside pocket of his jacket. "I own the Griffin Gate Spa Hotel. We're all about the finer things in life, which as someone from New York, I'm sure you're used to. I'd love it if you'd come by and give my little place a try one day. All complimentary, of course, as a welcome to my new neighbor."

Amber flipped open the brochure. Although she'd expected tacky and over the top, it was actually quite beautiful. The grounds were landscaped rather than empty horse or cattle fields, with fountains and mazes of flowers. The spa itself looked like it could rival any she'd been to in New York, or even the ones she'd been to in France when she was playing in that crowd. The prices were similar too. "You get people in this area willing to pay East Coast prices?"

"Damn right I do." His smug smile showed too-white teeth. "In fact, we're so busy we're booked right through to Christmas."

"Impressive." Amber closed it and pushed it back toward him.

"It is that." He nodded and took another sip of his coffee. "But it could be even better."

It was the kind of marketing lead-in she was used to back in the city. The sales pitch was coming. She waited, not wanting him to think she was genuinely interested.

"See, I've been wanting to put in a golf course, which would bring me a whole new market, and people around here would love it. But I'm short a few acres."

"That sounds like a you problem." Amber's skin crawled as he'd leaned closer.

"Well, you could solve that problem. A nice New York girl like you doesn't belong down here in Kentucky, and if you'd be willing to sell me Honeysuckle, you'd have an awful lot of money to spend living somewhere you'd be more comfortable." He frowned at Fran as she took his coffee away, still half full.

"You have no idea where I belong, what I want, or what would make me comfortable. People making assumptions like that really pisses me off. And I'm not looking to sell, at least not for a while." She stood and looked at Fran. "That pie was amazing. You should add that to my order for tomorrow."

"Hey now. I didn't mean to offend, and there's no need to get uppity." Jimmy stood as well. "You should at least hear my offer."

"Uppity?" Amber rounded on him after handing Fran her credit card. "Mister, you've never seen uppity if you think me telling you to back off is even close. And if you're that desperate, then I imagine your offer will be a hell of a lot better if and when the day comes I want to sell."

"Two million dollars." He crossed his arms, his expression neutral. "You can't tell me you couldn't use that money."

Amber shrugged. "That's a lot to *you*, Jimmy. I worked with five times that in an hour in New York. If you're going to try to play with the big kids, I suggest you learn some things." She turned to Fran, whose smile was so wide it looked like it might actually hurt. "Thanks again for this. If you'll give me a pen, I'll write down my number in case you need to get hold of me." She accepted the pen and scribbled down her number for Fran. "But I'm staying at Rowan's until the house is ready."

"Why bother to rebuild it if you're not going to stay?" Jimmy asked. "That's a waste of time and money. We could just finish tearing it down after you sell and move on." This time the look in his eyes wasn't even fake friendly. His eyes were hard, his jaw set.

Amber stepped closer and realized he wasn't much taller than her. "Listen carefully, you oily, creepy cartoon of a human. If you want to intimidate me, you're going to have to try a lot harder. Better yet, accept no for an answer and move on," she said, imitating his accent and turned away. "See you soon, Fran."

She ducked and hurried through the rain, which was still

coming down hard and fast. Rowan's explanation of the heart of the storm came back to her as she watched Jimmy stare at her from the doorway of the diner as she put on her seatbelt. Was she the cold air clashing with everyone else's hot air down here? Her mom wanted the property, or at least money from it. Jimmy wanted it for his golf course. No one other than Rowan seemed to care in the least what *she* wanted.

On impulse, she typed the Griffin Gate into her GPS. The long, winding drive had solar lights along the way, and it opened into a beautiful open area complete with huge fountain and valet service. The spa itself was enormous, taking up what she guessed would be at least two acres, if she'd understood the measurements right. She drove off, her curiosity satisfied. She wouldn't be taking Jimmy up on his offer of complimentary services, but she felt better having seen the place for herself. Even if she wanted to sell at some point, she'd rather sell it to just about anyone else.

Back at Rowan's, she spent the rest of the afternoon curled up in front of the fire looking at new kitchen fixtures, beds, and curtains. It was odd to be shopping without wondering if she actually had the space for it. Even a new vase needed to be thought out for her loft. Now she found herself wondering about having a room just for books. She hadn't had the time to read one for ages, and it felt like a good time to get back to it.

The front door opened, and she glanced at the time. "Shit." She jumped up and ran past Rowan. "Sorry! I lost track of time. I'll get dinner going now."

Rowan held up her hand. "Amber, it isn't like I expect you to cook for me. And I need to shower anyway. There's no hurry."

Amber watched her walk to the stairs. Her shoulders were hunched, and she moved awkwardly. "Are you okay?"

Rowan nodded and started climbing the stairs slowly. "I got thrown by a horse a few years ago and hurt my back. Still acts up now and then, that's all. Be right back."

Amber moved quickly and had the leftovers heated and waiting by the time Rowan came back downstairs, and although she still looked tired, she didn't seem to be moving as gingerly. "Here you go. Gourmet reheating, done all by myself."

"Well done." Rowan grinned and sat down. "I've been looking forward to this all day."

"Leftover Thai? Or dinner with me?" God, did she really say that? How needy could she sound?

"Both." Rowan made an appreciative sound as she started to eat. "You do the shopping you wanted to do?"

Amber nodded and decided there was no delicate way to eat the Pad Thai noodles. "I found lots of things. I have stuff in all kinds of online shopping baskets. I just have to make decisions."

"I'd like to see what you're thinking of." Rowan looked up when Amber didn't answer. "What?"

"It just occurred to me that no one has ever really been interested in knowing what I like." She stabbed at the noodles. "I don't know how to take it."

Rowan shook her head. "Don't overthink it. Share what you want to and know I'm interested. That's all."

That's all. Like it was that easy. Who didn't spend their life overthinking things? "I went into town today and ordered some food for the workers at Honeysuckle. Fran gave me some amazing pie."

Rowan laughed and took another helping of food, since she'd already wolfed down the first one. "Yeah, that's Fran." She glanced up. "You felt okay to drive?"

"Not a headache in sight."

Rowan nodded. "Great news."

"I did have a strange encounter though." She hadn't been able to get Jimmy completely out of her mind, and she wanted Rowan's take on it. "This guy came up to me and said he was my better neighbor."

Rowan grunted and shook her head. "Jimmy."

"If his breath hadn't warned me off, the way he spoke to me did." Amber cut her egg roll in half.

Rowan's head snapped up. "What do you mean? Was he inappropriate?"

"Whoa there, cowboy." Amber grinned and held up her fork. "You'll remember that I can handle myself. And he wasn't so much inappropriate as he was a dick trying to prove he has one. He asked me to sell Honeysuckle, and I said no. That's the gist of it anyway. What a piece of work."

Rowan's shoulders seemed to relax, and the lines around her eyes eased. "I'm glad to hear that you turned him down. He came around here for the same reason a couple times, and I had to set him straight. God knows he bugged the hell out of your grandparents, right up until your grandmother punched him."

"You don't mean my grandfather?" Amber could picture the slimeball bothering other people too.

"Nope. Your grandmother. She had a mean right hook, and when he threatened to tell Social Services that they weren't fit to live there on their own anymore as a way to get them off the land, she clocked him so hard, she knocked him clear onto his ass into a mud puddle. She said next time it would be a shotgun and not her fist." Rowan laughed and finally stopped shoveling in food. "Virginia was something else."

"Wow. I wish I could have seen that." Amber smiled at the image of some old Southern woman laying Jimmy flat. "He seems to think he can bully me the same way. Fran seemed to appreciate my response."

"I bet she did. Jimmy has been a thorn in everyone's side since he left town and then came back and bought that piece of land. No one wanted that resort here, but it was his land, so we had no say in it. At first, we thought it might be good for the town to have rich folks spending their money here. But then he made it so they could get everything they needed at the resort and not have to leave it at all. When they do come into town, they're rude and mostly just complain about everything. Now he wants to build some big housing development next to a golf course. He wanted the land next to his, which is yours, but he would have settled for mine. Something like that would change everything about our town." She pushed her plate away and wiped her lips with a napkin. "Thank you for that. I worked my ass off today, and I was starving."

Amber gathered a couple of the cartons, briefly pondering the fact that Jimmy had left out the housing element of his plan. "Seems like the least I can do since you're letting me stay here. In fact, I wanted to talk to you about paying rent."

Rowan jerked back slightly. "Why would you want to do that? I'm not charging you to stay here."

"But I *am* staying here. Using your electricity, your water. I don't want to take advantage of you." Amber laughed when Rowan's brow quirked and she grinned. "At least, not that way."

Rowan shook her head and closed her eyes as she rested her head back against the chair. "That's not how neighbors do things around here. If you want to pitch in here and there like you did tonight, that's great and much appreciated. But I'm not taking money." She cracked one eye. "Besides, aren't you paying for your place in New York too?"

"For the time being, yeah. But I have enough in savings to deal with life for a long time before I need to worry." She smiled wryly. "The benefit of working in high finance as a wealth manager is knowing how to manage your own money well. I've got enough investments and options to keep me going until I decide what to do next. Paying five grand a month for a place I don't even own seems excessive, I know—"

"Good God." Rowan's eyes snapped open. "Didn't you say it's tiny? Five thousand?"

Amber nodded. "But that's pretty typical in New York right now."

"Then why on earth hold onto it if you're going to stay here for a year?" Rowan almost seemed irritated.

"Because I might go back one day, when all this madness blows over. And I won't want to start from scratch when rental prices might be even higher. And if things don't work out here, then I've got a fallback option."

Rowan stared at her for a long moment. "Around here, we'd call that hedging your bets instead of going all in. Why not just commit to a path and make it work instead of assuming it will fail and having a way out?" She shook her head and stood. "Maybe it makes sense to you, but I think it just sounds like you're biding your time instead of actually wanting to stay."

"Is that so wrong?" Amber stood and faced her. "It isn't like I made a secret of the fact that this wasn't exactly my lifelong dream. Now that I'm here, I'm excited, sure, but that doesn't mean I'm going to settle down for the foreseeable. I like the theatre, and movies, and five-star restaurants. Watching horses run around a field all day isn't my idea of entertainment."

Rowan backed up a step and shoved her hands in her pockets. "Just when I think you might fit in here, you remind me that you'd be as out of place as a bull in a llama pen." She turned and headed to the stairs. "I'm wiped. Good night."

Deflated, Amber sank onto the couch. She'd been looking forward to showing Rowan the things for her new house. How had the conversation gone so wrong so fast? Forcing herself to her feet, she finished cleaning up the dinner mess and headed upstairs. She could hear Shift snoring from Rowan's bedroom, and she was tempted to crack open the door and call him over so she could have some company tonight. Instead, she went into her room and flopped onto the bed. The repairs on her place couldn't come soon enough. She needed space, away from other people's expectations and judgment. Rowan usually seemed to understand, but something about tonight had set her off. Why would she be upset that Amber had a practical plan in place? She always did; even when she'd moved in with a partner, she'd kept her own place. That way, when it went bad as it always did, she had somewhere to go. It worked and made things less messy and unstable. How was that a bad thing?

She flipped over, wishing she could punch something harder than a pillow. This new start wasn't nearly as shiny as she hoped it would be.

Chapter Fifteen

ROWAN SLAMMED HER OFFICE door shut so hard, the pictures on the walls rattled. The official office in the main building had a big, impressive desk, photos of race winners they'd stabled over the years, and a drink cabinet that made plenty of her clients happy to be there. Today though, she was ready to bust up everything in it.

The door opened, and Ted peeked around the edge. "Is it safe? Or am I gonna get a bottle upside the head that'll mess up my good looks?"

She gave him a warning glance as she poured herself a whiskey. "I won't promise anything."

"If you're still talking, then it's safe enough. It's when you go all quiet that we know a real storm is comin'." He came in and took one of the big leather seats. "You done frightened that poor new receptionist half to death."

"Fuck." Rowan slammed back a second whiskey and felt a little better. "Want one?"

"Nah. One of us needs to be sober if I have to call the police to put a straitjacket on you." He smiled, but his eyes were serious.

She dropped into her chair. "Just a bad day."

"A bad day around here is unusual, but a bad day that makes you lose your shit is like chicken's teeth. Talk it out so you don't take it out."

"That's a dumb saying," Rowan muttered as she toyed with an expensive pen she didn't even use. "I just heard that they're moving Tankard Jay to the Sullivan place. Apparently, they're giving people who come over from other stables a discount."

"And?" Ted shrugged. "That happens. Never bugged you this much before."

"And this." She shoved her phone across the desk to him and listened as he played the video of Craig telling an interviewer how his time at the Willows had helped him find his center again. "I asked him not to say he was here."

Ted pushed the phone back. "And he didn't. While he was here. No doubt he thinks he's doin' us a favor."

"Well, his favor means the phones haven't stopped ringing with people trying to book, people trying to wheedle their way into getting their horses stabled here, and even people demanding—demanding—that their horses be moved to better stalls because we can clearly afford better if someone like Craig is staying with us. It's utter nonsense, and I've told them so."

Ted got up and poured himself a drink. "Did you now?"

She sighed. "Not phrased exactly that way, no. But the essence of it, yes."

"So you don't want folks taking their horses elsewhere, but you're also going to tell them they're idiots when they call?" He sat back down and swirled the whiskey in the glass. "And you're upset that so many people want to come here that we'll have a waiting list for years?"

"They don't want to come here for the right reasons." She tapped the phone, hard. "They want to come here for celebrity bullshit, not because we're the best damn racing farm in Kentucky. They just want some way to be associated with someone famous, and that pisses me off."

"You smell that?" He looked around. "I smell manure being spread all over the place."

Heat rose inside her again. "I would think you'd agree with me."

"What's it matter to you what people's reasons are if they're bringing you business? When someone goes into a supermarket, do you care why they're there or what they're getting? No. You mind your own business and get what you need. This is the same. They want to pay your prices and go on a waiting list? Let 'em. At the end of the day, the Willows is still the best riding farm around, no matter what reasons people have for wanting to be here."

Rowan opened her mouth to argue but nothing came out. He was right. She was running a business, and Craig had just made sure a hell of a lot of people knew about it. And a farm with horses that won races might as well be housing celebrities. "Yeah. Okay."

"Now." He took another sip from his glass. "Tell me what's really put a spur in your underpants."

"Did you know Amber is still paying five grand a month for her apartment in New York? She figures she'll have it to fall back on if Honeysuckle doesn't work out."

He waited. "And?"

"And? That's ludicrous. She's throwing away good money instead of making a commitment to getting things right here." She was right, but why did it come out sounding so petulant? "It's frivolous, and I can't say a word about it, or she gets all cranky and says she's a grown woman who doesn't need my help."

Ted studied her for a long moment as he drank his whiskey. "Rowan, I've known you since you were playing in mud puddles in your birthday suit, so I'm gonna speak clear. I've never seen you so twisted up around a woman. Never seen you unfocused and paying so much attention to anyone other than a horse or an employee." He shook his head and held up his hand when she went to speak. "I'm your elder. Shut up, and let me talk. Now, I like Amber when she lets her guard down. But when that guard is up? Well, she's a lot like her mama, isn't she? Bet she'd spit fire if you told her that, and I'm not nearly that dumb. But it's true."

Her jaw ached from not responding, and it was a good thing the pen was palladium, or it would have broken between her fingers by now. "What's your point?"

"My point is you seem to want to control things that aren't

yours to control. What Craig said, what Amber does with her money or living situation, what an owner wants to do with their horse. Rowan, ain't none of these things your concern. You need to ease up your grip some, child, or you risk making the horse kick." His gaze softened. "I know how hard it was on you when you lost your parents, and they'd be damn proud of how you've kept this place going. But they'd also want you to live and enjoy what you've built, not hold on so tight you can't breathe. Maybe you like Amber and want her to stick around, and there's nothing wrong with that if she can settle. But that has to be her choice when she's ready to make it. Just like you can't break a horse that isn't ready to take the bit. You need to be patient."

Rowan didn't want to let go of the anger, but it melted like salt in a downpour. "How many people out there do I need to apologize to?"

"Maybe let's have a big crew meal in the barn tonight?" He stood and looked down at her. "You're a damn fine boss, a damn good rancher and business owner, and a damn fine friend. And if I needed someone to watch my back in a bullring, you'd be the person I'd choose. Now you just have to let go a little, so you don't break things that might be fragile." He turned to go.

"Ted, will you tell people we'll have dinner at seven in the barn?"

He waved and left without another word. Rowan crossed her arms on the desk and rested her forehead on them. Ted had been there when her mom had died and when her dad had left. He'd been there when she'd received the news about her dad's death. If anyone in the world really knew her, it was him. Ignoring his advice would be stupid, and she prided herself on being reasonably intelligent. She picked up her phone and sent a text to Amber.

Coffee break?

It took a few minutes before she got a text back.

I'm probably not great company right now.

Join the club. Let's be shitty company together. Rowan added a poop emoji and got a laughing one in response, along with a coffee cup. She grabbed her pile of paperwork and left the office. She stopped at the reception desk. "I'm sorry. I don't blow up like that often."

The young girl gave her a tremulous smile. "All good."

Rowan left, shame making her feel itchy inside. No one deserved to work somewhere they didn't feel safe. She'd need to do something to make it up to the girl, who couldn't be more than seventeen. She drove up to the house and smiled at the smell of fresh coffee.

"You moved fast," she called out as she walked through the kitchen. Strangely, Shift didn't run to meet her. She went into the living room and saw why. Amber was sitting in the middle of the floor, surrounded by what looked like letters. Her face was damp with tears, and a pile of used tissues sat beside her. Shift lay in the middle of the mess, his big head on Amber's lap. He looked at Rowan as though to explain his lack of fidelity. "Good boy," she said, and he huffed and closed his eyes.

"Would you mind pouring me a cup of coffee too?" Amber said, barely looking up from the letter in her hands, which were shaking. "I'm a little buried here. I made that pot about two hours ago."

Rowan nodded and headed back to the kitchen, where she made a fresh pot and studied the scene in the living room. A medium-sized red trunk with old fashioned clasps sat to one side, open. It looked like there were still things in it. Discarded envelopes were scattered among the letters, and there were a few yellowed photographs as well. And in the middle of it all, Amber's hunched shoulders and tears made her look incredibly small and alone.

Rowan poured the coffee and brought it back in, and she had to reach across the river of paper to hand Amber the mug. She sat down on the floor too and crossed her legs. "What's all this?"

Amber let the letter in her hand fall to the floor and wrapped both hands around the mug. "This is the final nail in the shitstorm of my life."

"You do come out with some weird sayings. What do you mean?"

Amber leaned back against the chair behind her. "I was going a little stir crazy. I've got everything ready for the house, and there's nothing more I can do until I can get it ordered and delivered. So I thought I'd look at some of the stuff my grandparents had stored in these great old chests." She nodded toward the open one. "I found a huge pile of letters. All of them were to my mom. All of them were returned, unopened."

Rowan looked at the scene of wasted emotion. "That's a lot of unopened mail."

"I found out what caused their fight." Amber scanned the letters, shoving some aside and flicking under others until she found what she was looking for. "She was pregnant with me before she left." She took a sip of coffee, which sloshed a little in her shaking hand. "My dad isn't really my dad. I doubt he even knows."

Rowan stared at her. "Go on?"

"She was dating someone they only ever refer to as Buck, which I'm guessing isn't his real name. She got pregnant, and he wanted to marry her, but she told him he wasn't good enough for her. That this town wasn't good enough for her. She stole money from their safe and left a note telling them she was going to New York and not to contact her."

Rowan whistled as Amber took a second to breathe. "Wow. I don't know how your parents kept that a secret. A teenage pregnancy around here isn't unusual, but everyone knows about it when it happens. And if the guy was from around here, then surely he or his folks would have told other people."

Amber nodded and looked at the pile of letters again, as though searching them for more answers. "The letters say something about him being willing to move here, so I'm guessing he was from nearby but not actually here. I haven't found any letters from my mom to them, but the first one says how good it was to hear her voice and thanks her for checking in and giving them her address. And for sending the baby picture of me." She set the cup down, still half full, and rested her fingers on a yellowed Polaroid. "But then they ask why she won't speak to them, they tell her about stuff going on here, and they ask over and over again if she'll bring me back to meet them, because they want to get to know their grandchild. They said that Buck would be willing to take me on, be a single father, if that's what she wanted." She pulled another tissue from the box.

"That must have been real hard on them," Rowan said. "They had pride, and it must've killed them to know how little she thought of them."

"It's so much worse than that though. They wrote to her when my grandmother got sick at some point." She shifted through the envelopes and then held one up. "Look. They wrote on the outside, so she'd see it and not just send it back again."

Neatly printed on the reverse side of the envelope as well as on the bottom of the front it said, *Urgent. Your mom is sick. Please read.* Below it, in red, messy scrawl, it said, *I don't care.*

"That's the last letter. They gave up trying after that one, and who could blame them?"

"Damn." Rowan watched as Amber dropped it back into the pile. "Is there any indication why she hated it so much here? Hated them?"

Amber shook her head and buried her hands in Shift's fur. "Nothing that I can find. I mean, they apologize for everything under the sun, and basically say they'll give her anything she wants if she'd just come back with me, but...nothing." She gave a humorless laugh. "And now I know I've got a father who wanted me and grandparents who wanted me. But instead, I got a mother who reminded me at every turn that I was a mistake and a father who looked at me like I was an alien he didn't quite know what to do with. He hadn't wanted kids but hey, his new wife was pregnant. She always told both of us that I was premature, obviously to cover up the fact that she was already knocked up."

"I take it you haven't called her yet?" Rowan asked, unable to fathom how that conversation would go.

Amber's laugh came out dry and coarse. "That's the other great thing about my day. I've received a text from her attorney asking me to come into his office to discuss the sale of the property."

Rowan blew out a long breathe, then downed the rest of her coffee and stood. "Come on. We're getting you some fresh air."

Amber looked at the mess around her. "What about this?"

"Well, we can hope the ranch imp will come in and clean it away, but I find he rarely does as he's asked." She took Amber's hand and pulled her to standing, much to Shift's annoyance. "Let's go."

Amber didn't even ask where they were going as Rowan told her to dress warm and comfortable. When she came down looking like she was carrying a mountain on her shoulders, Rowan took her hand and led her to the quad. Shift jumped in behind them, and she set off toward the staff stables. Amber sat quietly, not seeming to notice anything around them.

When they pulled up outside the stables, she finally looked up. "What are we doing?"

"We're going for a ride." Rowan took her hand again, and Shift raced ahead of them, occasionally stopping to stand at a barn door and touch noses with one horse or another. "Hey, Quin. Can you get Cloud saddled up for Amber? I'll take care of getting Willow ready."

"Sure thing, boss. You ever ridden, Amber?" Quin asked as she went to the tack wall.

"A horse?" She shook her head. "No. I'm not sure I'm going to now."

"Cloud is a training horse. She's gentle and knows what's she doing no matter who's on her. All you need to do is relax and not fall off."

Rowan smiled at the description, which was mostly accurate. She pressed her head to Willow's. It had been far too long since she'd been down to spend time with her childhood friend. "Sorry, girl." She took her out and got her ready, and the simple routine she knew by heart settled the fractious part of her soul. She mounted and waited as Quin helped Amber into the saddle.

"These are the reins, but you don't really need to do anything with them except if you're asking her to turn one way or another. Keep a loose touch, keep your feet in the stirrups, and just enjoy the ride."

Amber nodded, her lips pressed into a thin white line.

Rowan nudged Willow, and they left the stable. She waited until Cloud moved up beside her and was glad to see Amber's hands loose on the reins, with one of them gently stroking Cloud's mane. They rode in silence for the first mile as Amber got used to the cadence of the ride, and then Rowan turned toward the long outer path that would eventually take them to the lake.

"This is nice," Amber said after a little while. "I always pictured myself falling off and getting dragged under the horse."

"We can do it whenever you want." Rowan ran her hand over Willow's neck. "Or you can go out with someone else. Most of the staff have their own horses that we keep here for them for free. It's just a perk of the job. So there'd always be someone to go out with you."

"I'd like to stick with you, if that's okay." Amber gave her a soft smile. "Thank you for this."

"You're welcome. Also, I owe you an apology." Rowan swallowed at the feeling of shame that shot through her again. "I was reminded again this morning that I don't have a say in the way people live their lives. Nor should I. I was wrong to get bent out of shape about your plans."

"So why did you?" Amber asked. "I've been trying to work it out, but I can't."

Rowan let the sound of the horse's hooves on the soft dirt calm her nerves. "I think it just comes down to me wanting you to stick around. Knowing you have a fallback plan means you may not, and like you said, you never claimed you would. But..." Rowan sighed. "I guess after what happened with my parents, I like things to be absolute. As in, you're staying or you're leaving. Not in some limbo where you have the option to go any time things get tough." She grunted. "And even though we see the world through lenses as different as a spyglass is from a telescope, I can't help but feel like this is the best place for you. That you'll come to see it that way too. I guess I think you'll be happy here. Happier than you were back in New York."

Amber let go of the rein with one hand and touched Rowan's leg. "And that's the nicest reason you could give me. I really like the idea of someone wanting me around. But I also won't make you a promise I may not keep." She brushed at her eyes. "Rowan, my life keeps sending waves at me, and I can't swim. My footing is gone. I don't have anything to offer anyone right now. Maybe not ever."

Beside them, Shift whined.

"She's okay, buddy. Go chase something." Rowan watched as he darted into the forest. "I don't think that's true, but it isn't for me to say. What I will say is that I'm here if you want me. You may not feel like you've got footing in the storm, but you've got people around you to hold on to if you'll reach out." It took all her control not to make suggestions about how to move forward or what Amber should consider doing.

"Thank you."

They rode in silence again, laughing as Shift darted off and onto the path again, chasing things only he could see, his tail wagging so hard it was shaking his back end. When they got to the lake, he looked at Rowan and huffed.

"Go on. I'll need to give you a bath anyway."

He leapt off the path and into the water, swimming this way and that and occasionally barking at them as though telling them to come in. The air was crisp, the lake was quiet, and Rowan wanted more than anything to pull Amber from her horse and hold her close. And as a friend, maybe she could do that one day. But right now, she didn't want Amber to feel any pressure.

"Rowan, do you think Cornelius would help me with the legal stuff?" Amber asked quietly, looking far more relaxed now.

"I'm sure he would. He comes across as a good ol' boy, but let me tell you, that guy's a sharp tack." She watched Shift finally come out of the lake and give himself a huge shake, sending spray everywhere and making the horses snort. "And I think it's a good idea. No need to deal with that on your own. Let the attorneys hash things out."

Amber sighed and finally smiled at her. "I'm so glad you're around."

Rowan turned her horse to the path home. "And I'm not going anywhere." She didn't need to say out loud the fact that Amber, on the other hand, might be gone with the spring winds, a fact that made her chest ache.

Chapter Sixteen

WHERE DID ONE START when looking for a father named Buck in the South? Amber had no clue, and she wasn't entirely sure she should be looking for him anyway. Why should she care about someone she'd never met? Biology didn't create connection, after all. Plenty of people all over the world knew that.

She stared at the front door of Cornelius's office, located on a street with independent shops who all seemed to like cutesy, quirky things in the windows or outside the shop front. His, surprisingly, looked traditionally serious. C. Atticus, Attorney-at-Law looked as respectable as it would in New York, if a lot smaller and without a foyer full of plastic receptionists. It had been much the same the night before in the barn. The impromptu dinner Rowan had thrown for her staff had seemed to bring out even more people than had been there at Halloween. Although a little less excitement had been in the air, it had been more intimate. Conversation around the firepits had been relaxed, and Amber had learned more about Rowan's people, who told stories, shared news, and gave advice. There'd been tales of kids away at college, spouses working overtime in the fire service, partners in the military, and one person even talked about his wife who was working on the NASA project involving Jupiter. Amber's preconceptions had taken a serious hit, and after wishing Rowan goodnight and hoping for more than a long, meaningful look, she'd tossed and turned as she considered that her world view was way more narrow than it should be.

A tap on her window startled her, and she hit the horn by accident. "This fucking place. It's like they pop up out of the ground," she muttered, opening her car door and forcing Cornelius to step back.

"Sorry to make you jump," he said, tipping his head. "But you've been sitting in here long enough for me to worry your butt might have become glued to the seat."

"I'm not late, am I?" She checked her watch.

"No, no. You're early. I was across the way getting a bagel and saw you pull up." He held up a little paper bag already growing damp with cream cheese oil. "But I'm here now."

She looked at him and then across at the bagel place. Why hadn't she taken time to explore the town's little main street before? A fresh bagel would be heaven. "You let me sit in my car while you waited for it."

He motioned toward the door and unlocked it, then waved her in ahead of him. "I know it can take folks a minute to feel comfortable about going through my door."

That was astute in a way Amber hadn't expected, and she remembered Rowan coming to his defense several times now. "Thanks. But I don't need to be babied. I'm tougher than I look."

He went to a cupboard and pulled out two small plates and then set a piece of bagel on each. Then he moved behind his desk and handed her a plate. "New legal topics are always best discussed over food. I'm sorry I didn't think to get an extra, but I'm happy to share."

Her breath caught at the kind gesture, but it wasn't good to show weakness in front of any lawyer. But the smell of it made her mouth water, and she simply couldn't turn it down. "Thank you." She took a bite and closed her eyes. It was *almost* as good as the ones at home.

"I don't know what they do, but I haven't found a better bagel within two hundred miles." He patted his stomach. "And believe me, I've tried." He took a bite, and then followed it with a sip of coffee from a well-loved mug. "Now. Is this about Honeysuckle? Your text asking to chat was short on details."

"That's because whatever I said in text wouldn't be enough to cover it." The bagel stopped tasting as good when she thought of her mother. "Actually, because I want to eat this, can I ask an entirely different question first?" When he nodded, she said, "Have you ever known someone named Buck?"

He laughed and coughed as he choked on his bagel. "Amber, I've known about ten of them in my time. You might have to be more specific."

She finished her bagel before answering, and he seemed fine with letting her take her time. Did she really want to go down this path? Taking a deep breath, she told him what she'd learned from the letters in her grandparents' trunk.

He leaned back in his chair and folded his hands on his belly. "Well, damn. That's quite the twist in the twister, isn't it?" He tilted his head and stared at the ceiling. "There are plenty of people around your mom's age who are still in town. If Rowan's parents were still alive, we'd start there, since Rowan's beautiful mama knew her pretty well. But you know that story?"

Amber nodded. "She told me."

"Good. I'm glad she's opened up about it. She deserved better than what her daddy did to her, but that's in the past now." He turned to his computer, hit a few keys, and pulled something off the printer. "Before we move on, let's get this signed to say I'm your attorney, if you're happy with that. Then we'll talk about how to move forward."

Surprised, she picked up the pen. "It isn't like I'm about to admit to murdering anyone."

"Not yet, you aren't." He grinned. "I like to have all my ducks in a row to keep us all on the up and up."

Amber could respect that. In New York, she'd have needed to put down a retainer before even getting through the front door. She filled it out and handed it back. He set it aside in a tray without even looking at it.

"Good. Now. I can hire someone to ask around about

someone named Buck that your mama was seeing all those years ago. But if I do that, you need to know it'll get around that I'm looking. Not necessarily that you're my client, but it won't take a rocket scientist to figure that out when it comes to the connection to your mama." His eyes were serious as he seemed to scan her face. "Are you sure you're okay with that?"

"I..." Amber stopped and forced herself to focus on one thing at a time. "I don't know. I guess I was asking if you knew him, but I don't know if I'm ready to go beyond that." She shrugged. "Not because I care what anyone here might think of my mother, since that seems to go without saying, but because I don't know if I want that kind of entanglement with a stranger."

"It's good to think it through real well before you take that step." He jotted some notes down. "I won't do anything on it until you give me the green light." He settled back again. "Want to tell me what really brought you here?"

Amber swallowed hard. "You knew my mother?"

He shook his head. "I'm not much older than Rowan. I heard about her plenty from neighbors, but my mama would have whooped us all if we'd been caught listening to gossip. But you hear things."

She laughed dryly and cleared her throat.

He held up his hand. "Coffee?"

She nodded, grateful for the momentary reprieve. He picked up the phone, ordered two of them, and then motioned for her to continue.

"Whatever you heard, it was probably ten times worse after she married my father. She's a bitter, angry woman who has always felt like life owes her more than she has—no matter how much she has." She pulled up the text on her phone and handed it to him. "Her attorney has been in touch."

He read it and frowned as he wrote down the name and number on his notepad. "I wasn't under the impression you were going to sell, given the repairs you're making."

"I'm not." She took her phone back and tucked it in her pocket. "At least, not yet."

There was a knock at the door, and someone came in carrying their coffee, complete with a silver jug of milk and a little bowl with sugar cubes.

"Thanks, Darlene. Much appreciated." Cornelius handed a coffee to Amber.

"Anytime, Mr. Atticus." She threw a quick curious look at Amber and then left again.

"You were saying?" he said as they both fixed their coffee.

"I've decided to give myself a year to figure out my life, and this feels like a good time and place to do it. But my mother called the other day and said not only should I sell, but also that the property is rightfully hers, and she wants seventy percent of the money from the sale. I think she intends to bully me into handing it over to her."

"Could she?" he asked, his tone gentle. "Bully you into something like that?"

Amber wanted to scoff and deny it, blow it off like it was no big deal. But being dishonest with shrinks and attorneys never did you any good, and it wasted your money as well. "Yes. I'd love to say I'm stronger than that, but she's bullied me into doing what she wants me to all my life, and if she pushes me hard enough, she knows she always wins." Mortified, she blinked back tears and sat on her hands so he wouldn't see them tremble.

He set a box of tissues in front of her. "I bet that was mighty hard to say out loud. It hurt me just to hear it." He waited a moment, but she didn't respond. "Amber, the will was clear. That house was left to you. Not to next of kin. To you, specifically. And it was done properly. No loopholes. She doesn't have a legal leg to stand on, even if she wants to contest it."

Amber had figured as much, but it was still good to hear it. "Can you talk to her attorney and explain my position, and tell him I won't be meeting him to discuss anything, ever?"

He grinned, and there was something of the shark in his eyes. "I'd be happy to. Are you okay with me giving him a copy of the will?"

"Rowan says I can trust you." Amber finally gave in and grabbed a tissue, dabbing it at her eyes. At this rate, she'd have to find a better waterproof mascara. "So I trust you to do what you need to on my behalf. I just...I just want to be here and figure things out."

He nodded, looking as though he understood the levels of things she wasn't able to expand on. "And although it's a bit outside my purview, what are you going to do about your mama?"

"Dodge her calls, I guess. She can't force me to pick up the phone."

"True, true." He rifled through a desk drawer and then handed over a brochure. "Maybe this will give you some ideas on how to move forward."

She looked at it and blanched. "This is for abuse survivors."

"Well, Amber, there's a whole lot of types of abuse, and sometimes we have a hard time seeing it for what it is when we're too close." His smile was almost paternal in nature. "And sometimes it takes a whole new life away from it to be able to close the doors so the monsters stay out of reach. One of the suggestions I've made to other clients is a simple one. Change your phone number. Don't just block the number because she can call from a different one. Instead, change your number altogether. The peace of mind that will bring you will surprise you."

Why hadn't she considered that? "Cutting her off that way seems so extreme."

"It does. Sometimes extreme measures are called for in order to keep ourselves safe, both mentally and physically. And it seems to me you could use a bit of that safety right now." He tilted his head. "I'm sorry though, if I'm speaking out of turn."

She folded the edges of the leaflet. "No. No, I think you're right. I just need time to think."

"All right then. Is there anything else I can do for you?"

She recognized the phrasing that meant the meeting was over. "Not right now. Thank you for taking me on as a client. Do you want me to pay now, or will you bill me?"

He waved the question away. "I've got your email. I'll send you a bill when I need to. This was a consultation meeting to see if I was what you needed." He stood and held out his hand. "I'm awfully glad to say I think I am. In fact, I think we're all what you need right now, if you don't mind me saying. I had a feeling that was going to be the case from the moment I met you."

She shook his hand. "I admit, I'm not sure about all this yet, but I know I feel better and a little less like a target waiting for an arrow." She headed for the door, and he followed. "As for the thing with," she couldn't bring herself to say father, "with Buck, I'll get back to you after I give it some thought."

He stepped into the doorway. "I'll let you know how things go with the other matter. But there's no need to worry any further about it."

She was about to get into her car and then looked at the bakery. "I think I'll bring some bagels back to the farm."

"Excellent idea. Tell them they're for Rowan, and they'll put together her usual Sunday order, even if it isn't the Lord's Day."

She shook her head. "I don't think I'll ever get used to people knowing that kind of stuff about each other."

He laughed, a big booming sound. "You never know what you can get used to if you just relax and let life lead the way."

That sounded more ominous than he probably meant it to, but she got the gist of it. It still felt too corny to respond to without sounding bitchy, so she just gave a quick wave and headed into the bakery. She told them what Cornelius had said, and they put together two massive bags of mixed bagels along with three big tubs of cream cheese, two flavored, one regular. *And I was only going to get a dozen.* She was about to gather the bags into her arms and was mentally trying to figure out how she'd get them to the car when a teenager came around the counter and picked them up.

"I'll take them out for you, ma'am." He waited expectantly.

"It's the way of things in these parts," the woman at the register whispered. "He's just bein' polite, not callin' you old or anything."

"Sure. Okay." Amber was too worn out from her meeting to argue, and she led the way to the car. The kid put the bags in the back seat, and she was just about to get into the car when a shout stopped her.

The woman from the bakery came hurrying over. "Corn said you might like one of these for your drive back to Rowan's." She smiled and handed over a bag, then hurried back to the bakery.

Amber looked at Cornelius's office. He waved from behind the window and rubbed his belly. She couldn't help but laugh and then got in the car and drove off. At a stoplight, she inspected the contents of the bag. It was a muffin of some sort. She pulled off a section and barely caught the gooey yellow drip that came from its center.

Flavor burst from it as she took a bite of something with the tang of lemons and the sweet smoothness of cheesecake. She groaned out loud, now that there was no one to hear it. She couldn't keep eating this way and fit into her clothes, but she had to admit to enjoying food far more than she ever had back home.

As she ate, she contemplated that word. *Home*. What did it mean now? Home was where you lived, but wasn't it also a feeling of some kind? That's what all the sappy movies would have people believe. That didn't feel right, though. When she was growing up, home had been a place of vipers and snide remarks, of quick slaps and manipulation a dictator would have admired. Home hadn't been a good feeling then. But what could it be now? Her own home, a place she put together herself. A place that belonged solely to her. If the day came that she did sell it, the money would mean she could easily afford another home somewhere else. But wouldn't New York always be her home location? As she ate the almost too sweet muffin and drove along the wide, nearly empty roads lined with old trees, she couldn't help but wonder where it was she belonged.

Chapter Seventeen

ROWAN WENT OVER THE lists for the third time and finally set them aside. Her back ached, and she could eat the side of her desk she was so hungry. But with the Harvest Grand only two days away, she needed everything to be perfect.

"You should come see this," Pam said, popping past the office and not waiting for a response.

Rowan sighed. She didn't need another problem. Colic had made an appearance at the stable, and she'd needed to make sure the infected horse was being taken care of. Now they were on high alert for any other cases. She stretched and frowned slightly as a couple other staff hurried past, laughing.

She followed the group to the main reception area, which didn't have any visitors scheduled today. Word about whatever it was had obviously spread as staff started arriving from all over the ranch. She nearly tripped over a child when she stopped to stare.

Amber stood behind the reception desk with platters of bagels in front of her, cream cheese buckets on the side. She handed out plates because the reception desk wasn't quite big enough for the spread. Someone said something, and she laughed.

Rowan leaned against the doorframe, her knees weak. How could a woman possibly be that beautiful?

"You look like a lovestruck skunk about to go chasing tail," Pam whispered in her ear, and then took a big bite of cream cheese-smeared bagel.

Rowan pushed away from the door. It wouldn't do for the staff to see her looking in any way out of control. "Shut up and eat your bagel."

Pam blew her a cream cheese speckled kiss, and Rowan grimaced as she walked away to wait her turn in line. When she got to the front, she was glad to see that Amber's smile widened. She looked more relaxed, more at ease than she had since she got here. "What's all this?" Rowan asked, accepting a paper plate and choosing an everything bagel for herself.

"You've been so great about helping me and being there for me even when I told you where to stick your niceness." Amber gave a tiny shrug, and her cheeks turned pink. "I wanted to do something nice in return."

"Well, you can't go wrong with feeding this lot, that's for sure." She looked over the spread. "I'm guessing Corn told you where to go?"

Amber nodded and handed someone else a plate. "I mentioned it, and he told me what to say." She wafted a paper plate at her face, though it was anything but warm in the room. "I hope it's okay."

"More than okay. Thank you." Rowan wanted to touch her. She wanted to pull her into a hug and show her the kind of appreciation you didn't perform in public. Instead, she picked up a plastic knife and went for the cream cheese. Then she sat on a bench outside near the others. Soon enough Amber came out, sans bagel, and sat beside Rowan.

"Nothing for you?"

Amber rolled her eyes. "Before I left, she brought me some lemon concoction that would have made the best bakery in Manhattan weep with envy. I don't have room for more bread."

Pam leaned forward from across the table. "I told you the solution to that problem."

"Which was?" Rowan asked, looking between them.

"She told me I should just take my clothes off so I didn't need to worry about them fitting anymore." Amber said it almost like she was tattling, her arms crossed, a defiant look in her eyes.

Rowan cleared her throat at the image. "Trust you to take that road, Pam."

"I'm nothing if not practical." Pam shrugged and licked some cream cheese off the tip of her finger. She winked at Amber, who shook her head. Then she yelped when Rowan kicked her under the table.

"Ass." Pam reached down to rub her ankle.

"Then don't be such a tool when it comes to pretty women." Rowan eyed her and tried desperately hard not to notice the subtle scent of Amber's hair or the way it was brushing her forearm.

"At least I know how to enjoy them." She moved before Rowan could kick her again. "Amber, no offense meant, if you took any."

"I've got thicker skin than that. And as I told Rowan, I'm a big girl. If you pissed me off, you'd know it." A breeze kicked up, so Amber shifted slightly and pressed closer to Rowan.

Rowan very nearly groaned out loud. But she managed to hold it together, thanks to the knowing grin Pam sent her. "Don't you have work to do?"

"Don't you?" Pam backed away. "Or are you going to sit there chatting up the city girl while the rest of us break our backs for you?"

Rowan threw the last bit of bagel at her, and Pam ducked, then started chatting with someone else as they walked away. Relieved that they could finally talk, she turned to Amber, putting a minuscule bit of distance between them. "How'd your meeting with Corn go?"

Amber picked at a bit of loose wood on the table. "Better than I thought it would. He gave me some good advice." She pulled a piece of paper from her pocket and handed it to Rowan. "So good I acted on it the moment I got here. I've changed my phone number."

Rowan glanced at it and then tucked it in her pocket. "Makes sense. Is he going to help you look for your father?"

Amber peeled away the bit of table and watched it flutter to the ground before she began picking at another piece. "I've decided to give that some more thought. I don't know if it's a door I want to open."

"Fair enough." She gently placed her hand over Amber's. "I get the need to do something with your hands, but maybe you could find something other than pulling apart my tables piece by piece?"

Amber flushed and tucked her hands between her knees. "Sorry." She took a breath. "How has your day been?"

"Better, after this." She ate the last of her bagel. "We've got a big party coming up this weekend. I was hoping you'd come along."

Amber seemed to light up. "I love parties. What's the theme?"

Rowan tilted her head. "Well, no theme, really. It's exclusive and elegant, if that fits. It's called the Harvest Grand. We do it every year to raise money. Last year we raised more than a hundred thousand dollars to help kids with disabilities learn to ride and to help a local school with the costs associated with having two horses on the school grounds. This year we're raising money for Heroes and Hounds, an organization that helps veterans and ex-military animals adjust to civilian life." Rowan reached into her back pocket and pulled out a folded-up flyer, then handed it over. "On Saturday during the day, we've got falconry exhibitions, craft stalls, music, a petting zoo, and even a mechanical bull for the courageous. Then in the evening, we have the ball. That's when we invite the horse owners and other stables as well as the business owners who have given in the past. It's a three-course meal and live auction, and there's a silent auction set up in an adjoining room as well."

Amber looked over the flyer, which was geared toward the day attendees, not the evening ones. "It looks like it's going to be amazing. I'd love to come." She grinned. "I'll have to go shopping again."

"I don't know if Jess will be allowed to help." Rowan put the flyer back in her pocket and couldn't begin to imagine the kind of thing Amber might wear. "She's in trouble for failing one of her math classes."

Amber bit her lip. "I hate shopping alone." She looked at Rowan expectantly and pouted when Rowan shook her head emphatically. "I'll figure it out."

"I need a break from my office and horse problems. Want to take a ride out to your place to see how it's coming along?" In truth, there was plenty she needed to do, but she'd hardly had any time with Amber, and a quick trip to Honeysuckle wouldn't hurt.

"Yes!" Amber jumped up. "I was going to do it myself this afternoon, but it would be so much better if you were there." She stopped like she'd run into a roadblock. "Not that I can't do it on my own, obviously. I'm fully capable of handling it."

Rowan held up her hands. "No question about that. Having a ride-along doesn't mean you can't do things. Sometimes it's just nice to have a friend with you." *A friend.* Rowan rolled that phrase around in her mind a thousand times a day. *Just a friend.*

"Perfect." Amber headed toward her car, parked in front of the main building. "Let's go."

Startled, Rowan followed. "Right now. That's what I had in mind."

Amber laughed as she put on her seatbelt. "From the tone of your voice, I'm guessing it wasn't at all what you had in mind. But now that you've suggested it, I'm not letting you off the hook. You're all mine now."

Rowan shifted the seam of her jeans away from her crotch as they drove away. That wasn't the wording she needed to hear. A car was coming down the long driveway, moving way too fast. "What the hell?" It slowed only a fraction as it passed them, and she swore.

"Wasn't that the slimy spa guy?" Amber asked, looking in the rearview.

"Yeah. What the hell would he be doing at the farm?" Rowan turned to look over her shoulder, half tempted to tell Amber to turn around.

"Do we need to go back?"

Rowan turned around and leaned her head against the headrest. "Nah. My staff know how to handle Jimmy. Whatever he thinks he'll get, he won't." Still, it itched at the back of her mind. She didn't like him anywhere near her.

"Corn is going to tell my mom's lawyer that I have no intention of selling." Amber's hands were tight on the steering wheel. "She's not going to like it, but now that I have a new phone number, I don't have to worry about hearing her bitch about it."

That hard edge was back in Amber's voice, and Rowan wondered briefly if it would ever go away when it came to talking about her mother. "That sounds like a perfect solution." She waited, but Amber didn't say anything else. The drive to her place was quiet but comfortable. Several work trucks were in front of Honeysuckle, and Amber pulled up behind them. She was up and out of the car in a flash.

"Wow. Look at that." She stood with her hand shading her eyes, looking at the roof.

"Looks almost done." Rowan scanned it and approved. The new roof looked so good, you couldn't tell it had been a shell not so long ago. "Let's see if we can go inside." She winced. "I mean, if that's what you want."

Amber laughed and hooked her arm through Rowan's. "How hard is it to give up control?"

She looked down at her and smiled. "Easier than it should be when it comes to you."

"Hey there!" A call came from the roof. "Go on in if you want to. Just watch for the cables and equipment."

Rowan waved and let Amber lead them into the house. It was a little disappointing when Amber let go to wander around, but she couldn't blame her. Amber looked from room to room, commenting on the new walls being where she'd asked them to be and the removal of the ones she wanted gone. She looked lit up from the inside, like someone had flicked a switch on her soul. Her smile was wide as she talked Rowan through the ideas she had for the spaces, excitement emanating from her.

Rowan walked around with her hands in her pockets, happy to listen and give encouragement. Amber didn't need her advice or opinions. Just her support.

Amber stopped in front of the floor-to-ceiling windows facing the forest. The trees swayed, their leaves gone for the season, their naked branches seeming to reach for the cloudy sky like arms. Rowan shook off the strange feeling.

"Hey there," Peter said, coming in and wiping sweat from his brow with a bandana he stuck back in his pocket. "Glad you came by to see it, although I'm sorry to hear that you won't be living in it. Seems a shame after you went to the trouble of redesigning it."

Amber frowned and looked at Rowan, who shook her head. "What do you mean?" Amber asked. "Of course I'm going to be living in it."

He looked between them. "Jimmy came by and said not to worry too much because he'd change the fixtures to the ones the spa uses. He said you wouldn't be staying."

"Oh, did he now?"

If Jimmy had been standing there, Rowan wouldn't have given him a cat's chance in hell of surviving the next five minutes, based on Amber's expression. A high heel through the forehead would've been probable cause of death. She thought of him heading to her own farm. What the hell was he up to?

"Allow me to disabuse you of any notion he might have put in your head." Amber stepped forward, like a tiny tornado ready to tear down towns. "This is my house. I've told Jimmy in no uncertain terms that I'm not selling it, and even if I did, it wouldn't be to him. Believe me when I say I'll make it even clearer the next time I see him. And if you ever need clarification about what it is I want, I suggest you come to me. No one speaks for me."

He took a step back, and Rowan nearly snorted with laughter.

"I understand. I'm sorry, miss. He seemed so sure of himself, I didn't think to wonder if he was outright lying." He took another step back. "You can be sure we'll follow your instructions and only yours from here out."

"Damn right you will." Amber turned to look at Rowan. "What the hell?"

Rowan tilted her head toward the car. "Maybe we should head back to my place and find out if he's still there?"

Amber marched past her, keys already in hand. "If he is, he's going to wish he wasn't."

Rowan had no doubt of that at all. On the way back, she voiced her worries. "Thing is, Amber, what would make him so certain that he'd have your place? He'd have to know it would get back to you."

"Could he just be messing with me because I told him off?" Amber asked, not taking her eyes from the road. "I could see people in New York doing it as a retaliation thing."

Rowan considered that. "I don't know. He's that kind of snake, sure, but it seems awfully ballsy, even for him."

"Well, it pisses me off. Who the hell does he think he is?" Amber's knuckles were white on the steering wheel. "How dare he interfere and think he can go behind my back." She glanced at Rowan, her gaze one that could melt steel. "I've had my share of people telling me what to do. I'll be dammed if I'm going to let some sleazy country bumpkin do it."

Rowan nodded, hoping Amber didn't see her wince. The country insult still stung, coming as it did from a place of superiority. Would that ever fade? Every time Rowan thought they were making inroads, something came up that made her wonder if it were possible to take the city out of the girl. When they arrived back at the Willows, there was no sign of Jimmy's car. She sent Pam and Ted a text, and both arrived at the main building within minutes.

"Everything okay?" Ted asked, watching Amber pace beside her car.

"I saw Jimmy drive up as we headed to Honeysuckle. Any idea what he wanted?" Rowan asked.

Pam was watching Amber, who now seemed to be muttering to herself. "Yeah. He said the spa wanted to be a main sponsor of the event and then went into the main hall to buy a ticket for Saturday night."

Rowan rolled her eyes. "We don't have event sponsors."

"Which is what I told him when they called me over, knowing full well we don't want him around." Pam thumbed toward Amber. "What's that about?"

Rowan sighed and squeezed the bridge of her nose. "Jimmy told the guys working on Amber's house to ignore her designs because she wasn't going to be staying, and that she's selling to him."

Ted whistled. "That's awfully bold, even for him."

"What would make him think that?" Pam asked, continuing to watch Amber, who seemed to have slowed her pacing a little.

"The fact that he's a little man with a little penis and a big desire to be seen as someone important rather than the gutter rat he clearly is and will always be." Amber spun to face them, answering Pam's question.

"Sounds right," Ted said, looking thoughtful. "But bad apples are still rotten for a reason. Might be you need to keep your ear to the ground, Amber."

She nodded, her anger seeming to deflate a little. "I will. In fact, I'm going to let Cornelius know, just to keep him in the loop." She gave Rowan a quick smile. "Thanks for coming with me."

Rowan nodded and watched Amber drive away toward the house. "I wouldn't want to be Jimmy. She could kill him off and bury him in the woods just by looking at him. Did he end up buying tickets?"

Pam nodded. "Four."

"Why does Jimmy need twelve hundred dollars' worth of tickets for a benefit he knows he isn't welcome at?" Something about the whole situation smelled like a dirty stall. Neither Pam nor Ted responded, and Rowan sighed. "Okay. Like Ted said, keep your ear to the ground. Anything to do with him nosing around can't be good. How's the colic situation?"

She walked with Pam and Ted to the stables and listened to the update, but part of her mind stayed with Amber. Protectiveness washed over her, and she thought about hogtying Jimmy to find out what he was about, but that wasn't what Amber would want. Was it? Hell if Rowan knew what was best these days.

When she got back to the house in the evening, the fire was lit, and Amber was curled on the couch. The mess of letters was back in the trunk that sat against the wall, and she was reading something on her iPad. She smiled when Rowan came in.

"Hey there. Long day?"

"Always is around here." Rowan liked coming in to find Amber waiting for her. She shouldn't, but she did. Damn it all.

"I made myself a fruit salad for dinner. There's extra in the fridge if you want it."

"It'll hold me while I make real food." She smiled and pulled the bowl of fruit from the fridge, along with some hamburger meat. She went about making herself a simple pasta meal and finished off the fruit while it was cooking. "How was the rest of your day?" It was a simple question that felt far too easy, too personal, too intimate.

"Good. I calmed down after I talked to Cornelius, and he said he'd be sure to send a letter to Jimmy telling him to back off. I read some more of my grandparents' letters, but they were making me sad, so I turned to a book." She motioned with her iPad. "Also, I sent Jess a text. In return for me giving her some math lessons, she's allowed to go shopping with me tomorrow."

Rowan laughed. "You'll be the most beautiful math tutor she'll ever have." She flushed at the thought that came out of her mouth without her brain engaging first.

"Thank you," Amber said softly. "I'm glad you're home."

Rowan continued to cook, unsure how to respond. Finally, she glanced up. "Me too."

They continued to talk in front of the fire, but Rowan's yawns finally made it hard to keep chatting.

Amber laughed. "Looks like you need to get to bed."

Her gaze was soft in the firelight, an undeniable invitation in it. Fuck and damnation. Rowan wasn't so tired she couldn't take Amber to bed and make love to her the way she deserved to be loved. Not loved, no. That was way too intense. But not just fucked either, although Rowan knew that would be damn near perfect too. Something in between, something that meant she could look into Amber's eyes as she drove her fingers... *Stop.*

Rowan stood, nearly knocking over the table in her haste to halt the train of thinking that would derail what they were building between them. She didn't miss the flash of disappointment in Amber's eyes before it was hidden with a wry smile. "Bed. Yup." She nodded, backing her way toward the stairs and nearly falling over Shift, who huffed at her as he headed the same direction. "You enjoy bed too. I mean, sleep. Sleep well." She turned and rolled her eyes.

Amber's light laughter followed her upstairs. "Chicken," she said softly.

Rowan very nearly stopped and turned around, challenge accepted. But with willpower she didn't know she possessed, she made it to her bedroom and fell face first onto the bed. *She's going to kill me off and make me enjoy it along the way.*

Chapter Eighteen

"IF I WERE GAY, I'd totally go for you."

Amber laughed and turned sideways to inspect the way the little black dress hugged her butt. Was it too much? How much weight had she gained in the short time she'd been away from New York? "The gays would be lucky to have you," she said to Jess, who lounged in a chair, phone held in front of her, though she did look up every time Amber came out of the changing room. Jess had found her own dress almost right away. "You think it works? Or should I go with something less traditional?"

Jess tilted her head and really looked at her. "I mean, that's nice, but it's a little boring." She jumped up and held up her finger. "One sec." She returned a moment later with a bold red dress in hand. "Try this one instead."

"Won't I stand out?" Amber held it up, admiring the way it shimmered in the light.

"Don't you want to?" Jess grinned and pressed her hand to her heart. "Isn't there a certain farm stud you have your eye on?"

Amber rolled her eyes and went into the changing room. "No, there isn't. Rowan and I are just friends." She came out in the red dress and did a little twirl. "I think you might be right about this one."

Jess stood and circled her. "I didn't say it was Rowan. I meant Pam because she's always flirting with you. People forget I'm around, which means I totally hear things." She grinned. "Good to know where your head is at though."

Amber turned and let the calf-length dress swirl around her legs. The deep V-neck showed off an impressive amount of cleavage that might be enough to break even Rowan's steadfast willpower. The red seemed to bounce off her hair. "You're right. This is the one. I'll need a wrap or something to go over it though. It's too cold for straps like this." She wasn't about to respond to the thing about Pam and Rowan. Jess was sweet but giving her ammunition like that in a town like this one would be a bad idea.

Jess nodded. "I know a different store for that. And I'm starving."

Amber nodded and went back into the changing room. Before she took the dress off, she turned in it again, trying to imagine Rowan's reaction. She'd never considered whether a lover might like one dress better than another before. She'd simply chosen what she liked and assumed the partner at the time would like it too. What made this any different? Aside from them not being lovers...yet.

Sighing, she slid it off. Rowan made it all different. The look in her eyes when they talked, the way she practically bumbled around like a teenager with a crush, and the way she respected Amber's boundaries even though it was clearly hard to hold back with an opinion or offer of help... It was all Rowan. And tomorrow's event was important to her. On a whim, Amber pulled out her phone and sent Craig a text along with the event's website. Raising money was something she could do, something that made her old life worth it.

She took the dress to the counter and paid, then draped it over her arm. "Where to for lunch?" she asked. They'd driven an hour to Louisville to go shopping, and she wanted to take full advantage of the day out.

"Heart and Soy, for sure." Jess picked up her own dress, and they headed out to the car. "Rowan texted me to say you're a veggie, and my friends and I went there a couple months ago because two of our group are veggies too."

"It's nice that you went to a vegetarian place just for your friends." Amber pulled into the light traffic as Jess put the GPS on and pondered that. In New York, they'd have gone to the place everyone most wanted to eat at, even if it meant someone couldn't eat at all.

"Well, yeah. Obvs." Jess shook her head. "Why wouldn't you be cool with your friends that way? It's not like the rest of us can't eat food without meat in it."

"True." Amber noticed the amount of great stores as well as boutiques they were passing. This was a city like any other. Why couldn't she stop thinking of it as inferior to what she knew? "Are you looking forward to the party tomorrow?"

Jess shrugged in the way only teenagers could. "Kind of. I mean, it's always great to see money being raised, and the day events are a lot of fun. I'm one of the riders who takes kids out on a tour of the property and tells them about the horses. I love that part." She rolled her eyes. "The night party, not so much. I have to go with my parents because we stable there, and we're one of the rich families in the area. But it's so..." She waved her hand like there was a bad smell. "I mean, there's all this posing and one-upping, you know? Like, someone will ask how your horse is doing, or who the rider will be in the races next year, but they don't actually care. They just want to tell you about their horse and how it's going to be better than yours."

What would it have been like to be a teenager most concerned with people's posturing around horses? The thought made Amber smile a little. She'd been worried about far different things. Although the posturing of the rich crowd was something she knew a lot about. "The best way to get through those is to be overly kind. Tell them you hope their horse does as well as they think it will, that they're doing great. That kind of thing. People who want to brag don't know what to do when someone is nice and doesn't brag back. They don't know how to handle not having someone to upstage."

Jess nodded like it was wise advice. "Sounds like you've been there."

Amber turned into the café's parking lot. "Oh, I could tell you stories. I've been there and thrown in the towel." They went in, and Amber inhaled the aroma of spices. After they sat and ordered, she turned to Jess. "Now. Tell me about this math class you're having a problem with."

Jess groaned and looked at the ceiling. "I don't get it. And I swear, it's not like I'm not trying. Mom and Dad say I'm being lazy and just want to be with Fury, but that's not true. I've stayed after class, and I've even worked with tutors in the library. It just doesn't make any sense."

Amber put her hand over Jess's after she'd wiped away a couple tears. "Sometimes that's the case. I went to school with a lot of people who struggled. Show me what we're dealing with."

Jess tugged her backpack onto her lap and pulled out a few sheets of paper, then shoved them across the table. "This. What do I even need to know math for anyway? I have calculators and when the time comes, I'll have accountants. Like you."

Amber studied the sheets, memories of high school flooding back. "But you need to understand what the accountants are telling you, or you'll always be dependent on other people when it comes to your finances, and believe me, that way is the road to despair in the long run. You never want to depend on anyone when it comes to your money."

"Yikes."

She looked up at Jess's tone. "What?"

"You sound seriously bitter. Like, did someone mess with you that way?" Jess leaned forward. "Is that why you became an accountant?"

Bitter? Is that how Jess thought of her? She shook her head and took out a pen. "I went into finance because I like numbers, and I'm good at them. Plus, the type of accountant I was came with a lot of perks."

"Like, hot perks who took you to hot parties?" Jess's eyes went wide. "Like Craig Caswell hot?"

"You heard." Amber flipped to another page and studied it, working out the problems in her head. "Yes, that kind of perk. And Craig is a good friend who knew he needed to understand how his money worked so he'd never have to worry about landing on the street." She flipped to the final page. "I think I can make this easier to understand."

Their food came, and as they ate, Amber took each problem and helped Jess work through it. She asked questions when it was clear Jess didn't understand so that she could figure out where the gaps were in her understanding, so she was able to find another way to explain as well as another way to work out the problem. They'd finished all three sheets by the time they shared a piece of vegan bourbon cake.

Jess sat back, looking at the sheets of paper. There were tears in her eyes. "Thank you. I hate feeling stupid, and math always makes me feel dumber than a grasshopper talking to a bird."

Amber didn't quite get the metaphor, but she got the idea. "I think anyone who struggles with a subject feels that way. It just means you have to find a different way to understand it." She stood and stretched. "Now, let's keep shopping."

By the end of the day, they were both pleasantly exhausted. A two hour drive home would normally have put her in a bad mood, but the day had been so...nice. It was a bland word, but she couldn't quite figure out a better one yet. There'd been no drama, no snide or snarky remarks, no pretending that things weren't good enough. Just plenty of laughs and talks about clothes and the boy Jess had a crush on but was too shy to talk to. The only text to come through had been from Rowan, asking if they were having fun. Should she feel like Rowan was checking up on her? And even if she was, why did it feel good to know someone was thinking of her?

"Why won't you date Rowan?" Jess suddenly asked, as though divining the path of Amber's thoughts. "She's really nice, and for an old lesbian, probably kinda hot."

"First of all, she's not old, and there's all kinds of weirdness about your statement in general. As to why I won't date her...well, that knowledge is above your paygrade."

"You mean my age grade. Adults always use that as an excuse when they don't have an answer." Jess crossed her arms and turned to lean against the door so she could face Amber. "Rowan is awesome. When my parents are being extra, she's always there to listen. Last year, when they took off for three months to tour Europe without me, Rowan let me stay in one of the staff cottages. Not because I couldn't stay at my own house, but because she knew I'd be lonely, and she said I should have family nearby. Around here, she's what we call good people." She made a come on motion. "So give up the goods. She's amazing, and I really like you. What's the deal?"

"You're right. I don't have an answer." She glanced over and saw Jess's look of disbelief. "Okay, I do, but only kind of. My life is a mess right now. I have no job, I have no friends, I'm out in the country learning about family I didn't know I had, and I'm not sure what I'm going to do next." She blinked back tears. It definitely wouldn't be cool to cry in front of a teenager. "I'm not ready to get into any kind of romantic entanglement. Especially with someone as together as Rowan."

There was a moment of silence as Jess seemed to think about Amber's response. Finally, she shifted to look back out the windshield. "That's lame."

It wasn't the reaction Amber thought she'd get. "I think it's pretty responsible."

"It's lame. I mean, isn't everyone's life a mess all the time? And dating her doesn't mean marriage and babies." Jess drew circles on the condensation of the passenger window. "You told me I should take the risk and talk to Ben, and it's not like I have my life all mapped out."

"It's a little more complicated when you're my age." It was a weak reply, and Jess's eye roll made it clear she thought so too.

"You're not supposed to have your life mapped out. You still have all your mistakes in front of you. I'm in the middle of mine."

"So why can't she be part of making the mistakes better? Like, moving on or whatever?"

It was a good question and once again, Amber didn't have an answer. "I just know that I don't want to hurt her." They drove for several miles in silence as Amber continued to think about Jess's questions and her answers.

"I think you don't want to get stuck here," Jess finally said without looking at her. "I think you're worried that you'll like her too much and end up staying in the country, which you'd totally hate. I don't blame you. If I could move to New York and keep riding, I'd do it in a heartbeat."

"You could," Amber said absently. "There are plenty of places to go by train outside the city. You could go to college in the city and be with your horses on the weekend." Was she right? Did it come purely down to being afraid of being stuck in one place? They'd acknowledged that Amber would be leaving, moving back to New York at some point. Or somewhere else, somewhere that wasn't middle of nowhere Kentucky. But maybe it was a little more nuanced than that. A relationship meant putting down roots. It meant believing someone would stay and not see you as a burden.

They pulled up at Rowan's, and Jess jumped out of the car. Rowan was standing on the porch, as though she'd been watching for them. Jess ran up the steps and pulled Rowan into a big hug.

"Thank you for being you," she said, then turned, ran back down the steps, pulled her shopping bags from the backseat, and loped off to her car. "See you tomorrow!"

Amber laughed at Rowan's look of bemusement as she made her own way up the stairs, shopping bags in tow. She let Rowan take a few off her.

"What was that about?" Rowan asked, following Amber inside.

"She's a teenager. Who knows what was going through her head?" Amber had no intention of telling Rowan about their conversation or the mixed emotions it had brought up. "If we hadn't spent so much time talking about the guy she has a crush on, I'd have thought she had one on you." She set her shopping bags at the bottom of the stairs. "But there's no question there's some hero-worship going on there."

"When it comes to kids and horses, they're easily influenced by people being kind. Both of them can get their fill of people who don't appreciate them." Rowan shrugged and shoved her hands in her pockets as she watched Amber move into the kitchen and get out the wine. "Did you have a good day?"

"Great, actually." Amber poured a large glass of white wine and tilted the bottle toward Rowan in question. She shook her head, and Amber put it away. "Shopping with her the other day was fun, but I feel like I got to know her better today. She's got a wise head on those young shoulders."

"She does. She's still a pain in the ass sometimes, but she's a good kid." Rowan glanced at the bags.

Amber moved in front of her, placing her palms on Rowan's chest. "Oh no, you don't. No peeking. You'll get your show tomorrow."

Rowan's eyes darkened, and her hands moved in slow motion to cover Amber's. "Yeah?"

Amber stood on her tiptoes and tilted her head back. "Yeah," she whispered and pressed her lips to Rowan's.

Rowan barely responded at first, and then she moved her hands to Amber's hips and pulled her closer as she deepened the kiss. Amber moaned softly at the feel of Rowan's hard body against her. God, it felt so right. So hot. So perfect, like a fire meeting a perfect piece of tinder.

She broke the kiss and rested her forehead against Rowan's shoulder. They were breathless, and slowly, so slowly, Rowan's hands eased their grip on Amber's hips.

"That was unexpected," Rowan said, her voice low and husky.

"But not unwanted," Amber said, making it more of a question than a statement.

"No. Not unwanted." Rowan moved back a little and looked down at her. "But it could be complicated." Her eyes moved to Amber's lips and then back to her eyes.

"Yeah." Amber stepped back and slid her hands away from Rowan's chest, letting her fingertips skim her nipples. Rowan's soft hiss made Amber want to press forward again. "But maybe less complicated than I've been worried about."

"Maybe." Rowan swallowed hard. "Want me to take those up for you?" she said, nodding toward the bags.

"And have you enter my bedroom?" Amber gathered them and grinned over her shoulder. "We both know you wouldn't leave with your modesty intact."

Rowan laughed, breaking the tension. "My modesty hasn't been intact for a long time." She ran her hands through her hair. "Dinner?"

"I'd like that. I'll be down in a minute." Amber felt Rowan's gaze on her all the way up the stairs, and when she glanced back, Rowan gave her a small smile, clearly not caring that she'd been caught watching her. Amber winked and then went into her room. She dropped the bags but quickly hung up the dress. Yes, it would be perfect for tomorrow evening. And, if she played her cards right, maybe it would end up on the floor by the end of the night, right next to whatever Rowan was wearing.

Chapter Nineteen

ROWAN SAT ON THE top of the fence, coffee in hand, watching it steam into the frosty morning air. The sun's rays were just starting to brighten the horizon, making the mountains in the distance loom like sentinels rising from the earth. Light and dark, night and day, shadows and bright spots. That felt a lot like her life with Amber under her roof. Which one of them was the dark and which the light, she wasn't always sure. Poetic thoughts like this definitely weren't the norm, but Amber made her think about life in words she wouldn't normally use.

And that kiss last night. Damn. Words hadn't been invented yet for what that had made her feel.

Dinner had been full of undercurrents strong enough to drown an alligator. Sure, they'd talked about shopping and Louisville and Jess's math issues, but beneath the mundane chatter had been a river of lava, ready to burst through the fragile foundation of their relationship and bust it all into a lusty volcano. When it had come time to say goodnight, she'd stayed rooted to her chair. If Amber had held out her hand, if she'd extended the invitation, nothing short of wild bulls would have kept her from carrying her up the stairs and fucking her senseless. And it would have been fucking, of that there was no question. She was so amped up and ready, and the look in Amber's eyes made it damn clear she was in the same space. But Amber had simply given her a look that would have melted ice cream on an iceberg, and then headed off to her room.

And Rowan had grabbed a beer and sat on the porch in the cold until she cooled down enough to think clearly. Well, she'd cooled down, but all night long, she tossed and turned, wanting to cross the hallway to Amber's room, throw open the door, pull back the covers, and brace Amber's legs over her shoulders. When her alarm went off at three, she'd been glad to get out of bed and out of the house.

Footsteps sounded, and she didn't turn, knowing who it'd be.

"You ready for today?" Pam asked as she climbed onto the fence, her own steaming coffee in hand.

"I think so. Vendors will start showing up about seven to get set up. The conference center is done. Looks real nice. The caterer will be here by three to get set up." Rowan ran through the list of things she'd need to watch out for today, of which there were about a thousand.

"Ted and I were talking."

Rowan took a sip of her coffee. "That's never a good sign."

"Yeah, well, we made a decision. You're going to delegate this year. Give each of us a section to be in charge of. Not just have us wander and help like everyone else. This is your one and only chance to use me and tell me exactly where you want me." Pam grinned and sipped her coffee, also watching the sunrise. "You won't give over control, so we're demanding you do it, or we'll revolt. We'll start an uprising and a coup and all that shit."

Rowan's heart swelled a little at the show of friendship. "You're demanding I give you more work? I feel like you might have been kicked by a horse too many times. It's rattled your brain."

"We're demanding that you untighten that butthole of yours a little and let people help." Pam laughed at Rowan's expression. "Seriously. You have people you can trust. It's time to let them step up and take some of that load off those bulky shoulders of yours."

Rowan nodded, letting that sink in. "Do you really have a thing for Amber?" she blurted.

Pam chuckled. "I should've known that would be eating at you. Even on a day like this, you're thinking about her? She's got you good and twisted."

Rowan shot her a look. "You haven't answered the question."

Pam looked back at her evenly. "No." At Rowan's narrowed eyes, she shrugged. "Yeah, she's hot. And under different circumstances, I might have been serious."

"You flirt with her constantly." Rowan winced at the petulant sound of her voice.

Pam nodded, looking back at the sun which had crowned the mountaintops with a sherbet halo. "I do. Mostly just to mess with you, but also because you need to see how you feel about her, and thinking I'm after her makes you pay attention to your own feelings about her. I think if I didn't, you'd be like a turtle after a hound. This way, you're more like a stud scenting a mare in heat."

"You're an ass," Rowan murmured, finishing her coffee.

"I'm your friend." Pam jumped down from the fence and dumped the dregs of her coffee in the dirt. "And as your friend, it's my duty to push you into the arms of the hottest woman you're likely to ever have interested in you."

"It's complicated," Rowan said, jumping down beside her and walking toward the stable, where farmhands were already showing up to muck out stables and take care of the horses. "What if I let my heart loose and then she takes off? Heads back to New York or goes to LA or something?"

Pam shrugged. "Then you get your heart broken. Not like it hasn't happened before. It'll probably happen again. Doesn't mean you can't ride that bronco right to the bell and then remember what a helluva ride it was."

"Hmm." Rowan wondered if that was true. Amber had made it clear she wasn't in a place to be involved with anyone. And Rowan had respected that, but it was becoming torturous, and that kiss last night hadn't helped. Had Amber changed her mind?

"Now." Pam turned in front of the stables and Ted wandered up to join them, giving a small nod. "Give us our own shit to do."

She looked between them for a minute as she considered.

"Pam, when the vendors get here, make sure they get set up where they need to be and that they have power and all the stuff they need. They've all been assigned their spaces, so don't let them talk you into putting them somewhere else."

Pam saluted and laughed when Rowan rolled her eyes.

"Ted, if you can spread out the staff to make sure we have people at the gates and at all of the stands, that would be great. But mostly, keep an eye on the horses and the tour groups. Make sure everyone is up to speed on where to go and how long to be out. Keeping track of the groups takes me a lot of time and mental energy."

He nodded. "And where will you be?"

Now that she'd handed off two of the biggest jobs, she wasn't sure. "I'll wander. I'll probably get underfoot with the catering and sound people for the event tonight. I want to meet the guests when they arrive. And I'll check all the stalls to make sure they look like they should cost the amount they do."

"Will you be wearing a new evening gown tonight? I'd hate to clash," Pam said, flipping her non-existent hair over her shoulder.

"Fuck off to work and let me know if anything at all goes wrong," Rowan said, and paused. "Thanks for making me let go of the reins a little."

Ted nodded and swatted Pam upside the head when she looked like she was going to say something pithy in return. "Good luck today," he said and led Pam away like a naughty child.

"Okay," Rowan said, turning and looking over the grounds. Now what? She lifted her face as the wind kicked up a little and then shifted to look at the sky behind her. Thin gray clouds scudded across the sky, their edges turned coral by the rising sun. She pulled out her phone. No storms had been forecast. According to the weather app, none was still forecast, though the wind speeds had changed. Experts or not, she could smell rain on the breeze. All she could hope was that it would hold off until after the event tonight. The moneyed crowd didn't like having to go out in their expensive clothes and cars when it rained. With that in mind, she headed to her office. Amber wouldn't be awake for a couple more hours, which meant Rowan didn't need to consider heading back to the house for coffee or any other reason she could think of.

The breeze kicked up again, and she pulled her jacket tighter. On impulse, she decided to check the storm shelters she'd had built for the horses should a tornado come through. The two long buildings were basic but had all the feed and water they'd need for a couple days if the stables were destroyed. She checked the canned food and water for the people who'd be in there too and was satisfied. It seemed like a waste of time on a busy day like today, but things like that often got left off the list because of work, and then it could be a catastrophe when it was needed.

That done, she grabbed a quad and headed to the far side of the property. The cows were out to pasture and the fields had been worked so the massive bales of hay, most of them wrapped in plastic, stood like strange sentinels in the middle of shorn fields. She stopped to chat with the crew and enjoyed a laugh, glad energy was high and that many of them planned on attending the festivities during the day. There was plenty of good-natured teasing about her shaking people's hands until the money fell out of their pockets at the auction, and she didn't mind it in the least.

Her radio squawked with someone calling her name, and she answered.

"Boss, can you come to the main reception? We've got something to run past you."

Her heart sped up just a touch. There was always something to deal with, and with Pam and Ted taking things on, she actually had the time to deal with them. "On my way."

When she walked into the reception area, she was surprised to see Steve, who was never up this early, Sally, and a couple of the other staff looking at the main computer. "What's up," she asked.

Steve pointed toward the computer. "We can cancel tonight's auction. We've already raised all the money we need."

She frowned and moved around the desk, and the others made room for her. "What are you talking about?"

Sally looked up, her frown lines deep. "We sold another one hundred tickets overnight. That takes us to capacity. Rowan, I accounted for a hundred meals, along with that number of staff. The catering company can't possibly handle this by tonight."

Rowan grabbed the mouse and scanned the names but didn't recognize a single one. "Do we know who these people are?" She looked at Steve. "Has there been anything on social media?"

He shook his head and held up his phone. "Nothing that hasn't been from us or about us by the usual followers." He brightened. "You think this has something to do with Craig Caswell?" He looked back at the list of names. "He isn't listed."

Rowan closed her eyes. She had a feeling it definitely had to do with Amber, if not Craig. "Okay, folks. We've got this. I'll call the event company and get the chairs and tables taken care of. Sally, call the catering company and see what they have to say, and then we'll go from there. The rest of you, call any friends and family you have who might be willing to pitch in tonight as waiters."

Everyone looked relieved at having a role to play, and they began to disperse.

Steve hesitated and then lowered his head. "Rowan, we don't have a ton of silent auction stuff. I mean, we had enough for the hundred people coming. But for double that number?"

Rowan groaned. She hadn't considered that. "I'll get on it. Thanks for mentioning it." She was about to walk away, and then stopped. "Steve, can you send discreet messages to our biggest donors and let them know the event has expanded rather suddenly, and that we'd welcome any items people might want to donate for the auction?"

In his element, Steve looked ready to burst. "God, yes. I'm on it."

Hoping she hadn't made a mistake, Rowan went to the back office and started making calls. She could hear her team making theirs, and it was good to know everyone was ready to help. Within half an hour, the tables, chairs, makeshift tunnel in case of rain, and catering had been handled. Staff, however, was coming up short. The last thing Rowan wanted to do was a buffet, but at this rate, she might not have a choice.

A knock sounded on the door frame, and Amber walked in. "Looks like there's a commotion."

At the twinkle in her eye, Rowan knew her guess had been right. "I have a feeling you're behind it."

Amber grinned and perched on the desk, right beside Rowan's hand, as though tempting her. "I might have sent a text or two about the event." She seemed to sense Rowan's mood. "But...maybe I shouldn't have? I just thought it would help you raise money."

Rowan leaned back in her chair, away from temptation. "And it was a sweet thought, really. It's just that we had the numbers pinned down and planned for, and now we've had to make some pretty quick changes."

"It worked? More people are coming?" Amber asked, her eyes alight.

"A hundred more people. Hell, there might have been more if it weren't for the fact that it hit the limit of how many we can hold in the conference center for a meal." Rowan didn't want to burst Amber's happy bubble, but it was hard to feel overly enthusiastic with all that could still go wrong. "I kind of wish you'd told me what you had planned."

Amber winced, and her shoulders dropped. "Sorry. Can I help with anything?"

"Not unless you know about thirty waiters."

Amber bit her lip, clearly thinking about the question Rowan had meant to be rhetorical. She suddenly jumped from her seat on the desk. "Be right back."

Rowan let her go and took a second to close her eyes. All she wanted to do, really, really badly, was close the office door and take Amber right there on the big oak desk. And that should be the furthest thing from her mind right now.

Amber came in looking like she'd won the prize at the state fair. "Your waiters are taken care of."

"How on earth did you manage that?" Rowan asked, dubious.

"I called Fran at the diner. They're going to close early and have all their staff come over here for the night. Plus, she knows a couple other restaurant people and said she'd get them to help too."

Rowan shook her head and picked up the phone. She relayed the information to Sally on speakerphone, her gaze never leaving Amber's.

"Well, damn. I should've known you'd figure it out," Sally said. "The catering team said they'd pull in extra staff and hope they can manage."

"Actually, Amber figured it out." Rowan smiled at Amber's look of surprise. She was probably used to people taking credit for anything she did. "Sounds like it's all coming together." She hung up and leaned back, looking Amber over. She wore artfully ripped jeans, a tight long-sleeved shirt that showed her breasts to perfection, and a leather jacket that Rowan very much wanted to take off.

"Keep looking at me like that, and your employees are going to get a very audible lesson on what sex should sound like." Amber leaned against the wall, the invitation clear.

"I'm sure there's a sexual harassment issue in there somewhere." Rowan's voice was raspy, and she cleared her throat. "Did you need something?"

Amber sighed a little dramatically and pushed away from the wall. "I'm going to my house to have a look around. I want to get the furniture ordered now that the changes have been made."

Rowan's stomach turned a little. What did she expect? That Amber would change her mind and want to move into her place when they hadn't even had sex yet? It was simply that she'd gotten used to having someone in the house. "Sounds good."

Amber waved as she headed for the door. "I'll be sure to text you if I get stuck in a flood or a basement or blown into a tree or something."

"I'd appreciate that." Rowan wanted to ask her to stay and work with them on the event. But that was absurd. Amber wasn't part of this crew, and it would be good to remember it. "There's a spare house key next to the front door. You should grab it before you go. I don't lock up usually, but with the amount of people who will be around today, it makes me feel better."

Amber paused at the door. "Do you think I could take Shift with me? I'd like the company." At Rowan's obvious look of surprise, she held up her hands. "Sorry, that's probably too weird, taking your dog—"

"Sure, go for it. He loves being in the car, and I won't have to worry about him as the vendors arrive. There's a portable water bowl by the back door on the third shelf up."

Amber laughed. "Of course you know exactly where things are. My place is almost small enough to touch both walls at once if I really stretch, and I still can't always find what I need." She blew Rowan a kiss and winked. "See you later, handsome."

Rowan rested her head on the desk and took a few deep breaths. Whatever was about to happen between them was going to be electric. She just hoped she was strong enough to handle what it would do to her heart in the long run.

Chapter Twenty

AMBER SAT AGAINST THE wall in the empty living room. Some of the furniture had been salvaged, including the gorgeous, enormous dining table. The couches had been toast, but that was okay, as she'd ordered some that were more her style: reclining ones that meant she could relax and look out the windows at the world beyond. She'd ordered all her furniture and arranged for delivery, and she couldn't wait for it to come now that the house had her stamp on it. With it being Saturday, the work crews weren't around, and she and Shift sat in the big, empty house on their own.

It was strange how different it felt from the first time she'd been there, not so long ago. Then it had felt like another world, a place where strangers had lived and died. Now it felt like a tiny piece of her puzzle, one that was helping create a picture of who she might be. She ran her hands through Shift's fur, and he rumbled against her leg.

"It's pretty great, isn't it?" she said, and his ears twitched in response. Maybe she needed to get her own dog. It wasn't like she could keep borrowing Rowan's whenever she wanted company, although she was becoming attached to the giant beast of love. Together they'd roamed the whole house, and she noticed small things she hadn't before. She'd even taken the time to sit in each room to get the feel of it and to imagine her things in it. When the delivery truck had arrived, she'd been able to tell them exactly where to put the new pieces. More were yet to arrive but having new things in her new space made it feel a little more real. She couldn't wait to show Rowan when it was all done.

How could she feel so at home in a place she'd barely had a chance to step foot in? Did change really happen that quickly? Shift huffed as though answering her silent question. Maybe it was just the difference in location that was giving her room to breathe. The thought of her tiny apartment made her feel almost claustrophobic as she relaxed in the big, open space. How could she go back? And why would she? The career she'd chosen out of necessity was squashed, at least for the time being, and it wasn't like she had anyone other than Craig to miss, and he was often away shooting movies. Here...

She shook her head and sighed. Here she already knew people she liked talking to and spending time with. Here she had a big home, plenty of space...and Rowan. "And what am I going to do about your boss, eh?" she whispered, playing with Shift's ears. She'd crossed the line with that kiss the other night, and Rowan had reluctantly, and then willingly, crossed it with her. And if Amber had her way, they'd leave that line far behind them tonight.

Because maybe she didn't have to leave after all. Maybe she could find her way out here. It wasn't like she was a tree, rooted to one spot. She could move, go places, travel. Maybe she could even convince Rowan to travel with her a little, leave the farm running to the others occasionally. She snorted, making Shift look at her. "Like she'd give that up for me," she said. "Okay, buddy. Let's get back so I can see if I've still got what it takes to seduce someone."

Shift trotted toward the door and Amber followed, locking up behind him. When she turned, he was in the yard, sniffing something and growling softly. Cautiously, she moved up beside him, not wanting to see if it was a snake or something. It wasn't. It was some kind of small yellow flag, planted in the ground. She glanced up and saw several more in a line going all the way to the trees. She plucked it and spun it in her fingers. Was it something to do with the crew working on the house? Maybe a plumbing thing showing where pipes were?

She called Shift, and they got back in the car. She tossed the flag on the seat, and Shift nudged it off and onto the floorboard. "That suspicious, is it?" she said, heading back to Rowan's. When she got there, she smiled at the controlled chaos. People were streaming in, and cars were parked down the sides as well as on the patch of land designated for cars. She rolled her window down and smiled at Ted. "Looks like a good turnout."

He grinned back, his thumbs stuck in his belt loops. "Real good. Everyone turned up on time, and I hear we have you to thank for saving the dinner."

Amber bit her lip, unused to praise. "Well, someone had to step up, right?" She looked at Shift in the rearview mirror, who was panting and had a paw pressed to the window. "Should I let him out with you?"

Ted laughed and opened the back door. "Come on, hound."

Shift jumped out and Amber drove slowly to the house, recognizing how strange it felt to wave at the strangers who waved to her as she passed, and yet, how right it felt too. Once she was back at the house, she let out a relieved sigh at not having run anyone over. Famished, she headed to the kitchen and sent Rowan a text letting her know she was back. How odd it still felt to check in with someone. Warmth spread through her at the return text.

Glad you're back. Missed having you here.

You'll have me later plenty.

Amber bit her lip and actually giggled at the brazen text. She laughed when a video call came in.

"Why?" Rowan said, looking at the phone and then looking around her. Fairground music played in the background. "Why would you do that to me when I'm surrounded by people?"

"What better time to mess with you?" Amber asked, biting into an apple. "What time should I be ready tonight?"

"Depends on what you think you're getting ready for." Rowan's gaze turned back to the phone, and her lips quirked in a crooked grin. "Do you mean dinner or dessert?"

Amber's knees went weak, and she sat on a stool. "Oh, you came to play, did you?"

"I play to win." Rowan waved at someone off camera. "You should be ready to head to the conference center at five if you want to go with me, although it will be before the guests arrive because I'll be there checking things. If you want to make an entrance, then be there at six." She looked at the camera and gave Amber a look that could have melted New York steel. "I'll see you soon. Bye."

Amber shivered at the promise coming their way. Tonight was a tipping point, and she was going to look fucking spectacular for it. She made herself a cup of coffee and headed upstairs. A long bath, followed by getting ready leisurely would mean she'd knock Rowan to her knees later. It was an image worth pondering.

***

Amber smoothed the red dress over her hips and twirled. Paired with a black silk shawl which still wouldn't be warm enough but was better than nothing, and four-inch black heels, she knew she looked exactly the way she wanted to. And yet, a moment of doubt wriggled its way in. What if this wasn't a look Rowan liked? What if she liked a more earth mama type, in flowing skirts and Birkenstocks? *Well, that isn't going to be me in this lifetime.* The alarm on her phone chimed softly, letting her know it was time to head downstairs.

After a final look in the mirror, she took a deep breath and left her room. But at the top of the stairs, she stopped, fully and completely distracted from thoughts of herself when she saw Rowan standing at the bottom, waiting for her.

Dressed in a tux, complete with bow tie and shiny shoes, she looked like she could walk a runway with the most gorgeous models in New York, regardless of gender. And that would have been more than enough to make Amber swoon. But the look she was giving her made it hard to walk at all.

"Damn," Rowan said, her voice hoarse. "It's like the Devil himself made you to tempt angels to their destruction."

"Except I happen to know you're no angel, and it's only you I'm hoping to tempt," Amber said, slowly coming downstairs, taking her time so Rowan could appreciate her outfit fully.

"Consider me fallen." Rowan placed her hands on Amber's hips and whistled softly. "You look incredible. There aren't even words for the way you look."

Amber reached up and pulled Rowan's head down for the briefest of kisses. "I've never said this to a date, but I think you might look even better than I do."

"A date, huh?" Rowan's eyes were dark with desire, and her hands grew a little tighter on Amber's hips. "I like the sound of that."

"For fuck's sake. It's like walking around rabbits in heat."

Amber laughed and looked past Rowan to see Pam in the doorway, also in a tux. "Well, don't you look handsome too."

"We look like giant country penguins," Pam said, tugging at the bowtie. "If I didn't think Rowan would fire me, I'd take all this off and just attend in my boxers and sports bra. That would bring in money too."

Amber shook her head. "Well, I think you both look dashing. Should we go?"

Rowan held out her arm. "I'll be the luckiest s.o.b. there."

The three of them made their way outside to the car, and Amber gasped as the wind caught at her shawl, making it flap hard as it caught a gust. She ducked into the car and smoothed out her hair. "I didn't realize it was so windy. It wasn't that way earlier."

Rowan frowned as she peered through the windshield, which was quickly covered in small drops of rain. "Weather's been weird all day. I just hope it keeps until after the party."

They pulled up beside a walkway with a tent covering it all the way to the entrance. "Did you have this planned beforehand?"

"Honestly, no. I just had a feeling you'd be pissed if you got wet coming tonight."

Pam's laughter filled the air around them as she got out of the car. "So to speak. And I don't think pissed is the right emotion."

Amber flushed and tried to school her expression so she didn't give Pam the satisfaction of having embarrassed her. "You're right. Too bad you'll have no idea what that emotion would be like in action." She sashayed past them and into the venue, smiling when she heard Rowan laugh and say she'd told Pam where to stick it.

Amber put her hand to her chest as she took in the venue from the entrance. "Wow. It's so...elegant."

Rowan draped her arm around Amber's waist. "I did say that was the tone, didn't I?"

Amber nodded, taking in the large chandeliers that cast soft light over tables decorated in black and white. Crystal glasses and jugs of water were already on the tables, along with wine buckets and wine already cooling on ice. Table numbers made of ice sculptures sat in bowls that looked like marbled obsidian, dry ice smoke curling around them. "You did, but I didn't think—"

"You didn't think we could do this kind of thing way out here in the sticks?" Rowan said, looking down at her with a wry smile. "It's good we can keep surprising you."

A staff member came over and said Rowan was wanted in the kitchen, and she lightly kissed the top of Amber's head. "I'll be back soon. Keep Pam on her leash, will you? Don't want her scaring the nice rich folk."

Pam made an obscene gesture, and Rowan walked away, laughing. "Want to sit down?"

Amber nodded, already feeling the soreness creeping into the balls of her feet. "These shoes aren't really made for standing still."

Pam looked down and grinned. "I'd say what they were good for, but I promised Rowan I'd stop flirting with her girl."

"Sorry, what?" Amber looked at her, eyebrows raised.

"Not that she said you were her girl." Pam backed up a step, glancing at Amber's heels. "I just know she likes you, and it appears you feel the same."

Amber laughed. "Do you look this scared when a horse charges at you?"

Pam blew out a breath and pulled out a chair for Amber at a table at the front of the room. "If a horse was as scary as you I might."

Satisfied, Amber sat down. "Is there anything we can do to help?" she asked, looking around.

"Are you kidding? Rowan just wants people doing what they're told to do or completely out of the way tonight." Pam looked over Amber's shoulder, and her face lit up. "My date is here. I'll be right back." She jumped up and hurried away.

Amber turned to look and was surprised to see it was the judge from the pumpkin contest. Rowan had implied that Pam was a love 'em and leave 'em type, but Pam seemed to really like this woman. And from watching them, it was clearly mutual.

"Hi there," the woman said when they reached Amber's table. "Isn't this place just the fanciest thing you've ever seen?"

There was a time, not so long ago at all, that Amber's response would have been cutting and just this side of snide. But less and less that was feeling like the right way to be toward people. "It really is beautiful. I'm Amber." She held out her hand.

The woman's hand was calloused, her nails unpainted but neat, and her grip firm. "Julie."

"I love your dress," Amber said, once again surprising herself. The dress, clearly inexpensive, was pretty in a simple way. In New York, Amber would have sworn it was homemade and made some caustic remark about it being from some religious cult.

Instead, she made Julie smile, and it warmed her in turn.

"Thank you so much," Julie said, running her hand over the neckline. "I haven't bought something nice for myself in so long, and it felt like an indulgence, but..." She smiled at Pam, and her cheeks turned a cute shade of pink. "Well, it seemed like a special night."

Pam smiled and kissed Julie's hand. "It is now that you're here."

Amber could picture Craig making a gagging noise as he opened the wine and started in about provincial tastes and the social ineptness of people in love. But then she pictured the way Rowan had looked at her as she'd come down the stairs, and it banished Craig and his bougie attitude. She liked the honesty of these people and the way they said what they were thinking and feeling without worrying about how it would make them look. She liked that they could be genuine and easygoing without thinking it made them look less than or weak.

Maybe that was what home felt like.

Chapter Twenty-One

ROWAN WAS ALREADY TIRED of playing the game, shaking hands and pretending to like people she didn't care for in the least. But the influx of new faces in clothes that cost a damn sight more than what was usually worn to this event made it a little more interesting. What was even more interesting was the amount of people Amber seemed to know from the new crowd and watching her was like watching a professional ice skater in a competition. She flowed from person to person, smiling, looking stunning, and clearly in her element. Rowan had barely had any time with her and was beginning to get frustrated, but it wouldn't be long before they took their seats, and she could feel Amber's thigh pressed to hers.

She excused herself from a couple who might as well have dressed in dollar bills instead of actual clothes and moved up behind Amber, who had stopped at their table to take a drink.

"You are extraordinary," she whispered, lightly brushing Amber's hair from her shoulder and making her shiver.

"You're not so bad yourself," Amber murmured. "I had no idea you were so smooth."

"Don't worry, you'll find I still have my rough side." Rowan lightly kissed her shoulder, though her eyes never stopped scanning the room.

"Promises, promises." Amber turned, forcing Rowan to take a step back. "Have you looked at the auction room?"

Rowan laughed and put her hand on Amber's waist, needing to touch her. "I did. And you outdid yourself. The amount of things that have come in is insane. Not to mention that bidding on some of the items is more than my employees make in a year."

"That's what I like to hear. Rich people parting with their money for a good cause." Amber laughed and drew her fingertip down Rowan's jaw. "And you can find creative ways to thank me properly later."

"You can count on it." Rowan's gaze dropped to Amber's cleavage. "Have I mentioned that you look beautiful tonight?"

"Once or twice." Amber winked. "But you can tell—"

"Trust you to wear the boldest thing in the room so everyone notices you."

Rowan frowned at the woman who came up behind Amber, and she felt Amber stiffen under her hand. She looked at her face and quickly pulled her close. She'd gone so pale, she looked like she might faint, and she seemed to weave slightly. She looked over Amber's shoulder again and saw Jimmy, standing there with a man who looked bored, and another guy she didn't know, who seemed to be scanning the room like an appraiser would a herd of cattle. The pieces began to come together.

"You okay?" she asked, looking into Amber's eyes. "I'm here."

Amber took a shaky breath, pasted on a smile, and her eyes turned to steel. She turned. "Mother. What a surprise." She looked past her. "Father."

"It wouldn't have *been* a surprise if you'd taken my calls. Thankfully, Jimmy saw fit to let me know about this cute little barn party so you and I could have a talk, and I could meet your new... friends." Amber's mother looked at Rowan like she might be mud on her mink coat.

Gently, Rowan pulled Amber back a little so she was right beside her. "I've heard so much about you. I'm Rowan Payton, owner of the Willows." She held out her hand, and Amber's mother returned it with a kind of limp fish handshake.

"Bea. Don't believe anything Amber says. She's always been prone to being overdramatic and needy." She looked Amber over again and then turned her attention to the crowd. "Fred, I need a drink."

He seemed to sigh and nodded. "Nice to meet you, Rowan." He held out his hand, and she shook it. "Amber, it's nice to see you looking happy." He turned and went in search of a drink. Probably more than one.

"And Jimmy." Rowan put her arm around Amber's shoulders as she felt the slight tremble in her body. "I saw that you'd bought four tickets, but I didn't think you'd be quite this devious. Shame on me for underestimating the lengths a snake will go to in order to get a meal."

His smile didn't reach his eyes. "I'm just a man who gets what he wants, Rowan. Let me introduce you to Baxter Anderson. Baxter is my partner at the spa."

Baxter frowned ever so slightly before he held out his hand. "I'm his backer actually. The spa is doing well, and Jimmy explained that we'd be able to discuss the new land expansion this evening." He looked between Amber and her mother. "That's with you ladies, if I'm not mistaken."

Before Rowan could say anything, Amber shook her head, her hand gripping Rowan's tightly. "I made it clear to Jimmy, as I did to my lawyer and *her* lawyer, that I have no intention of selling."

Baxter looked at Jimmy, whose face flushed. "I believe your mother has come to talk some sense into you. The amount we're willing to pay for your land is far and away more than it's actually worth. That money could let you live anywhere in the world, and Lord knows you don't belong here."

Amber's mother laughed, a grating, almost angry sound. "Although looking at the way you're dressed tonight, maybe that's not true. And you've clearly been eating like you can afford to gain weight. We both know that isn't true, and you were awfully brave to wear that dress. How charming."

Before Rowan's eyes, Amber seemed to shrivel. Her shoulders dropped, and she looked at the floor, her throat working as she clearly tried not to cry.

"Excuse me," Rowan said. She squeezed Amber's hand. "Is it okay to say something?" she asked quietly.

Amber tilted her head but didn't look up. Rowan wasn't sure that was a go ahead or not, but she took it as one. "The fact that you'd say something so vile makes it quite clear you don't deserve the title of Mother. Perhaps you should go take your seats so Amber can continue to help me raise money for this event without having to listen to the acid flowing off your tongue. Unless, of course, you'd like to leave, given that your presence might lower the tone of the evening."

Amber let out a sound somewhere between a gasp and a laugh, but still she kept her eyes down.

"Now I see why Amber likes you." Her mother's eyes flashed with fire. "She's always liked a lower class of person, mostly because no one with taste would have her." She shrugged. "But we'll sit. And Amber, you and I will discuss the sale of the house before I leave tonight." She walked away and Baxter followed, looking distinctly uncomfortable.

"It's for the best, Amber," Jimmy said, his tone soft and patronizing. "You don't belong in this world. You're better off with your own people back in the city. I'm sorry I had to resort to bringing your mother here, but if anyone can talk sense into you, it's her."

Amber frowned. "The weird little flags outside the house. You were measuring for the new housing development because you're so sure it's going to be yours."

Rowan took a half step forward, putting herself in Jimmy's personal space. She smiled so it would look like a normal conversation to anyone watching. "If we weren't surrounded by people I respect and admire, and we weren't trying to raise money for charity, something you damn sure know nothing about, I'd lay you out cold and when you woke, you'd have wished I'd hit you hard enough to make it so you didn't." She let the menace fill her voice and took a bit of pleasure in him taking a step back.

"Consider yourself lucky I don't take you out back right now and bust you to pieces."

He tilted his head, jaw working, and walked away quickly, joining Amber's parents and the finance guy at their table.

"Come on," she said, taking Amber's hand and leading her away from the crowd. She closed the door to the smaller conference room down the hall behind them.

Amber gave a soft sob and fell against Rowan's chest. She held her and let her cry, rubbing soft circles on her back. Finally, she stepped back and looked around. Understanding, Rowan strode to the bathroom across the hall and brought back a handful of paper towels.

Amber took them gratefully. "I'm so sorry. I never fall apart like that. I don't know what came over me."

"Seems to me that when a snake bites you, you don't ask why you feel sick when the poison spreads." Rowan lightly caressed Amber's hair. "And that woman is a snake."

Amber nodded, still looking crestfallen. "I was having such a good time. I convinced myself I could be happy, that she'd leave me alone." She dabbed at her eyes, grimacing at the eye makeup on the paper. "I should have known better. She never gives up when she wants something."

Rowan wanted to take charge. She wanted to have the foursome thrown out and banned from ever entering the town again, not that it was possible. But the last thing Amber needed was someone else telling her what to do. "How can I help? How do you want to handle this?"

Amber closed her eyes. "Thank you for asking. Honestly, I don't know. I think...I think I just want to avoid her for as long as possible. I don't want a scene tonight. If she's still here tomorrow, I'll deal with her then."

Rowan nodded, thinking and planning. "Okay. Then that's what we'll make happen."

Amber looked up at her, eyes still shiny. "You've got so much to do tonight. You can't babysit me."

"No. But fortunately, we've got a team of people who can run interference like you wouldn't believe." Rowan grinned and looked at her watch. "We're about to start the speeches and such. Let's get you to the table, and I'll make some rounds and then join you."

Amber took a deep breath and smoothed the dress down, though now it looked like a self-conscious motion instead of a self-confident one. "Thank you for helping me."

Rowan tilted Amber's chin up and kissed her softly. "I'm here. Whatever you need." She took Amber's hand, and they walked back into the conference room. People had begun to take their seats and as promised, she got Amber set up at their table with a glass of wine, and then she went in search of her team. A quick whispered conversation without unnecessary detail was all it took and quickly, their table was full of people Amber could consider friends if she allowed herself to. Feeling better that Amber was being watched over, Rowan continued to make the rounds and then made her way to the podium at the front.

"Thank you for coming," she said, her voice carrying through the room via the microphone. The screen behind her lit up with the images they'd use of the items for the live auction as well as to tell people about the charity. "There are many people here who have come to the Harvest Grand celebration year after year, and I've also met many new supporters tonight. I'm guessing more than a few of you might have been bullied into coming by mutual friends of ours. Craig and Amber can be quite persuasive, it seems."

General laughter confirmed her suspicion, and she smiled. "Well, we're glad you're here, and we hope you continue to come back year after year as well." She continued her speech, giving details about the ranch and about the money they'd raised the year before. Then she introduced the head of the Heroes and Hounds charity and took her seat as he began to talk about the work they did.

Amber remained tightly coiled, like she was waiting for the moment to dart off, but she seemed to relax a little as Rowan draped her arm over her shoulders. Applause followed the speaker, and the auctioneer for the night took his place. There were plenty of jokes and some light banter, and the bids on various items were higher than she'd anticipated. She noticed that Amber's mother bid on an exclusive spa package offered at Jimmy's place, and her father bid on a golf trip in Scotland. The likelihood of her mother coming to use that spa, in a town she hated, was as likely as Rowan putting on Amber's dress and heels, but she figured it was more of a statement than anything. And if she were married to her, she'd want to go off to Scotland too.

By the end of the live auction, they'd already raised more than they had in total the previous year.

Rowan took to the stage again, though Amber had seemed reluctant to let go of her hand as she'd left the table. "Wow. Your generosity tonight is exceptional. I know Heroes and Hounds will be able to put your money to good use. Don't forget that the silent auction is open for an hour after dinner. Don't put your wallets away just yet."

She left the stage and watched as the servers began bringing out plates of food, swarming from the kitchen in perfect timing before people could get up from their seats after the auction. She noticed where ice buckets needed to be refilled, which tables might need someone to help start a conversation, and who looked like maybe they needed water now instead of booze. Within seconds, people were coming up to talk to her, and though she wanted to get back to Amber, she couldn't be rude to the guests. She had to trust that her team would watch out for her.

By the time she made it back to their table, her food had long since gone cold. "Where's Amber?" she asked, looking at Pam and then around the room. Her mother wasn't at her table either. Rowan's stomach dropped.

"She said she had to go to the bathroom," Pam said, her arm draped around her date. "We thought she'd be okay to do that on her own."

"Damn it." Rowan started toward the door but was blocked by Amber's father.

"Can I have a moment?" he said, his hands clasped behind him.

"That depends. Is Amber with her mother?" she asked, glad she was an inch or so taller than he was.

"She is. But Amber is tough and her mother...well." He shrugged a little. "But this is about business. I may not like the way she's gone about it, but Bea is right. Selling the house and land to Jimmy makes sense. You're a businesswoman, and one who clearly knows what she's doing." He finally unclasped his hands and motioned at the room. "What you've done here is impressive, and I understand why you won't sell to Jimmy as well. That would be ludicrous. But what's more ludicrous is Amber holding onto real estate she has no idea what to do with when she could make far more by selling it."

Rowan crossed her arms. "But that's her choice and her money. Why, exactly, do you and her mother have any say in it?"

"Because she's Bea's daughter. She does what she's told, and she always has. I don't know much about Bea's life here, but it sounds like she's owed something." Now he sounded far less convinced.

"Then maybe you should find out the truth before you start giving advice. Your daughter doesn't owe either of you anything. In fact, you both owe her an apology for the way you've treated her. But that's not for me to say. You should know that she'll have the full backing of the Willows to fight you, if that's what she wants to do." She lowered her head so her words wouldn't carry. "But make no mistake that I will have you thrown out in the rain if you make her cry again or try to take advantage of her in any way. You should leave."

He grunted, but to his credit didn't look cowed the way Jimmy had. "You'll find that Bea is a lot like a rottweiler when she wants something. She'll lock her jaw and squeeze the life out of something before she lets it go."

"And you'd let that happen to your daughter, would you?" she asked.

He looked at her for a moment, his gaze calculating. "I suppose that would depend on whether or not she was really my daughter." He tilted his head and stepped back. "We'll be going just as soon as Bea comes back. I'm sure our business will be concluded."

Rowan narrowed her eyes. He knew he wasn't Amber's father then. But what about business being concluded? She turned toward the bathroom, but before she could head that way, Amber's mother came in, a sickening smile on her face.

Shit.

Rowan nearly ran to the bathroom, but Amber wasn't there. She went back into the conference room and hurried up to them before they could leave. "Where's Amber?" she asked, stopping just short of grabbing her mother's arm.

"She left," her mother said, looking Rowan over. "She understands her place and will do as she's told. And rather than embarrass herself any further trying to fit in with the local yokels, she's gone home to gather her things. We'll sign the paperwork tomorrow and then she'll come back to New York, where she belongs." She fluffed her hair out of her coat. "I'm sure you can find yourself some cowgirl to plough instead. And anyway, Amber may not be much, but she's still better than you."

Rowan had never in her life hit a woman, but she was sorely tempted to now. As though sensing it, her father gripped her arm and pulled her outside with a quick glance at Rowan. Jimmy and Baxter were already gone.

Rowan looked back at the room full of people and swore silently. She couldn't leave, but Amber shouldn't be alone. But then, had she really left? She went to the valet and got it confirmed. Amber had asked to be driven back to her own house and one of the staff had obliged.

The wind gusted, slamming into the tent and making it snap loudly. Trees were blowing and the air was oddly warm. Frustration welled, and she wished she could punch something. Amber shouldn't be alone right now, but this was Rowan's livelihood and reputation, and disappearing wouldn't look good. She had to trust that Amber would be okay until she got home in a little while. She took out her phone and sent a text.

I wish you hadn't left. Are you okay?

The reply came back quickly.

I'm going to go to sleep. Enjoy the rest of the night.

Rowan sighed and pinched the bridge of her nose. Tonight had held so much promise. Now it held only heartache and questions.

Chapter Twenty-Two

EVERYTHING HURT. FROM HEAD to toe, Amber ached with grief, impotent rage, and the sense of darkness that she'd grown up with. She'd taken a couple painkillers and stripped off the night's outfit, which she'd felt so good in, and which now looked like a sad heap of crumpled hope. Lying in her new bed under fresh new sheets, she should have been happy that she had her own space. But it wasn't going to happen. She should have known.

She'd avoided leaving the safety of the table at the event for as long as possible, but the need to pee had finally outweighed her fear of being alone. Pam and Julie had been locked in a whispered, probably dirty, conversation if their expressions were anything to go by, and the others had been taken away by other guests. So she'd hoped she'd make it to the bathroom and back without being accosted.

No such luck.

Every time Amber went to replay the conversation, a new flood of tears began, making her headache that much worse. Her mother's cruelty had reiterated everything she'd been told growing up: that she was weak, spineless, useless, and stupid. Not to mention unattractive and always trying too hard. And underpinning the whole thing had been that Amber was incapable of living in the middle of nowhere with people who would only ever tolerate her presence as an outsider. No one would ever really like her, and a successful woman like Rowan could do better.

Bombarded and beaten down, Amber had finally given in and said she'd talk to the lawyers in the morning. Her mother was right. She had no business being here, and she simply had to lick her wounds and go back to the office to grovel for her old job. It would be humiliating, and if her old boss didn't take her back, she'd just have to go job hunting. That was the world she knew.

So why did it hurt so bad? She'd never intended on actually staying here, had she? Sure, she'd given herself a time frame to work out her life, but... *Stop lying to yourself.* She wiped away a few stray tears. The last few days had made her think that maybe this was where she belonged after all. But she didn't belong anywhere. She was an outsider no matter where she went.

Something banged against the window, making her jump. Heart racing, she got out of bed and looked outside. A tree branch lay on the ground below, but not for long. Suddenly it was swept away in a gust of wind that rattled the window. She backed away, a strange foreboding coming over her, and the eerie wail from her phone set her heart racing even faster. She leapt for it.

NWS: TORNADO WARNING in this area til 3:00 a.m. Take shelter now. Check media.

She began to shake. Why was she here? Why had she left New York? She grabbed a sweatshirt, coat, and thick socks, her mind skittering from one thought to the next. *Purse. Laptop.* She grabbed them and shoved them in a thin canvas bag she'd bought in Paris and never shown anyone because it was so touristy. The windows rattled harder, and it sounded like half the forest was hitting the house. Shelter. That meant the white door outside, the one tucked into a mound. Was it unlocked? Did she have a key? What if it got blocked, and she ended up entombed in the hill like some weird fairytale character?

Glass broke somewhere in the house. "Shit fuck damn fuck," she yelled, trying to overpower the fear. She just had to hope the shelter wasn't locked. She grabbed her things and ran to the back door without waiting to see what was broken. It wouldn't be her house much longer anyway.

She flung open the door, and wind and water slammed into

her, knocking her backward. Sirens wailed through the darkness like banshees singing a song of death. She held her bag to her chest and walked forward into the storm, bracing herself and occasionally slipping back, unable to watch her step as the ground quickly became a pond. The roar of the wind was matched by the creaking and snapping of the trees, an orchestra of fear and fury. The journey to the shelter felt like it took forever, and she was shaking, her muscles straining when she finally reached it. Holding her bag tightly in one arm, she reached out and yanked on the door handle.

It didn't budge.

No matter how hard she pulled or which way she turned it, it didn't move. Tears were blown off her cheeks to mix with the pounding rain, and she sobbed, letting her rage and despair mix with the storm's. Just as she was about to turn and make a run back to the house, a large hand covered hers.

"Hold onto me," Rowan shouted.

Amber hadn't heard her arrive, but the fact that she wasn't alone made her nearly collapse with relief. She watched through slitted eyes as Rowan reached around the side of the door, moved something, and then turned the handle. The door swung inward to reveal a ladder leading into the dark. Rowan reached in and flipped a switch next to the door, and the darkness ahead was banished.

"Go!" Rowan moved aside and pushed Amber in front of her.

Clumsy and still shaking, Amber descended the ladder, her bag slung over her arm. Above her, Rowan entered and slammed the door shut. It was like a blanket had been thrown over the world as the storm was reduced to a dull rumble. She moved away from the ladder and looked around, barely taking it in as her heart thudded and panic continued to make her want to bolt, though there was nowhere else to go. Cold, shaking, and wet, she didn't know what to do next.

"Hey," Rowan said, gently pulling her into a hug. "You're okay.

You're safe. Breathe."

Instead, Amber's shaking intensified, and the sobs rose once again. She felt Rowan move them to a sitting position but never lifted her head from Rowan's chest. Rowan let her cry.

Eventually, too tired to cry anymore, she raised her hand and smiled wanly as Rowan handed her some wadded-up tissue. "No one has ever seen me being such a snotty mess before."

"I don't doubt that."

Finally, Amber looked up and gasped. "You're bleeding."

"Am I?" Rowan shrugged. "I can't feel it. Must not be too bad."

Amber shook her head as she looked at the inch long gash on Rowan's temple. The blood had dried, so it probably wasn't deep. She looked around for the first time. "Is there a first aid kit?"

Rowan pointed. "That yellow box there."

Amber went and got it and knelt in front of Rowan. "Why in the world did you come here?"

Rowan flinched a little when Amber rubbed the alcohol wipe over the cut. "I was seeing off the last guests, and I was going to text you to see if I could come over. But then the sirens started, and I knew you wouldn't be prepared for a tornado warning, and it would probably scare the pants off you. You didn't answer your phone, and I had a feeling you'd be headed this way but that you also probably had no idea how to get it open."

Amber gently placed the bandage over the cut and then noticed that Rowan was still in her tux. "I don't know what to say," she said softly, cupping Rowan's cheek. "You shouldn't have put yourself in danger for me. I'm not worth it." The last words came out like slivers of ice over her tongue.

Something hit the door, and she jumped. The faint sound of a siren continued like discordant background music and what sounded like baseballs hit the door. Probably hail. She rested her cheek on Rowan's knee and sighed at the feeling of her hand in her hair.

"Amber, after meeting your mother, I can't even fathom what

you've been through. I thought that kind of villain was something made up for dark fairytales, not something in real life." She tugged gently on Amber's hair, getting her to look up. "All I can tell you is that everything she says is a lie. It's all wrong and clearly comes from a place of evil." She ran her thumb over Amber's cheek. "You're beautiful, intelligent, kind, and funny. And tonight, you looked more beautiful than the stars on a clear night, like the moon came down and took human form."

Amber gave a shaky laugh. "I read a book like that once. The moon in female form. Sometimes she was full of life and laughter, sometimes she was shadowy and distant."

"A woman who experiences every aspect of life." Rowan reached down and pulled Amber up to cradle her in her lap. "You're going to have scars on your soul for a long time. Maybe forever. But you don't have to let her give you new wounds." Her hand caressed Amber's lower back. "Tell me about your tattoo."

"Remember when I told you about that trip to Hawaii? I spoke to a guy in the marketplace. He was making these beautiful wood carvings of animals covered in tribal symbols. The sea turtle one was so stunning, I had to have it. But we talked about it first, and he told me about all the things the sea turtle represents there. Stability, strength, endurance, perseverance, and guidance. All the aspects of life I wanted. Even then I knew I'd lose the carving one day, but I could have the tattoo to remind me of what to strive for." She brushed away a tear. "I should have gotten it somewhere I can see it every day. I forget it's even there."

"I'll remind you." Rowan pressed her fingers to it. "I won't let you forget again."

Amber pressed her lips to Rowan's, kissing her with all the passion and desperation she'd felt over the last several days. Rowan's arms tightened around her, and she returned the kiss, her tongue demanding entrance. Amber moaned and Rowan stood, turned, and gently placed Amber on the thin bed. She threw the tux jacket aside, pulled open the bowtie and then unbuttoned her shirt, never taking her eyes from Amber's. That bit of clothing landed with the tux jacket, leaving her in a white sports bra and her tux pants. She knelt between Amber's legs and Amber rose, eagerly ridding herself of the sweatshirt and tank top beneath it.

"I'd hoped to look different for this," she murmured, wincing at the sweatpants Rowan tugged off her hips.

"You think I give a damn what clothes I'm pulling off you so I can see this?" Rowan asked, her fingertips skimming lightly over Amber's stomach. "That's just wrapping, baby. This is the gift."

Amber lifted her hips, and her underwear joined the pile of clothes on the floor. Naked, she thrilled a little as Rowan lowered herself, still half dressed, onto Amber's body. The power Rowan exuded combined with Amber's vulnerability and created a deep throbbing at her core. Rowan's hard thigh pressed against her clit and she cried out, arching against her.

"Please," she whispered. "Make me forget everything but you."

Rowan growled softly and kissed her hard, palming her breast and pinching her nipple. "Oh, I can do that."

Her mouth was hot and firm against Amber's skin as she made her way from her neck to her breasts, sucking one nipple and then the other until Amber was writhing beneath her, one hand in Rowan's hair, the other pulling, pressing, digging into her shoulder. Incoherent with need, all she could do was let her body ask for what she wanted and hope that Rowan understood.

Rowan cupped her pussy and squeezed, making Amber moan. "Tell me you want me," she said, her husky voice dripping with desire. "Tell me."

"Please," Amber whispered, "please fuck me the way you want to."

"To fuck you all the ways I want to, we're going to need a far different space." Rowan nipped at her thigh and drew her thumb through Amber's wetness to her clit. "But I'll make a start."

Amber moaned as Rowan pressed two fingers into her, deep and slow, and then began fucking her in a steady rhythm while she continued to lavish attention on Amber's nipples. She was everywhere and as promised, Amber forgot everything but the way Rowan felt on top of her, inside her. And when Rowan added a third finger and picked up the pace, fucking her even deeper and harder, Amber rose to meet the thrusts, raking her nails across Rowan's back and crying out as she came, over and over again. Rowan didn't let up, slowing down only to take her over the edge again. Then she pulled out, flipped Amber onto her stomach and pulled her to her knees, so she could enter her again from behind, with one arm wrapped around Amber's waist as the other fucked her into an ecstatic kind of high. The final orgasm left her limp in Rowan's arms.

Gently, Rowan shifted to let Amber lay down. She pulled a blanket from a storage box and draped it over Amber before taking off her shoes and trousers and climbing back under the blanket and pulling Amber against her. "You're so beautiful," she murmured against Amber's hair. "So perfect."

Amber couldn't have said words even if she could think of any. For the moment, she was safe and content in a lover's arms and that was all that mattered. She let herself drift to sleep, the storm outside continuing to rage.

When she woke, she had no idea how much time had passed.

"You okay?" Rowan said, lightly brushing her hand over Amber's shoulder.

She shivered and smiled. "Better than okay. And it sounds like the storm has stopped."

"Could be. But I heard it was a big one, so we're probably in the eye of the storm, when it goes quiet before it lets loose again."

Amber sighed, weirdly glad that it might still be too dangerous to go out. At least this way she had a little more time with Rowan before... She pushed away the thought. It would wait until they were back out in the open.

"Do you know why my parents planted willow trees?" Rowan smoothed the hair away from Amber's cheek.

"I guess I assumed they'd always been there. Do people put a lot of thought into trees?" Amber raised up and rested her chin on her fist so she could look into Rowan's eyes.

"Some people do. My parents did." Rowan raised up to kiss her before settling again. "We have two main types of tree on the property. The line of willows by the driveway, and the oak in front of my house."

Amber nodded. "That oak tree is huge." She'd often admired the swing bench that swayed in the breeze below it.

"The willows were a reminder that if you stand too rigid against a storm, like this one, then it will blow you down, break you apart, uproot you. But if you bend with the wind, holding just firm enough to stay where you are, then you'll be okay. It'll have less power to hurt you."

Amber rolled her eyes, which remained sore from all the crying. "Subtle."

Rowan laughed and tweaked her nipple, making her jump. "Yeah, well, I don't think you're big on subtlety."

"And the oak?" Amber asked, splaying her hand over Rowan's stomach. It wasn't rock hard or terribly defined, but it was flat and she could still feel the muscle beneath it. She continued to stroke and liked the way Rowan's eyes flickered closed.

"The oak is about our family. Strong, solid, forever. A place of beauty. If my parents fought, they'd go out there to work it out, even in the rain or snow." Rowan laughed and then caught her breath when Amber slid her fingertips under the band of her boxers. She put her hand gently over Amber's. "Believe me when I say I'm going to explode, but I get a little in my head about receiving." She smirked down at Amber and ran her finger over Amber's lips. "I need to be relaxed and in my own bed. A little boring, maybe, but I'm happy to give anywhere and everywhere, so I hope that makes up for it."

Amber dragged her nails lightly over Rowan's stomach before snuggling back in against her. It was disappointing, as there might not be a second time, but she wouldn't let herself focus on that right now. "Good to know."

"But if you still have some energy," Rowan said, pulling Amber up to straddle her. "I'm more than happy to continue."

Amber was about to protest that she was more than sated, but Rowan's big, calloused hand cupped her breast and stroked her nipple in just the right way, and she shut up. Instead, she pressed herself against Rowan, rocking her pussy over her abdomen and holding herself up by putting her hands back on Rowan's thighs. It pushed her breasts forward, giving Rowan open access.

She took quick advantage of it, sitting up to take Amber's nipple in her mouth as she slid her hand between Amber's legs and entered her, this time quickly.

Amber ground down on her fingers and rode them, her breasts on fire under Rowan's touch. She fell into the sensations and lost herself, letting go of everything but the way Rowan made her feel. She came, and Rowan thrust deep and held still until Amber relaxed and collapsed on top of her. Rowan pulled the blanket up over them and wrapped her arms around Amber.

"So fucking perfect," Rowan murmured, stroking her back.

Amber drifted off, beautifully exhausted.

The next time she woke, there was a freight train roaring over them, throwing itself against the door of the shelter. She gasped and pressed back into Rowan, who was asleep behind Amber, her arm around Amber's waist.

"Tornado," Rowan said, coming awake and rising up on one elbow. She seemed to listen. "Big one."

"What about your horses? All your animals?" She turned to look at her. "Oh God. Is someone with Shift?"

Rowan gave her a small, sweet smile. "The horses are in their own shelter, as are all my animals. No shelter is perfect, but they should all be fine. Pam went and got Shift the moment she knew

I was coming to you."

"I'm sorry I didn't think to ask sooner." Amber listened and shook her head. "And just after I rebuilt the house."

"Hey now." Rowan kissed her shoulder. "Tornados move in funny ways. They can demolish one side of a street and leave the other untouched. Hell, they can jump one house and hit the next. Try not to worry about it until we can see what the trouble is."

"Are you worried about your place?" Amber asked, calmed by how unperturbed Rowan seemed.

"Sure. And I'm worried about all my people, and the town. But there's nothing I can do from here. And truth be told," she said, placing a longer kiss on Amber's shoulder, "there's nowhere I'd rather be right now."

Amber lay down facing her and sighed happily at the feel of Rowan's arm around her. She'd treasure the memory of that feeling. "Me too."

Rowan's gaze seemed to search for the answer to a question she hadn't asked, and Amber wasn't about to have this special moment in the midst of the storm ruined. She kissed her softly and then turned over, pushing her butt into Rowan's crotch and eliciting a soft groan that made her smile. "Thank you for coming for me," she said.

"Well, I haven't yet, but here's hoping." There was a smile in Rowan's voice and then she squeezed Amber close. "I'll always come for you, if you let me."

There was deep nuance to the double-edged words, and Amber blinked back the tears. She wouldn't ruin this one, perfect moment that would have to sustain her later.

Chapter Twenty-Three

ROWAN WOKE FEELING MORE contented and relaxed than she had in years. Amber breathed softly, her naked skin a temptation Rowan didn't want to resist. She kissed Amber's shoulder and watched her eyelids flutter as she woke.

"Is it over?" she asked, covering her mouth as she yawned.

"I think so," Rowan said, nibbling Amber's earlobe. "Want to bring in the day the right way?"

Amber grinned, then grimaced. "Much as I'd love to...there isn't a bathroom down here, is there?"

Rowan laughed, only mildly disappointed. There'd be more time later. "Of a sort, but I don't think you'll like it." She shuffled off the end of the bed and pulled the covered bucket from under the steps.

"Nope. Uh-uh." Amber pulled the blanket up around her like a shield. "I'd rather die of holding it."

Rowan laughed and bent down to pick up their pile of clothes. "Then maybe we'd better go see what the world looks like this morning." There was no phone signal in the shelter, and that was something she should look into getting fixed for Amber. Hopefully she'd never be alone in it during a storm, but things happened.

She stepped back into her tux trousers and put on the shirt. "I haven't done the walk of shame in a hell of a long time," she said and laughed.

Amber pulled her sweatshirt over her head. "Well, I'm glad I don't have to put that dress back on right now."

There was something about Amber's body language.

Something about the way her eyes flicked to Rowan's and then away again. "Are you okay?"

"Of course. I had a magical night in an underground box with a hot cowboy. Why wouldn't I be okay?" Her smile was tight and didn't reach her eyes.

"Amber—"

"Come on, before I burst." She motioned toward the stairs and pressed her legs together.

"Right." Rowan climbed the steps and opened the door slowly, lest any debris be settled against the door and about to fall on them. A bit of dirt rained in, but they were greeted with a bright blue sky. She climbed up and held out her hand for Amber, but she bypassed it and shot past her toward the house, which was, thankfully, still standing.

Rowan followed at a more leisurely pace, letting Amber have some privacy. She called Ted. "Hey. How is everything?"

"Well, we're all okay." He hesitated. "But we've got a couple more cows than we should. In the potato patch."

Rowan laughed. "And they're in one piece?"

"Don't even seem upset." Ted's disbelief was obvious. "Me and Shift checked your place, and it's all good too. Horses are spooked and restless but fine."

"Cattle?" Rowan entered Amber's place and headed for the bathroom herself.

"About to head down there now. Amber's place made it, guessing by your tone?"

"I haven't had a good look yet. We just came out of the shelter, but everything seems to be in place." She noticed the broken glass in the kitchen. "Maybe a couple of broken windows, actually."

"All right. Let me know when you're back, and we'll start moving the horses back to the stables. Police are asking folks to stay put so they don't get in the way of rescues. I'll let you know if I hear anything important from town."

"Thanks." She hung up and made use of Amber's small

downstairs bathroom, taking the time to freshen up as best she could. She smiled as she looked in the mirror. *What a fucking night*. She hadn't felt that kind of sexual connection with anyone in a long time. That kind of total giving yourself over, where it felt like your souls started to intertwine like coral honeysuckle vines, wrapping around each other. Amber had let her guard down, and she'd been the most beautiful, most breathtaking thing Rowan had ever seen. The image of her straddling Rowan's lap and riding her hand would be burned into her memory forever. She couldn't wait to see what other memories like that they could create.

She washed her hands and made her way back to the kitchen, where she could hear Amber sweeping up the glass. "Need a hand?" she asked.

"No, I'm good, thanks." Amber looked up. "Is your place okay?"

Rowan nodded, leaning on the counter. "Ted says everything is fine, but I want to go check it all out myself." She looked at the busted window. "Have you looked around? Is that the only one?"

Amber nodded, dumping the broken glass into the garbage. "I think so. I'll need to really have a good look to make sure. I'll call Peter and see if he's available."

"Depending on who got hit, you might be last in line. I can bring over some wood to cover it in the meantime." Rowan stretched. "Want to come to my place? We can—"

"Rowan." Amber took a deep breath and put her hands on the counter. "There's no easy way to say this, so I'm just going to say it. I'm selling the house. My mother and I are going to split the proceeds, and I'm going to buy my own place in New York. I'm supposed to sign the papers at Cornelius's place today."

Rowan's chest hurt like she'd been kicked by a horse. "What? Amber, you can't let her win. You can't...you can't..."

"Don't tell me what I can and can't do." Amber's eyes grew glassy with tears, and she held up her hand when Rowan stepped toward her. "She's right. As amazing as you are," she swallowed and glanced up, "and you *are* amazing, I don't belong here. I knew it the moment I stepped in horseshit outside that café my first day here. I knew it when I took a fucking hay ride to a country fair."

"And did you know it in my arms last night?" Rowan asked, her stomach churning. "Did you know it when I was fucking you into a stupor?"

Amber's breath was shaky, her hands white as she pressed them to the counter. "That's the only thing right about me being here, and it isn't enough. I belong back in the city, and taking a year out was a stupid idea. I have to get off my knees and show them all that I'm not a waste of money or time. That I'm still damn good at my job. This place...it isn't me."

"Not enough?" Rowan backed toward the door. "She's really done a number on you, hasn't she?" There was no fucking way on earth she'd let Amber see how much it hurt to hear that it had all been a charade. "Okay, Amber. Let her take it all away from you, yet again. If what we shared last night isn't *enough* to show you that you belong here, then I don't know what else I can do. And to agree to sell to Jimmy, after all you've seen. After all you've *said*. When you know what he's going to do to the land, to the community. To your family home." She turned and opened the door. "I hope you find some peace, Amber. I hope you get to a place where you can move beyond what she's done to you. Because..." Her voice cracked, and she didn't look back. "Because you're missing out on something pretty fucking special."

She left, slamming the door behind her and heading for her truck. Before she could leave, she had to clear branches off the cab and out of the bed, and it made her feel better to throw them as hard as she could off to the side. But the ache of betrayal and loss suddenly hit, and she leaned over the bed to vomit. How could this be happening?

She wiped her mouth with the back of her hand and got in the truck. She threw it in reverse and caught sight of Amber standing at the window, her arms wrapped around her like she was trying to keep from falling to pieces. Well, that was her choice. Rowan turned and sped out of the driveway, leaving her vision of the future behind.

***

"Enough." Pam slapped her hat against Rowan's shoulder. "Slow down, and let your poor horse breathe."

Rowan dropped the reins and Willow instantly slowed to a walk, her head hanging, her sides puffing. "Sorry, girl," Rowan said, patting her neck.

Beside her, Pam's horse was breathing hard too. "Let's stop at the lake."

Rowan followed them to the lakeside water trough. They tethered the horses to let them rest and graze, and she joined Pam on a bench. She accepted a bottle of water gratefully and closed her eyes, her face tilted toward the afternoon sun. After checking the fields and with her crew, she'd thrown herself into working in the stables until Pam had suggested a ride before everyone who worked for her quit thanks to the vibe she was throwing off. At first she'd been reluctant, but then the idea of getting away from it all had set in, and she couldn't get the horse saddled fast enough.

"Now." Pam took a long swig of water. "What has you all knotted up?"

"Amber's selling the farm to Jimmy. She's signing the papers today." The words were bitter on her tongue. "Not just that, but she's leaving for New York as soon as that's done. Buying a place there because she doesn't belong in a place like this with a person like me." She leaned forward, the pain of those words stabbing her in the chest.

"But..." Pam swirled her water bottle. "What the fuck? She had all that work done on the house. She seemed happy. You guys looked so good together." She blew out a breath. "Her mom is a real floating turd, isn't she?"

"Yeah, well." Rowan sat back, swallowing hard. "Amber's going to have to learn to stand on her own, isn't she? You can't save someone from themselves."

They sat in silence for a while, the horses munching, an occasional puffy cloud sliding slowly across the sky, and Rowan feeling like she'd fallen into a black hole and was still falling, despite the world around her looking solid.

"You know," Pam said, breaking the silence. "It seems to me that Amber has been standing on her own for a long time. I know what you mean, that she needs to break the chains, but after listening to her mother last night? I don't know if I'd be that strong either. And it seems like maybe Amber is stronger than she thinks. If only she had someone to lean on who didn't walk away." She raised her eyebrows and shook her head dolefully.

"Fuck off." Rowan rubbed at the back of her neck, the muscles in her shoulders screaming with tension. "Last night, in the shelter, was fucking magic." She rolled her eyes at Pam's low whistle. "If she couldn't tell how I feel about her from that, then there's no other way she'll understand."

"That's a load of horseshit." Pam tapped Rowan's head with her water bottle and grimaced when Rowan grabbed it and threw it into the grass. "Sex is great and all, but sticking with her and talking things through is better."

Rowan shook her head slowly. "Pam, she knows how we feel about her selling that land and letting Jimmy expand. She *knows*. And she said she understood. If she can get derailed with a single visit from her mother, then who's to say she won't just up and sell later anyway? She'd stick around, I'd let my heart get involved, then she'd leave, and I'd be left wondering where the hell it all went wrong. I already know how that works, don't I?"

"Ah." Pam turned toward her. "Rowan, not everyone is going

to leave the way your dad did."

She hadn't made the connection, but hearing Pam say it out loud made her slump on the bench. "He loved me, Pam. He was the most important person in my life, and I wasn't enough to keep him here." Tears blurred the scenery into a green and blue mire. "If he couldn't stick around, then why would Amber? She said outright that I'm not enough, so it's not like it would be a surprise down the road. It's better that she leave now, before I fall for her, than when she could break me to pieces."

"*Before* you fall for her. Right." Pam stood and clapped Rowan on the shoulder. "Sounds like maybe it's time to talk about this shit with a professional, buddy. You've held onto it long enough. Amber or no Amber, this baggage with your dad will weigh you down."

They were silent on the ride back, allowing Rowan to ponder the painful epiphany. She didn't even know she felt that way about her dad leaving the way he had. She was sure she'd put it in the past. But Amber had dredged up old dirt, and now that she was leaving with a large chunk of Rowan's heart, she felt like she was losing someone precious yet again. At what point would she be enough for someone to want to hang onto her? When they got to the stables and took care of the horses, she punched Pam's shoulder. "Thanks."

Pam rubbed at her shoulder. "Asshole. You're welcome." She rested her hand on her horse's neck. "For what it's worth, I'm really sorry about Amber. She was a pain in the ass, but I thought she'd come around. Like she found her place." She shrugged. "But, buddy, her baggage and yours are very separate things. And I'll always be on your side."

Rowan swallowed against the ball of emotion. There was way too much of it today. "Thanks."

They were walking back toward the stables when Rowan heard a quad approaching from behind them. Ted drove up, his face flushed. "Come on."

Without question, they got on, and he turned back toward the house. "What's wrong?" Rowan asked, her first concern about Amber.

"Cornelius's place got hit by the twister. They found him and his wife. The girls are still missing."

Rowan and Pam exchanged a glance, and Rowan went into planning mode. "Get as many of our staff as you can down there. Use the trucks and take them all in a group. Cancel all our tours and meetings. Call Fran and get food over there for the workers and emergency crews. Tell her to put it on our tab, and we'll take care of it."

Ted dropped them at Rowan's truck and sped off to follow her orders. She and Pam got on the road to Cornelius's place. "They used to shelter at Grant and Virginia's place. They must not have felt like they could go there now that it belongs to Amber."

"Damn," Pam muttered as they turned onto Corn's street.

There were probably better words, but Rowan couldn't think of them right now. The F4 tornado had ripped a half-mile gouge behind the main town, and it looked like it had played a game of hopscotch with the houses. One hit, one fine, two hit, one fine. One a pile of scrap wood mixed with the detritus of people's lives, one still standing as though it was any normal day.

Cornelius's house was one of the ones that now looked like matchsticks. He sat in the back of an ambulance, his head wrapped in a bandage that was already showing blood. When he saw Pam and Rowan drive up, he went to stand but the medic gently pushed him back down.

Rowan jogged over and pulled him into a hug. "How can we help?"

"They took Marge to the hospital," he said, his voice hoarse. "But I won't leave till we find my girls." He turned to Rowan, tears trailing through the dirt on his cheeks. "My girls, Rowan."

She squeezed his hand and looked over her shoulder at the truck arriving full of her crew. "We'll find them, Corn."

He nodded and looked toward the truck. "Thank you," he whispered.

Rowan jogged to the truck and shouted to be heard by everyone. "We've got two little girls missing. One ten, one eight. Stay out of the way of the first responders and do what they tell you to. But time is of the essence, so listen carefully, watch where you step, and shout if you think you see or hear anything at all. Let's go."

As a group they moved to what had once been a large, four-bedroom home with a wraparound deck. Now it was hard to distinguish what had been a room and what might have been dropped there by the tornado. A teddy bear lay face down, arms torn and head askew. Rowan prayed like hell the girls hadn't been anywhere near it.

This could have been Amber's house. We could have been searching for her body instead. It hadn't been, and it wasn't. But maybe...maybe there was a slim chance she was right. Maybe she didn't belong here, where this kind of thing could happen. New York got snow, and that was about it, wasn't it? *No.* Try as she might, she couldn't think that Amber would be safer anywhere that Rowan wasn't. Would Amber have come to help if she'd known about this? It bothered Rowan that she wasn't sure. But she was supposed to sign the paperwork at Corn's office today, and he clearly wasn't there. So where was Amber?

A car drove up, and Rowan saw Fran get out with some of her staff and begin setting up a table with hot drinks. Maybe Amber would have helped with that part. Or maybe she wouldn't have been there at all, saying that it was the first responders' job, and they should just stay out of it. City people were well known for not helping each other. The bottom line was that she wasn't there. For all Rowan knew, she was already on a plane back to New York. She tossed the thoughts away with a piece of lumber.

"Here!" Jess, whom Rowan hadn't even seen, yelled from a pile of rubble. "I can hear something!"

Rowan and the others scrambled over and began shifting debris beside the firefighters. And then a pink shoe appeared, and she knelt down, careful about how she moved the wood.

"Rowan?" said a small voice. "I'm scared."

"I know, sweetheart." Gently, Rowan lifted Cornelius's oldest daughter from the wreckage. "Is your sister with you?"

"We were holding hands, but I let go." She whimpered, tears sliding down her cheeks. "I let go."

"Shh," Rowan said. "We'll find her. It wasn't your fault." She carried the girl to the ambulance where Corn stood crying, his arms open.

"Thank you, God," he said, dropping to his knees and pulling her into a hug.

Rowan returned to the group still searching and told them what the child had said. The fact that they'd been pulled apart wasn't good. The smaller child could have been taken by the tornado. Night was closing in, and it was getting colder. Spotlights were set up in preparation. Rowan moved around the edge of the wreckage as she headed over to the table to get a drink, but movement caught her eye. A piece of wood shifted ever so slightly and then settled again.

"Here!" she yelled and was quickly surround by help. Beneath a pile of timber, Corn's younger girl lay on her back with her hands and feet in the air, like an overturned turtle. She'd been pushing against the boards, but they'd been too heavy to get off her.

Once again, Rowan reached down and plucked the child from the debris, and she wrapped her arms around Rowan's neck. Cheers went up, and the word went around that the last child had been found, and people could go home. When Rowan rounded the corner to take the child to Corn, she nearly tripped.

Amber stood at the drink table, handing out cups of steaming liquid as well as blankets for people to wrap up in when they took breaks. She met Rowan's eyes and put her hand to her chest as she took in the child resting in her arms. Rowan gave her a weak smile and continued on to Corn, who held her to him as he sobbed quietly.

"I thought I'd lost you," he said.

The child looked up at Rowan. "When you taught us to ride, you said the best riders never give up, even when they're hurt or scared. And I'm the best rider my age, so I did what you said."

Rowan and Corn laughed, and she wiped tears from her eyes. "Well, you certainly proved that you're the best, didn't you?" She looked up and saw Amber watching, her expression tender and thoughtful.

"Rowan, we can't thank you enough for bringing your people down. It's a hell of a town, isn't it?" Kelly came over and thumped Rowan's shoulder. "Maybe I'll come by one night and give you a hero's celebration," she said with a wink.

Rowan felt her face flame and looked over her shoulder.

Amber was gone.

Chapter Twenty-Four

SNOW FLUTTERED PAST THE window of Amber's loft, drifting lazily, caught by an occasional gust, and then swirling frantically. *I'm a snowflake in a storm.* She sat curled on her sofa with a mug of coffee and her TV set to show a fire in a fireplace. It was an absurd parody of the real thing, but it felt right to have that kind of falseness around her right now.

The devastation at Cornelius's house had turned her knees to water. They'd waited for a while outside his office until someone had finally come by to tell them the news. Her mother and father had been irritated by the delay and said they'd find some other way to get it done. Baxter had looked thoughtful, while Jimmy had looked like an animal trying to find a way around a trap. Jimmy's place had gone unscathed, and her mother had complained bitterly about having to spend the night in the basement area without any catering or entertainment.

Amber had stayed silent throughout, replaying her final conversation with Rowan over and over in her mind. The look of betrayal in her eyes would haunt Amber forever. But her mother had made a few more remarks about Amber getting back to the gym and laying off the carbs, and she'd shut down altogether, refusing to think about anything at all.

But when they'd decided to head back to New York and deal with the legal situation from there, Amber had balked. She simply couldn't bring herself to get in the car, like a magnet being pulled toward its counterpart. She thought of Cornelius's laugh, his pride in his kids, the pamphlet he'd given her... And she'd told them she'd see them in New York the next day, that she was going to help.

She snorted softly as she remembered the expression on her mother's face. Disbelief and disgust were etched into every frown line, and she'd told Amber she'd better be back in time to sign the paperwork when it was ready. Jimmy and Baxter had left in their own cars, and Amber couldn't help but wonder how Jimmy could be so callous about the people he'd grown up around.

But then, he didn't care in the least about what they wanted. And she was going to help him prove it.

When she'd shown up at the wreckage, it had broken her heart. She'd recalled Corn showing her around the house that first time, and the pregnant pause when he'd mentioned that they sheltered there with her grandparents. A pause she'd intentionally left open. Was it her fault that they hadn't felt able to run for shelter?

Fran had called her over to help, and Amber had gladly jumped in, even though she felt more like an outsider than ever as she watched the community work together to save their own. And watching as Rowan had delivered that little girl into Cornelius's arms had been the most beautiful thing.

But then Kelly had gone over and offered her services, and Amber was brutally reminded that she and Rowan had come to a dead end.

Tears slid down her cheeks, and she didn't bother to wipe them away. Why did it all feel so awful? So messy?

Her doorbell buzzed, and she forced herself off the couch. "Yes?" she said, holding down the button.

"Let me in. It's freezing out here."

She smiled a little and hit the release, and Craig was shaking snow out of his hair a moment later in her kitchen. "I thought you were filming in Brazil."

"I was. But they're working through some scenes I'm not in, so I thought I'd come home for a bit and see how my bestie is doing." He looked her over. "I'll order takeout, and you can tell me all about it."

She curled up on the sofa again and only vaguely listened to him place the order. Then he chucked off his shoes and maneuvered his considerable muscle into a cross-legged sitting position beside her.

"Start with after I left."

She shook her head. "It feels like a billion things happened. But in such a short space of time that it seems surreal." The explanation took them through the receipt and eating of their meal and into wine after. "And here I am. A coward, alone in her loft the weekend before Thanksgiving, with fuck all going on in her life."

He sipped his wine and stared out the window for a moment without responding. Finally, he looked at her. "Don't think. Just respond. One, two, three. Did you love that house?"

"Yes." She swallowed hard.

"Good start. Now. Do you love this loft?" He motioned with his wine glass, nearly spilling some.

"No." She sighed. "I like it. I like living in the city. Or I thought I did. But when I got back, it felt...cramped. Not just my place, but the city itself. Like we're living in a beehive, all on top of each other. It was hard to breathe."

"And you're selling to Sleezebag McDuck, who's going to bulldoze that house and build a golf course and a ton more houses over it, because your mother bullied you into it."

There was no question there, and no judgment either. "Not just that. She said some things that made sense. About me not fitting in there, and not being right or good enough for Rowan." Tears started again, and she grabbed the half-empty box of tissues and held it to her chest.

"Oh, honey." He pulled her into a hug. "That evil bitch wouldn't know who was right for anyone, let alone for you. *She* didn't fit in there, and therefore she doesn't want you to either." He brushed the hair from her face. "Amber, we've known each other for a long time. And I've never seen you as happy and relaxed as you were there."

She pulled away to blow her nose. "I really was," she whispered.

"Then what are you thinking?" He looked genuinely upset for her. "Babe, I know you're lost. I know you think this is what you have to do. But all you need to do in this life is find the path that makes you happy. That's it. And you found your yellow brick road, Dorothy." He twirled his hand, motioning forward.

"That was Kansas, not Kentucky." She smiled and sniffled. "But my mom is supposed to know me best, right? What if it's true?" Her voice broke. "What if I'll never fit in anywhere? What if I really am a waste of space?"

This time, the sobs were almost violent. She wrapped her arms around herself and shook, letting out the grief, despair, and loneliness that had been threaded through her soul from the moment her mother had started talking to her when she was born.

Craig held her, rocking her, and let her cry herself out.

Exhausted, she rested her head against his shoulder, her eyes sore and her head aching. "I don't know what to do."

He tugged on her ear. "Obviously."

She looked at him, and he smiled gently.

"But no one can give you the answers either. You've got to make some decisions, babe. You need to decide what you want your life to look like going forward. You can live believing your mother's lies and vitriol, or you can leave her in the dust and find out who you really are. But that choice is up to you."

"It doesn't sound like much of a choice when you put it like that." Amber shuffled to the kitchen and pulled out a tub of ice cream she'd felt insanely guilty about even buying, let alone actually wanting to eat. Now, it seemed like the perfect way to flip off her mother.

She handed Craig a spoon, and they dug into the vegan café oat marshmallow concoction together.

"I'd ask what you want to do about Rowan, but it seems like you have other stuff to figure out first." Craig waved the spoon at her. "But if it were me in your little lesbian heels, I'd be on that hot butch's doorstep before she could even think about that fire lady."

"But that's the other thing, isn't it? Kelly is tall, and gorgeous, and local. Why would Rowan want this when she could have that? It'd be like having tofu instead of steak."

"If she was so into this Kelly person, why isn't she with her?" He rolled his eyes. "You and I have had enough flings to know how that works." He set the spoon down on a coaster and took her hand. "The damage your mother has done to you is going to take a long, long time to repair, and it can only be done if you cut the cord and make the decision to let the healing begin. If you keep submerging yourself in poison, you're not going to get it out of your system."

She pointed the spoon at him. "Where did my non-emotional, sarcastic friend go? Who is this deep, sweet man I see before me?"

He picked up his spoon again. "I'm the real thing. The other guy is for public consumption."

"Do you get tired of being both?" she asked, settling back against the cushions and letting him have the tub.

"Of course. And that's why balance is important. Having you in my life means I've got a tether to something real, to someone who isn't just hanging out with me for my charm and money." He grinned. "Of which I have inordinate amounts of both."

She laughed, the anchor of despair lifting from her chest. "I miss Rowan," she said softly. "I wish I was with her right now."

"I'll try not to be offended." He got up and put the mostly empty ice cream back in the freezer. He checked his watch. "Okay. I need to head home and get some sleep. Let's have brunch tomorrow." He frowned. "You haven't signed the papers for the sale yet, have you?"

She shook her head. "Cornelius hasn't been back in the

office, so everything is on hold. Mother is going apeshit, but that's nothing new. Why?"

"Seems to me you should make use of this little gap in motherly mayhem to see a pro about your mental meanderings." At her raised eyebrow, he laughed. "My character in the new film has a really good vocabulary." He leaned down and kissed her cheek. "You'll be okay. Just...take care of you."

She waved from her place on the couch as he left and then she pulled the blanket up around her chin and stared at the fire flickering on the TV. He was right, of course. *Everyone* who said she needed to stop listening to her mother was right. So why was it so hard? Why did she continue to allow that poison into her system?

She grabbed her phone and pulled up Google to look for a therapist who could work wonders quickly. It was time to make some changes. Hopefully, she could fix things before she lost Rowan for good.

***

The café was crowded on Friday morning, and the windows were steamed up. Amber sat in a booth at the back, her nerves on fire and her stomach swirling.

"What a strange place to meet." Her mother slid into the booth opposite her. "I know a couple celebrities come here, but it's still so...quaint." She motioned to the passing waiter. "Coffee, black, and a croissant, warmed." She turned away without bothering to notice if he'd heard her. "Now. Did you bring the paperwork? Is that why you dragged me down here?"

"No." Amber took a deep breath. "I wanted to have a discussion."

"Always so dramatic. What about now?"

"About my father." Amber didn't miss the twitch of her mother's eye or the way her fingernail dug into the table.

"What about him? He's getting ready to leave for that trip to Scotland." She tutted. "I don't know why you'd play golf in the snow with a little white ball, but whatever. It gets him out of my hair for a while."

"Not him." Amber didn't look away. "Buck. My biological father. The one who wanted me and would have raised me if only you'd given me up."

Her mother sat back and didn't acknowledge the arrival of her coffee and pastry. "Where did you hear that?" she hissed.

"My grandparents kept all the letters they sent you. Every single one of them from what I can tell. I learned a lot." Amber allowed the anger to rise, something she'd never done in front of her mother. "I learned that they wanted to meet me, and they would have been great. I could have been with people who loved me instead of someone who loathed me."

"What do you know?" Her mother leaned forward, fire in her eyes. "They were hillbilly nobodies. I raised you to be someone. I gave you a life I dreamed of having, you ungrateful shit. It isn't my fault you blew it to pieces."

"No. No more." Amber kept her voice level and firm, pulling on the strength the therapist assured her was in there somewhere. "No more name-calling. No more gaslighting. Who was he? I want a name."

"What, so you can rock up at his door all these years later and expect a big hug from your long-lost daddy?" Her mother sneered and waved her hand, long nails clawing at the air. "You're just like them. No sense, no ambition. You had a piece of something and threw it away. But if you'd stop being a brat for a moment, I could probably help you get back on track."

"Name." Amber folded her arms, doing everything she could not to give in, not to allow the hurt child within to wither.

Her mother stared at her, lips pressed to a paper-thin line. "Jeff Crossley. A nobody. His father was a coal miner, and Jeff wasn't ever going to be anything better. And now that you know, you'll see that he isn't worth your time, just like he wasn't worth mine."

Jeff. She had a name, and now she could start looking properly, when she decided to do so. "Do you know what city he lived in?"

"Is that stupid bit of information all you wanted?" Her mother said, finally taking a sip of coffee and glaring at Amber over the rim. "He won't be glad to see you, you know. You'll just be a reminder of the woman he loved who was too good for him. If you want any other information, you'll have to dig it up yourself."

"I guess I will." Amber pressed her boots against the floor to ground herself. "There's something else. I'm not selling the land. Or the house."

If her mother had looked angry before, she looked apoplectic now. "You little bitch. Listen to me—"

"No." Amber slapped the table, making the silverware clatter and coffee slosh over the side of the mug. "*You* listen to *me*. I'm done with you, Mother. Completely. From this day forward, I'll have nothing to do with you. Tomorrow, you're going to be served with a restraining order that requires you to stay away from me. I wanted to let you know in person and to say goodbye so I can close the door."

Her mother's throat was working like she wanted to say something, but the words were stuck. Her eyes were wide. "How dare you? After all I've done?"

"All you've done is deride, shame, and demean me. You've taken out your anger and bitterness on me, someone you should have protected and loved. You're an abusive, bitter woman, and maybe one day I'll forgive you for the way you've treated me. But probably not." Amber stood. "If you ever want to get in touch, talk to my attorney. But under no circumstances am I selling that land, and you have no legal right to it, which means you have no need to speak to me, ever again." She picked up her purse and really looked at the woman she was walking away from. There was a beautiful, utter absence of feeling. "You nearly broke me.

But thanks to the people who actually care, I'm going to be okay. I'll find my way in a world you haven't tainted with your poison. Goodbye, Mother."

Her mother reached out to grab her, her nails raking Amber's wrist as she pulled it away. "Don't you dare walk away from me. I'm your mother, and you don't get to just leave. Amber! Amber, come back this instant!"

The shouted demands slid off her coat like melted snow, and she left them behind in the café. Outside, she took a deep breath of cold, cleansing air and tilted her head to the sky. All the tears leading to this moment had already been shed. It was time to let the storm pass and see what waited on the other side.

Chapter Twenty-Five

"GOD, I LOVE THE smell of pumpkin pie." Pam leaned over the tray of pies and inhaled. "Can't I have a tiny piece?"

Rowan shoved her away from the countertop. "No. Check the turkey, will you?"

Pam grumbled and did as she was told.

Rowan's house was alive with the sound of people getting ready for Thanksgiving dinner. She was grateful for the distraction. Work had slowed as the snow had moved in, and the stables were set up for the winter. Groups and tours had stopped for the holidays, and she was left with paperwork that did nothing to quiet the deep, cold sadness lodged in her chest, like the snowstorm had started there and moved to her surroundings. She hadn't heard from Amber since she'd walked away, and Corn said he'd had plenty of calls from Amber's mother as well as her attorney and Jimmy, but he hadn't returned them. The message on his voicemail said he was away dealing with a housing issue, and he'd get back to folks as and when he could. But he hadn't heard from Amber directly.

Rowan looked into the living room and smiled a little. Corn and his girls sat on the floor with Ted and Shift, and the game of Jenga didn't seem to be going to plan, since Shift kept sticking his big nose against the bricks and knocking them over. Corn saw her watching them and gingerly got to his feet and shuffled into the kitchen. The head wound had been superficial, but the bathroom sink that had landed on his hip meant he wasn't getting around very well.

"I can't thank you enough, Rowan." He leaned on the counter

and accepted the glass of eggnog Pam thrust at him. "You've truly gone above and beyond by bringing us into your home."

"Corn, it isn't like I didn't have the room. And you need to stop thanking me. What's said is said and done is done, okay?" She tapped her glass to his and they drank. "Marge okay?"

He nodded, looking tired. "I imagine she'll be up soon. We're both waking up with nightmares and going to check on the girls at night."

Rowan knew it was true since she could hear them up and wandering every night. "It'll pass eventually. When you go through what you did, it's gonna take time."

Julie came in, laden down with bags. "Hey, y'all! Happy Thanksgiving!" She set the bags on the extra table. "I brought some Kentucky bourbon cheesecake, homemade buttermilk biscuits, and some honey roast ham. Pam said I didn't need to, but what Southern woman shows up empty-handed? I mean, really." Julie smiled and gave Pam a loud kiss on the cheek.

"Well, we've got enough people here to make a good dent in it." Rowan smiled and gave her a quick hug.

Ted and Shift came into the kitchen, making it crowded. "You got any of those biscuits now?" He peered into the bags of containers. "Rowan's making us wait till my stomach turns inside out to have dinner."

"It's four in the afternoon, Ted." Rowan rolled her eyes and opened the fridge. "Here." She shoved a plate of cheeses at him. "The crackers are over there, under the square silver lid."

He tossed a piece to Shift as they made their way to the crackers, and Corn and the girls quickly joined him.

"Locusts," Rowan mumbled, opening the oven to check the turkey and then moving to put the ham from Julie onto a tray. It wasn't long before everything was cooking and there wasn't much else to do, so they all headed to the living room. Drink in hand, Rowan smiled as they laughed and teased one another. Shift came over and put his big head on her lap, looking up at her with soulful eyes. "I know, buddy. I miss her too," she murmured as she scratched his ears.

She might have been projecting, but she didn't think so. She'd seen Shift sniffing at Amber's old room and the blanket she liked to wrap herself in on the porch, and then he'd whine and walk away, tail down. If she had a tail, hers would be down too.

"So," Corn said, placing a piece into a puzzle they'd been working on haphazardly for two days. "I got an interesting message from Baxter today."

Rowan frowned. "Why would Jimmy's finance guy be calling you?"

"Seems he wants to know what the real situation is. Said he could tell things were messy with the sale, and according to Amber's mom's lawyer, the land isn't for sale anymore after all. Jimmy is telling him differently, saying it's just a matter of time and patience." Corn looked up at Rowan, his eyes narrowed thoughtfully. "Strange, isn't it?"

Rowan didn't answer. She got up to check the food, her mind racing. Strange didn't quite cut it. Intriguing did though. Had Amber changed her mind? Why would she, when she'd been so adamant when she'd actually left? She looked at her phone and considered calling. But to say what? Amber had walked away, even after what they'd shared. And she hadn't called once since she'd left. Surely that meant they were really over.

Suddenly, she wanted to send a text. What was Amber doing today? Was she spending Thanksgiving with her vile parents? Or was she alone? Or maybe with Craig and his crowd? Rowan closed her eyes against the idea that Amber was sitting alone in her loft. Plenty of people spent the holidays alone, but that didn't mean it wasn't lonely.

"Snow's getting deep," Pam said as she popped a cracker with a mountain of cheese on it into her mouth. "We may all end up sleeping here."

Rowan shrugged. "The couches are comfortable, and I have

plenty of blankets." She grinned. "But remember there are kids in the house. No noises their parents will have to explain away in the morning."

Pam choked on her cracker and thumped at her chest. Face red, she said, "As if I'm going to have sex in your house. A thought of you would intrude, and I'd suddenly be impotent for the rest of my life."

"Pretty sure that's not how it works, but we'll go with it." Rowan opened the oven and wafted the steam away from her face. "I think we can eat in about thirty minutes."

Ted rolled onto his back. "I might make it," he said, holding his stomach and groaning, making the girls giggle.

Rowan's phone buzzed, and she took off the oven gloves. It was an unknown number, but she had plenty of clients who weren't contacts. "Hello?"

"I don't suppose you have snow tires? I don't, and I'm stuck in a snowdrift. Because that's what you get for driving in the country where apparently you don't use snowplows."

Joy, sweet and electric, swept through her. "Amber, for a woman who doesn't like to be rescued, you seem to get yourself in a lot of scrapes." Rowan motioned to Pam, who shook her head and picked up the oven gloves. Rowan grabbed her keys and pulled on her coat. "Any idea where you are?"

"I'll text you a map pin of my location." Amber's voice grew distant for a second. "And I'm coming around to the idea of you being my rescuer in any and all physical ways." She hesitated. "I'm sorry. I know you're busy—"

Her phone pinged, and she checked the map. "Save it until I get there. It's going to take me about twenty minutes to get to you. I'm going to need my hands and concentration, so we'll talk when we're together, okay?"

"Bossy. Drive safe." Amber disconnected.

Rowan pulled her snow chains out of the utility room and got them on quickly before she set off. No sense in getting stuck herself. She spent the twenty-minute drive wondering what the hell was going on, and more so, what the hell she was feeling. How could it feel so good to hear Amber's voice after the way they'd separated? She'd been thinking a lot about the stuff she and Pam had talked about, and she'd even made an appointment in Louisville to talk to a shrink. With or without Amber, she clearly had some issues to deal with.

With Amber. She took a shaky breath that fogged up the windshield, forcing her to slow down even more. Was that really an option? Could she trust that Amber wouldn't spook and throw her off again? She looked at the GPS and rolled down her window, hoping to get better visibility by looking outside, since the snow was coming down so hard and so fast the wipers weren't doing a lot of good.

Flashing yellow lights lit the snow like a ghostly call for help, and she carefully turned the truck around in the middle of the street, backing up until she was level with Amber's car. Her mouth went dry, and her pulse was likely going so fast she'd have a heart attack.

Amber stood beside the car, her bright blue jacket a beacon against the whiteout. Snow created a winter crown in her hair, and if Rowan had been a believer, she would have sworn Amber was a snow angel come to life.

Rowan hopped out of her truck, leaving it running, and ran around to open the passenger door. "Need a ride?"

Amber smiled, but her eyes were searching, as though looking for any recriminations or anger. Whatever she saw, her shoulders seemed to lower, and she stepped forward, grabbed Rowan's jacket, and pulled her down for a hot, long kiss. When she finally let go, Rowan let out a whoosh of air.

"Well, damn. I'm going to ask you that question all the time if that's the answer I get."

Amber's expression remained serious. "Thank you for coming. I have so much to say—"

"Maybe you should say it in the truck?" Rowan motioned for her to get in. "Otherwise we're going to be snowmen in about two ticks of the clock."

Amber nodded and turned back to the car. "Let me grab my bag."

Rowan waited but saw that Amber was struggling to lift the enormous case from the trunk. "Can I help?"

Amber grimaced. "Thanks."

"No problem. Get on in, and I'll get your bag." Rowan lifted it out and grunted at the fact that it really was heavy. And then she saw two boxes and a shopping bag. She put them all in the back seat of the truck, hope feeding a fire that had been about to go out.

Once she was back in, she turned the heat to full blast and set off slowly. "That's a lot of stuff for a woman who's about to sell her house and move into a city shoebox," she said, keeping her eyes on the road but wishing she could look into Amber's eyes as she responded.

"Isn't it?" She laughed when Rowan frowned. "I'm staying. I have a lot to share with you, but I need to say something important first." There was a slight tremor in her voice, and her hands were balled into fists. "I'm a mess. I have a ton of baggage, and I'm going to start working through it. But that night with you was the best night of my life, and I'm really sorry I fucked off back to New York. You deserved better, and I'm really hoping you're open to giving me another chance."

Rowan nodded, waiting to see if she was done. "Another chance at what, Amber?" She finally glanced over. "I thought maybe we had something, but it wasn't like we'd said we were going to start dating or anything. What is it you want? With me, and from me?"

Amber bit her lip and stared out the window. "Honestly, I don't have a great answer to that. I know I want more of you. I haven't stopped thinking about you since you drove away that day. I feel weirdly empty without you, like I haven't had enough food or water to sustain me. Only, it isn't that. It's you. Being around you has made me want a life I didn't think existed. So..." She shrugged. "I guess I'm asking if you'll date me. That sounds really lame."

"I like the sound of that." Rowan wished she could let go of the steering wheel to take Amber's hand. "We'll work out the rest." Suddenly, she realized her mistake. "Damn. I assumed you'd be coming back to my place. Do you want me to take you to yours?"

Amber took in a shaky breath. "Would it be okay to go to your place? I don't...I don't want to be alone. And I've missed you."

Rowan laughed, the knot of loneliness slowly but surely unraveling in her chest. "Baby, you can come to my place any time. But you should know, I've got a house full. Corn and his wife and kids are staying with me until they get their house back, and Pam and Julie and Ted are there too."

"Your chosen family," Amber said softly. "I'd like to be part of that."

Chosen family. That was something she'd need to ponder in a bit, after the shock wore off. Maybe the chosen ones were the ones who didn't leave you behind. They pulled up to Rowan's place. "I'll come get your bags in a while, if that's okay?"

Amber nodded and put her hand on Rowan's leg. "Will you kiss me?"

Rowan leaned across and wrapped her hand in Amber's hair. "Any time, any place." She kissed her, softly at first, and then harder, pulling her closer.

"I'm going to intentionally burn the turkey!" Pam yelled from the doorway.

Rowan sighed and leaned her forehead against Amber's. "Rain check?"

Amber smiled. "You bet."

Rowan followed Amber into the house, and they shook away the snow. Everyone welcomed her as though nothing had happened, as though she'd been there the whole time. Cornelius came over and pulled her into a hug.

"Glad you made it. I was worried when I heard the storm was going to be worse than they thought," he said, holding her at arm's length. "You're okay?"

She smiled and hugged him again. "I'm fine. You're the one who had a house land on you."

"That I did!" He laughed and shook his head. "But thanks to Rowan, we made it out okay."

"You knew Amber was coming." Rowan narrowed her eyes at him. "Didn't you?"

He raised his hands. "Hey, now, don't shoot the non-messenger. She wanted it to be a surprise."

Amber grinned. "Surprise!"

Rowan pulled her against her, needing to feel her body, needing to know this was real, and she wasn't a mirage sent to torture her.

"Burning. The. Turkey," Pam said, smacking Rowan in the head with the pot holder. "If you don't feed us, I'm just going to burn the whole place down."

"That makes no sense at all. You could've just started without me." Rowan let Amber go and started gathering the dishes. "Everyone to the table."

They sat at the formal dining table Rowan only used on holidays, and as they passed around the dishes and commented on the smell and taste of everything, Rowan felt tears well up. *Chosen family*. Amber was right. These were her people, and Amber wanted to be one of them. She held Amber's hand under the table, still not quite believing that she was really there. She looked around, more thankful on this Thanksgiving than she'd been in a long, long time.

Later, full and pleasantly exhausted, they watched a movie, though Rowan paid no attention to it at all. She couldn't take her eyes off Amber, and it wasn't long before frustration began to set in. She wanted to be alone with her, but there was no chance of that tonight.

Ted leaned over the couch. "I put the bigger snow chains on the truck. Just in case Amber wanted to sleep in her own bed tonight." He yawned and sauntered away.

Amber's cheeks pinked a little, but there was hope in her eyes. So she felt the same way.

Rowan stood, pulling Amber to her feet. "Right. I'm taking Amber back to her place. See you for brunch in the morning."

Knowing looks were sent their way from the adults, who didn't say anything out loud because of the kids, who seemed to pick up on everything.

Rowan couldn't get her winter gear on fast enough and helped Amber get her coat on. "This might be a little hairy, depending on how bad the road is. Sure you want to go?"

Amber got on her tiptoes and brushed a kiss on her lips. "If it means I can swear and blaspheme while you fuck me senseless and give me something to really be thankful for tonight, then I don't care how long it takes us to get there."

Rowan kissed her a little harder, then held her hand as they made their way out to the truck. The snow was already up to Amber's knees, and their laughter made it harder to get through the snow to the truck. Amber was soaked when they got in, but her eyes were lit with a carefree glow Rowan had only just begun to glimpse before she left.

The drive to Amber's was agony. Not just because of the snowy roads, but because Amber kept tracing a hot line up Rowan's thigh with her nails. By the time they got there, Rowan was ready to throw her into the snow and take her right there beside the truck.

Amber leapt out and into a snow drift, nearly disappearing. "Help!"

Rowan laughed and pushed through the snow, then lifted Amber out. "You look good in white. And maybe it will cool you off a little."

Amber pulled her house key from her pocket and shoved it into Rowan's hands. "Cornelius had one of the workers come by this morning and turn on the heat and hot water. Off you go."

Rowan shook her head but forged forward and got the house unlocked. "After you."

Amber dropped a mountain of snow at her feet inside the door and shivered. She threw off her coat, and then yanked off her sweater. "Ready?"

"For what?" Rowan said, mesmerized as Amber's clothes continued to add to the pile until she was down to a deep blue panty and bra set.

"So I can show you how grateful I am that you're not the kind to hold a grudge." She backed toward the stairs. "Unless you were just dropping me off..." She yelped and laughed, dodging as Rowan lunged toward her. "Get those clothes off!" she yelled over her shoulder as she ran up the stairs.

Rowan tripped on her pant leg, hopping as she tried to get her boots off. Nothing shifted as quickly as she wanted it to, but she managed to leave a trail of clothes on the stairs. The water was running, and Amber was already in a hot shower, water sliding down her body, steam rising around her.

Rowan stopped to take in the view, and also because her legs had gone weak.

Amber turned so her back was to Rowan and looked over her shoulder. "Coming?"

"Damn right." Wild horses wouldn't pull Rowan away. They had things to work through and plenty to talk about, but right now, all she needed was to hear Amber calling her name as they created magic between them once again.

Chapter Twenty-Six

AMBER STRETCHED AS MUTED daylight streamed in the window, her body gorgeously sore from the night's activities.

"Good morning," Rowan murmured, pressing a kiss to her shoulder. "That was the best Thanksgiving I've had in a while."

Amber turned over to face her. "It better be the best one you've *ever* had. A girl doesn't like to hear you've had better, you know."

Rowan laughed and pushed her leg between Amber's, making her gasp. "Well, maybe you need to remind me what it was like." Her calloused hand caressed Amber's breast and lightly pinched her nipple.

Amber pushed into her touch, unable to get enough. She rolled back, tugging at Rowan to come with her. There was something so hot about Rowan's weight on top of her, pinning her to the bed. When she shifted and pushed her hand between Amber's legs, she spread them wider, inviting her in.

"Tell me," Rowan said, her eyes dark with desire. "Tell me you want me."

Amber grasped the metal rail in the headboard with one hand and Rowan's shoulder with the other. "I want you so bad it hurts. Make it better."

Rowan grinned and pushed three fingers into her, making her cry out and arch into her as she began to thrust hard and deep, just the way Amber had begged for it all night long. She kissed her neck, her chest, and then bent to take Amber's nipple in her mouth. She sucked hard, and Amber writhed and begged in repetitive phrases as Rowan made her come over and over again until Amber went limp.

Rowan lay back, and Amber curled against her, resting her head on Rowan's shoulder. "Thank God for cowboy stamina," she said softly, unable to open her eyes and feeling so physically contented she never wanted to move again.

"Well, if that's how you feel..." Rowan shifted like she was going to start again, and Amber thumped her arm.

"You don't want to kill me off just yet, which you'll definitely do if you fuck me any more this morning."

Rowan laughed and settled again. They lay there quietly for a while, and Amber's mind started up again, thoughts swirling in lazy circles. She raised up on her elbow and looked into Rowan's eyes. "Can I touch you?"

Rowan's eyebrow twitched, and she looked thoughtful. "Yeah. But outside only."

Pleasantly surprised, as she'd expected to be turned down, Amber slowly moved on top of Rowan, straddling her the way she had for a long time last night for an entirely different reason. She bent and pressed hot kisses over Rowan's collarbone and then down her stomach until she was kneeling between her legs. Rowan's arms were tucked under her head, her eyes half-lidded as she watched.

Amber lay between Rowan's strong, muscular thighs and felt her own excitement ramp up again. She flicked her tongue over Rowan's clit and smiled when Rowan groaned, her head falling back on the pillow as she reached out to grab the metal in the headboard.

Amber took her time, flicking soft circles and then increasing the pressure as Rowan's moans became more urgent and her thighs flexed and began to shake. Her hand moved into Amber's hair, holding her in place, and Amber thought she might come again from how incredible it felt. Rowan came, her hand tightening in Amber's hair, her hips thrusting toward her mouth.

"Fuck me backwards." Rowan released her grip on Amber's

hair, and her hand flopped to the bed.

Amber rested her cheek against Rowan's thigh. "I take it that's a good thing?"

Rowan glanced down and motioned. "Come up here and let me hold you."

Amber slid up her body, allowing her almost over-sensitive nipples to brush her skin. Rowan growled and flipped Amber onto her stomach and was back inside her in the blink of an eye. "Feels like you think it was a good thing too," she said into her ear as she fucked her fast and hard from behind.

Amber pushed back against her, begging incoherently once again until she came and dropped her face into the pillow. "No more." She groaned as Rowan pressed her fingertips to her clit.

"You're so beautiful." Rowan lifted off her and lay on her side, pulling Amber's back against her. "You're like something out of a fairytale. Is that the world you came from? You're not from New York, are you? That's just a portal where fairy creatures like you come through."

Amber sighed, too contented to think of a response. "You've fucked me stupid. No words now."

Rowan chuckled. "Coffee?"

"You never need to ask. That answer is always yes, even if I already have one in my hand." She grimaced. "My clothes are still in my suitcase in the truck."

"I'll grab them and everything else if you'll start the coffee."

Amber sat up. "But I don't have anything to wear."

Rowan grinned and stretched as she got out of bed. "You mean you'll have to make coffee naked? That's a travesty." She laughed as she left the room and headed downstairs.

Amber shook her head and draped the sheet around her toga-style, and she rather liked the feeling of the sheet trailing behind her as she made her way downstairs. Snow glittered outside the kitchen window, and the trees bowed with the weight on their branches. Hints of blue sky peeked through the dark clouds, and a feeling of rightness settled into place in her soul.

She jumped when Rowan kissed her shoulder.

"You're miles away," Rowan said. "Want to share?"

"I do, but this first." Amber got the coffee brewing and then went to the suitcase Rowan had left by the stairs.

"Do you have to?" Rowan asked. "I really like that just out of bed look you've got going on."

Amber bit her lip and turned. "Well, I suppose it's the least I can do given the number of orgasms you gave me."

Rowan, dressed in her jeans and sweatshirt from the night before, moved toward her, the look in her eyes suggesting they weren't going to have that coffee any time soon. "Speaking of..."

"Nope." Amber raised her hand in a half-hearted command for her to stop. "I'm so sore you won't be able to use me again for at least an hour."

Rowan looked at her watch. "Countdown has begun."

Amber giggled and poured the coffee. After handing a mug to Rowan, she made her way to the new couch that sat in front of the floor-to-ceiling windows. "Will you start a fire?"

Rowan knelt and got one started quickly, then joined Amber on the couch. "I really love the changes you made to the house. You updated it but kept the original feeling." She went to sit down.

"You're overdressed." Amber looked pointedly at the outfit. "I can't be the only one naked here."

Rowan grinned and looked her over. "I don't know. I think it's pretty hot, me dressed and you waiting to be ravished."

Amber rolled her eyes. "Come on, cowboy. Off with it."

Rowan stripped down to her boxers and white tank top. "Better?"

"Much." She watched as Rowan relaxed into the opposite end of the couch and sipped her coffee. "Thank you. For giving me another chance."

Rowan's expression turned serious as she looked at Amber over the coffee mug. "My heart didn't give me a choice. But I admit, my head is a little wary."

Amber swallowed. That was fair, even if it hurt a little. "Tell me more?"

Rowan stared out at the blanket of white beyond the windows for a moment. "I told you about my dad. Turns out, you leaving that way brought up some stuff about not being enough to keep someone around."

At no point had Amber ever considered that, and she winced as she thought of what she'd said as she left. "I'm so sorry."

Rowan nodded slowly and ran her hand over her face. "I know, and you've said as much so we can let that go. You came back, and I'm really hoping you'll stick around." She set her cup down and wrapped her hand around Amber's ankle. "Can you tell me what brought you back?"

"It turns out that not only do I belong here, but..." This was it. She had to say it out loud. "My heart is here too. I'm in love with you. I want to be with you, and I promise that you're enough." She wiped the tears from her eyes, emotions she wasn't familiar with too huge to keep inside. "You're more than enough. You're everything."

Rowan let out a long, slow breath, her gaze searching Amber's. "I love you too," she said quietly. "Please don't break my heart."

Amber launched herself across the couch and into Rowan's arms. "I promise," she whispered as Rowan's arms tightened around her. For the first time in her life, it was a promise she knew she'd keep.

***

They walked into Rowan's house hand in hand, and Amber felt a little like a teenager coming home late as everyone looked up from the breakfast table.

"Well, don't you look freshly fu–" Pam winced. "Ow!" She

scowled at Ted, who nodded toward the kids. She looked momentarily chagrined and then winked at them. "You get the idea."

"Crass." Rowan kissed Amber's knuckles and then let go and headed toward the stove. She held up a plate in question, and Amber nodded. She proceeded to fill their plates with eggs, but she skipped the bacon on Amber's and added toast to both.

"All good in the world?" Julie asked, looking between them.

"All good." Rowan grinned and started wolfing down her food. "All good here?"

"We did all the morning work for you, don't worry." Pam motioned between them with her fork. "You sticking around, Amber?"

Amber nodded, wondering how Pam felt about her treatment of Rowan. If she was pissed, it didn't show. "I am. And it looks like you two have settled into more than pumpkin contest fixing?"

"Okay." Ted folded his napkin and put it on the plate. "C'mon, kids. Let's go make snowmen while the couples talk about couple things."

Amber watched as the kids jumped up from the table, but before they went to get their winter clothes on, both stopped and gave Rowan a strong hug, then they ran upstairs.

"Corn and Marge are taking the opportunity to sleep in, now that they've got built-in babysitters," Ted said. "I expect you four to take your turn. Don't leave this old man to do all the heavy lifting." He whistled as he left the room to Pam and Rowan teasing him about not busting a hip while building snowmen.

"In answer to your question," Julie said, her cheeks turning pink. "Yes, we're a couple. To be honest, we'd already like to move in together in true U-haul style, but my place is too small, and the bunkhouse isn't really a great place for us." She shrugged. "We'll find something right. It's just...Pam's place is a little small for us."

A thought began to form, but she needed to talk to Rowan about it first.

Pam began to clear the plates. "Any plans for your future, Amber?"

Amber took a deep breath. "First of all, I'm really sorry. I owe all of you an apology. My mom is out of the picture now, and I've done what I can to make sure she won't bother me again. I'm not selling the house or the land, but I have no idea what to do with that many acres, so I'm hoping you guys will help me figure that out down the road." She took Rowan's hand, drawing strength from her. "And I have my dad's name."

"You do?" Rowan's eyebrows raised. "You didn't say that earlier."

Amber winked at her. "We were a little occupied with other things."

Julie laughed. "So, what's his name?"

Rowan looked at Pam. "I'm not sure you were supposed to share Amber's story."

"No, it's fine." Amber shook her head and touched Pam's hand when she looked embarrassed. "Honestly, I understand how things work around here. His name is Jeff Crossley, but Mom didn't know, or at least she wouldn't tell me, where he lived."

There was silence around the table, and Amber saw the way they looked at each other. "What? Do you know him?"

"First of all, have you decided how you want to handle that? Do you want to find him?"

Amber nodded slowly. "If I want a real picture of who I can be, I need all the pieces of what came before me. And that includes finding him. Do you know him?" It was nice that Rowan hadn't simply taken charge, that she'd asked what Amber wanted. It meant a lot.

"Let's put a pin in that and come back to it in a minute. Trust me." Rowan held up her hand to keep Pam from talking. "I know you said you don't need to work. But do you want to?"

Amber smiled as she thought of the option she'd come up with. "I think I might want to be a teacher."

Pam choked on her orange juice. "What now?"

"I really enjoyed teaching Jess how to get around the math problems she was struggling with. I know it seems like it's out of left field, and maybe I need to think about it some more, but..." She shrugged. There was a strange energy around the table, and it was making her antsy. "What aren't you guys saying?"

Pam and Rowan shared a look and then Rowan got up. "I'll be right back. Don't share any life-changing information while I'm gone." She kissed the top of Amber's head and left the room, pulling her phone from her pocket as she did.

"This is irritatingly mysterious." Amber folded her arms.

"That's the way they are, I think." Julie stood and went to the oven, where she pulled out enormous cinnamon rolls. "Do you want kids yourself, Amber?"

"Christ." Rowan tripped as she came back into the kitchen. "She only came back yesterday, and you've already got her pregnant."

"That's your job." Pam grinned and pulled Julie onto her lap as she set the buns on the table. "We want three. An older one to take charge, a middle one to feel left out, and a young one to run wild."

"Pretty sure that's not what you should be aiming for." Rowan shook her head, but the look she turned to Amber had a tentative feel. "But I mean, do you? One day? Want kids, I mean?" She flipped Pam off when she chuckled at Rowan's ineptness.

"I don't know, honestly. I never have before, no. But my life is going to be so different from what it was, and I don't want to say no to anything right now."

Pam gave Rowan a wicked grin. "Lucky bastard."

Julie rolled her eyes and covered Pam's mouth. "Ignore her, Amber. I think you're right where you need to be mentally."

Rowan's phone pinged, and she read a text then checked her watch. She looked at Pam and Julie. "Want to come along?"

Pam nodded, and Julie shook her head, making Pam pout.

"We'll stay behind. This isn't a moment for extra folk to gawk."

"But I want to gawk. I like gawking." Pam hugged her tighter and whispered something in Julie's ear that made her blush and giggle.

Amber looked at Rowan. "Are you going to clue me in?"

Rowan held out her hand. "Come on. It'll become clear soon. Better you see for yourself than have it explained."

Amber huffed and took Rowan's hand. "It's a good thing I love you."

Pam whistled, and Julie put her hands over her heart. It was good that they knew how she felt about Rowan. She wanted everyone to know. Especially Rowan.

"Yeah, it is a good thing." Rowan tilted her head toward the door. "Come on."

They got back on the road, which had been plowed but was still slick. Rowan insisted she couldn't talk because she had to concentrate, but Amber knew full well she was just avoiding Amber's questions. "It isn't bad, is it?" she asked. "He's not some kind of right-wing nutter or in prison or something?"

Rowan shook her head slowly, a small smile on her lips. "No. Definitely not anything like that." She glanced over. "And I'll be right beside you."

Somehow that didn't make Amber feel any better. "Okay, if you're not going to answer my questions about him, I have something else to pass by you."

Rowan glanced over but didn't say anything.

"So, your house is really crowded right now. Mine is empty. Pam and Julie need a place of their own." Now that she was saying it out loud, it sounded absurd, but she plunged forward anyway. "We love each other, and I'm tired of waiting for my life to start. So I'm thinking you move into my place with me, and let Pam and Julie live in your place until they find one of their own."

Rowan was silent for a long time, and Amber chastised herself. Who was she to tell Rowan to offer up her house? "Or you and I could live in your place, and Pam and Julie could live in mine. I just thought, with Corn's kids in the house, we'd have more privacy at mine, but—"

"I think it's a great idea." Rowan reached over to hold Amber's hand. "You're right. Your place would suit us, and I think maybe I need some space from living in my parents' shadow. I don't have to live on the farm to work it." Her smile widened. "Wow. You really jump into things when you set your mind to it, don't you? Are you sure you want to live with someone already?"

"No." Amber laughed when Rowan looked confused. "I don't want to live with just anybody. I want to live with you. I want to wake up in your arms every morning and welcome you home every night, even when you smell like horse and whatever other animal you have out there."

Rowan laughed. "Sexy." She navigated her way past a huge, ornate metal gate. "We're here."

Amber looked around. "Is this a university? No one is around."

Rowan nodded. "The closest one to us. Lots of kids from town end up here, but they're gone for the holidays." She ducked her head, reading off the names of buildings as they passed them. "Here it is."

They got out, and Amber looked up at the beautiful brick building. "I don't get it."

Rowan looked up from her phone. "You will. Come on, beautiful." She took Amber's hand and led her up the stairs to the door, which buzzed before they even touched it.

Waiting inside by a wide staircase was a tall, thin man. When he saw Amber, he grasped the railing and sank onto a step, his eyes wide. "God in Heaven," he whispered. "You look just like my sister."

Rowan pulled Amber forward gently. "Jeff Crossley, Amber Archer."

Amber looked from Rowan to him. "I... Nice to meet you." She couldn't think of anything else to say.

He stood, still looking shaky. "Amber, I've waited decades for this. I never stopped hoping you'd find me one day, that somehow we'd find each other." He held out his hands, and she took them. "Darlin' girl, we have so much to catch up on."

The look of awe and genuine emotion in his eyes was almost too much to bear. Her own mother and not-father had never looked at her that way. "Thank you for meeting us today." Amber gently pulled her hands away. "Do you work here?"

He flicked a glance to Rowan, who shrugged. "I figured all the stuff you have to share should come from you."

He nodded. "Thank you, that's mighty kind. Why don't we go to my office?" He led the way, looking back occasionally as though to make sure they hadn't disappeared.

Amber blinked when she read the name on the door. "You're the president of the university?"

He smiled. "I am. I started out as a math professor and then made my way up here. I still miss teaching sometimes though." He gestured toward the leather chairs. "What do you do?"

"I'm in finance. Or, I was." Amber looked at Rowan, wondering what she thought of the connections. "I was thinking about becoming a math teacher."

He laughed, a big, open sound that made Amber's heart swell. "Guess a fondness for numbers runs in the family."

"Why Buck?" Amber rolled her eyes. "Sorry. My thoughts are moving faster than I can deal with. My grandparents called you Buck in their letters. Why?"

His smile turned a little sad. "Your mom and I took a ride when we were first dating. Mind, she didn't want anyone to know she was dating a coal miner's son, so we did it way out of town. One day, she rode up on a coyote that spooked the horses, and I got bucked off. From then on, she called me Buck and your grandparents took it up too. It felt like something they'd call a son." He tapped at the desk as though to ground himself. "I was real sorry about their passing. I hoped I'd see you at the funeral."

"I didn't know about them. Or you." Amber's chest hurt at the loss of connection she'd felt for so long and which hadn't been necessary. "I'm glad I do now."

Conversation over the next hour was mostly about how she'd arrived in town and what her plans were. It was overwhelming, and Amber needed time to process, and seeming to sense that, Rowan squeezed her hand.

"I'm sorry, but I have to get back to the farm to check on the horses."

Amber gave an internal sigh of relief. "Of course."

Jeff stood and shook his head. "I can't believe what a gift today has become. Can I get your number? Maybe we could have lunch?"

Amber nodded and wrote her number down for him. "I'd like that."

He stepped forward. "Do you hug? Your mom hated it."

Well, if her mom hated it... "I do." She stepped into his embrace and breathed in the smell of expensive cigar and subtle aftershave. It was nice. Comforting, even. She gave a little squeeze and stepped back.

He wiped at his eyes, still shaking his head. "I just can't believe it. My daughter, after all this time." He walked them back out to Rowan's truck. "I'll be in touch in a few days. Give you some time to settle in." He held out his hand to Rowan. "I can't thank you enough. If there's ever anything I can do for the Willows, just say the word."

"No need." Rowan shook his hand and then opened the door for Amber. "See you soon."

The ride back was quiet, and Amber was grateful for the time to ponder. Eventually she asked, "How do you know him?"

"The Willows has an agreement with the university. A lot of their students come in the spring to work with the horses and to get a sense of what it is to run a farm for their agricultural management degree program. I've known Jeff since I was a kid. He and my dad were friends, but they grew apart when Jeff went to college and my dad got busy on the farm. When he got in touch to ask about the Willows partnering with the university, I was happy to help." Rowan sighed. "So strange, how small the world really is sometimes."

Amber rested her head against the cold passenger window and stared out at the white blanket covering the world beyond. It was beautiful and serene, and it would be awhile before life poked through again, change happening beneath the surface until then. She, too, could take the time to heal and decide what she'd grow into come spring.

"I love you," she said, turning to look at Rowan. "Thank you for changing my life."

Rowan smiled and raised Amber's hand to her lips. "You're the one changing your life, baby. I just have a front row seat to the show."

They pulled up at Rowan's house but before they went in, Amber went up on her tiptoes for a kiss. "Thank you for that. For everything."

Rowan wrapped her arms around Amber and looked into her eyes. "Show me how grateful you are tonight."

The kiss was full of promise and passion and left Amber breathless. The future was hers, and whatever she made of it, Rowan would be there building it with her. The storm had passed, and she could see all the way to the beautiful horizon.

AUTHOR'S NOTE

Thank you for reading *Heart of the Storm*. If you enjoyed my hot cowgirl melting the New York ice queen, I'd really appreciate it if you would review it on Amazon for me! And if you haven't read any of my other books, maybe you'd like to try my Goldie-shortlisted *Fragments of the Heart*?

www.allymcguireromance.com
Follow me on Instagram, TikTok, Twitter,
and Facebook at AllyMcguireRomance

Other Great Butterworth Books

Fragments of the Heart by Ally McGuire
Love can be the greatest expedition of all.
Available on Amazon (ASIN B0CHBPHR6M)

Sanctuary by Helena Harte
Passions ignite and possibilities unfold. Welcome to the Windy City Romance series.
Available from Amazon (ASIN B0D4B42RRW)

Dead Ringer by Robyn Nyx
Three bodies. One killer. No motive?
Available on Amazon (ASIN B0CPQ8HFK7)

Medea by JJ Taylor
Who will Medea become in her battle for freedom?
Available from Amazon (ASIN B0CK2FB7GW)

Brave Enough to Love by Valden Bush
In a dance between truth and sacrifice, can they rewrite the rules of love?
Available from Amazon (ASIN B0CQP8PMVB)

Virgin Flight by E.V. Bancroft
In the battle between duty and desire, can love win?
Available from Amazon (ASIN B0CKJWQZ45)

Here You Are by Jo Fletcher
.Can they unlock their hearts to find the true happiness they both deserve?
Available on Amazon (ASIN B0CBN935ZB)

Green for Love by E.V. Bancroft
All's fair in love and eco-war.
Available from Amazon (ASIN B0C28F7PX5)

Stunted Heart by Helena Harte
A stunt rider who lives in the fast lane. An ER doctor who can't take chances. A passion that could turn their worlds upside down.
Available on Amazon (ASIN B0C78GSWBV)

Dark Haven by Brey Willows
Even vampires get tired of playing with their food...
Available on Amazon (ASIN B0C5P1HJXC)

Green for Love by E.V. Bancroft
All's fair in love and eco-war.
Available from Amazon (ASIN B0C28F7PX5)

Call of Love by Lee Haven
Separated by fear. Reunited by fate. Will they get a second chance at life and love?
Available from Amazon (ASIN B0BYC83HZD)

Where the Heart Leads by Ally McGuire
A writer. A celebrity. And a secret that could break their hearts.
Available on Amazon (ASIN B0BWFX5W9L)

Stolen Ambition by Robyn Nyx
Daughters of two worlds collide in a dangerous game of ambition and love.
Available on Amazon (ASIN B0BS1PRSCN)

Cabin Fever by Addison M Conley
She goes for the money, but will she stay for something deeper?
Available on Amazon (ASIN B0BQWY45GH)

Breakout for Love by Valden Bush
They're both running from their pasts. Together, they might make a new future.
Available from Amazon (ASIN B0CWHZ4SXL)

The Helion Band by AJ Mason
Rose's only crime was to show kindness to her royal mistress...
Available from Amazon (ASIN B09YM6TYFQ)

That Boy of Yours Wants Looking At by Simon Smalley
A riotously colourful and heart-rending journey of what it takes to live authentically.
Available from Amazon (ASIN B09V3CSQQW)

Sapphic Eclectic annual anthologies edited by Nyx & Willows
A little something for everyone...
Available free from Butterworth Books website

Of Light and Love by E.V. Bancroft
The deepest shadows paint the brightest love.
Available from Amazon (ASIN B0B64KJ3NP)

An Art to Love by Helena Harte
Second chances are an art form.
Available on Amazon (ASIN B0B1CD8Y42)

Music City Dreamers by Robyn Nyx
Music brings lovers together. In Music City, it can tear them apart. Available on
Amazon (ASIN B0994XVDGR)

Let Love Be Enough by Robyn Nyx
When a killer sets her sights on her target, is there any stopping her?
Available on Amazon (ASIN B09YMMZ8XC)

Dead Pretty by Robyn Nyx
An FBI agent, a TV star, and a serial killer. Love hurts.
Available on Amazon (ASIN B09QRSKBVP)

Nero by Valden Bush
Banished and abandoned. Will destiny reunite her with the love of her life?
Available from Amazon (ASIN B0BHJKHK6S)

Warm Pearls and Paper Cranes by E.V. Bancroft
A family torn apart by secrets. The only way forward is love.
Available from Amazon (ASIN B09DTBCQ92)

Judge Me, Judge Me Not by James Merrick
One man's battle against the world and himself to find it's never too late to find, and use, your voice.
Available from Amazon (ASIN B09CLK91N5)

Scripted Love by Helena Harte
What good is a romance writer who doesn't believe in happy ever after?
Available on Amazon (ASIN B0993QFLNN)

Call to Me by Helena Harte
Sometimes the call you least expect is the one you need the most.
Available on Amazon (ASIN B08D9SR15H)

What's Your Story?

Global Wordsmiths, CIC, provides an all-encompassing service for all writers, ranging from basic proofreading and cover design to development editing, typesetting, and eBook services. A major part of our work is charity and community focused, delivering writing projects to under-served and under-represented groups across Nottinghamshire, giving voice to the voiceless and visibility to the unseen.

To learn more about what we offer, visit: www.globalwords.co.uk

A selection of books by Global Words Press:
Desire, Love, Identity: with the National Justice Museum
Aventuras en México: Farmilo Primary School
Times Past: with The Workhouse, National Trust
Young at Heart with AGE UK
In Different Shoes: Stories of Trans Lives

Self-published authors working with Global Wordsmiths:
Steve Bailey
Ravenna Castle
Jackie D
CJ DeBarra
Dee Griffiths
Iona Kane
Maggie McIntyre
Emma Nichols
Dani Lovelady Ryan
Erin Zak

Printed in Great Britain
by Amazon

46294702R00165